NO HUMAN ENEMY

John Gardner

CHIVERS

British Library Cataloguing in Publication Data available

This Large Print edition published by BBC Audiobooks Ltd, Bath, 2008.
Published by arrangement with Allison & Busby Ltd.

U.K. Hardcover ISBN 978 1 405 64432 7
U.K. Softcover   ISBN 978 1 405 64433 4

Printed and bound in Great Britain by
Antony Rowe Ltd., Chippenham, Wiltshire

*For Trish,
again and always.*

'The blind impersonal nature of the missile made the individual on the ground feel helpless. There was little that he could do, no human enemy that he could see shot down.'

Winston Churchill on the V-Weapons

AUTHOR'S NOTE

This is the fifth volume of a projected six books set during the Second World War, starring the young policewoman Suzie Mountford.

It is also my 52nd book, and written in my 80th year—though I don't know what that's got to do with the price of eggs.

I should say that the Royal Marine NCOs, Colour-Sergeant 'Tubby' Shaw and Sergeant Harvey, who appear in the closing chapters of this tale, should not be confused with the late Colour-Sergeant 'Tubby' Shaw and the excellent, if taciturn, Sergeant Harvey, who whipped Y9 Squad through basic drill at the Royal Marine Depot, Deal, in the early spring of 1945. I should know; I was in Y9 Squad. At the time, the war was still being fought, yet at Deal we were even taught the ceremonial *Feu de joie*, which Tubby Shaw called the *Foo Dee Joy*, as all surviving members of Y9 will recall.

John Gardner,
Hampshire, 2006.

CHAPTER ONE

Suzie's brother James flinched as the explosion shuddered through the walls of his sister's sitting room high above Upper St Martin's Lane. The curtains puffed—windows open to stop bomb blast from shattering glass.

'Damn!' said the convent-educated WDI Suzie Mountford. Then to her brother, 'It's OK, Jim . . . Fine, don't worry.' Looking up from her teacup, concerned, glancing at the military style watch she wore on her left wrist.

Three minutes past twelve noon exactly.

'Bloody doodlebugger,' Tommy Livermore growled. 'Third today. That wasn't as close as it sounded. On a calm day . . .'

'Shut up, Tommy, we know. On a calm day the sound is carried over long distances causing the aural illusion of the explosion being closer than it really is.' Suzie spoke as though quoting from a manual.

Up to that point the conversation, when it wasn't about the fighting in Normandy, was about the V-1 doodlebugs, flying bombs. Failing that, in recent days the talk had been of the attempt to assassinate Hitler in his headquarters at Rastenburg in Prussia, a few weeks previously, on 20th July.

All of them, at that moment, felt the disturbing ripple under their feet. Suzie, sitting

1

near the door, felt it through her thighs and bottom as though someone had repeatedly pummelled her. It was not an unpleasant sensation.

For a moment, Lieutenant James Mountford, Royal Marines, thought he was back on Sword beach over a month before, going in with the second wave of 41 Commando on D-Day. He heard the explosions as he reached the surf line, the Sherman tanks with their flails slashing, clearing the mines from the sand: the heavy inhuman whoosh of the flame-throwers ahead. Then he saw the bullets kick up the sand and felt the terrible gouging drill into his right foot, suffered as the bones were snagged apart and again as a further bullet ripped like an electric shock into his left shoulder, spinning him down into the surf, rolling him as though he was a piece of driftwood, blacking him out and disorienting him until Marines Page and McDermott lifted him bodily from the foam and dragged him up to the dressing station already set up among the dunes.

This he relived in a fraction of a second, standing back from the window, right foot encased in plaster, left arm in a sling. He was in battledress, with the Royal Marines Commando flashes on his shoulders, the triangled dagger below, parachute wings and the Combined Ops flash on his right sleeve. He leant on a walking stick and looked sickly

2

white, his eyes sad as those of a frightened puppy.

It was Sunday—second week of August—and they had discharged him from hospital that morning, so he rang Suzie to find she was back in London: she'd been away on cases, twice with Tommy, in recent weeks: before D-Day up to Manchester, following and interrogating a soldier suspected of throttling a prostitute in London, in a flat above Beak Street, Soho. Then there was the case in Sheffield where a young housewife, Doris Butler, had been bludgeoned to death in her kitchen on the night of 5th/6th June. The husband had been on leave but had long gone back to his unit and by 9th June was dead in Normandy. Tommy told Shirley Cox and Laura Cotter to root around and look for a boyfriend; there had been some footprints and a lot of cigarette ends behind bushes at the far end of the woman's little garden, someone watching the house. 'Boyfriend,' Tommy reckoned. 'Boyfriend driven mad by the husband being home and sleeping with his wife. Came down most nights to watch them move around the house, put the blackouts up, go to bed. Hubby goes back to his unit and the bloke nips in. They have a fight—"You said he never touched you!" Bang! Over and out,' there, in Sheffield, the United Kingdom's steel capital. Tommy raised his eyebrows and corrected himself in a mutter, 'No, look for

3

boyfriend*s*, plural. I think our Doris rang the changes: had round heels.'

Later that day, James Mountford was going on to Larksbrook. Their mother, Helen Gordon-Lowe, was coming to collect him, together with the dreaded stepfather, the Galloping Major, who got petrol from God knows where. All the time.

Suzie found it odd that when the war had started her brother was still at school; now here he was in her flat, an officer wounded on the beaches of Normandy.

A Maren, as they called Wrens attached to the Royal Marines, proudly wearing a blue beret with the red flash and the RM Globe and Laurel cap badge, had picked up Jim in a jeep and driven him up from the military hospital on the outskirts of Oxford.

'Thought all the jeeps were in France now,' Jim said.

'Not this one, sir. Wouldn't float so they left it with me.' She glanced at him cheekily and liked what she saw. Marens often twisted young RM officers round their little fingers and other parts of their anatomies. By the time they got to Upper St Martin's Lane and Suzie's flat, Jim had discovered her name was Emily Styles. She came from New Malden, in Surrey, and he'd also got the telephone number of the Wrenery from her, plus her home number in case she was on leave. 'If the excuse is good enough I can always charm a

4

jeep out of the chiefy,' she told him. 'No problem. I'll just give your name—it'll be in the register for a month. I can easily tootle down to Newbury.' She would have taken him today, but he'd told her his mum was coming for him, so she had to make do with helping him up to his sister's flat, letting the back of his hand brush hard against her left breast as she did so.

Now, up in Suzie's living room, he felt dejected, could've been with the Maren instead of his fun-defying stepfather, Ross Gordon-Lowe, hero of World War One, firewatcher extraordinary, dull as a tarnished cap badge.

'Cheer up, Jim. You're a hero now,' Tommy grinned at him.

'Hero my arse. Commissioned for less than four months, commando course, parachute course then off to 41 Commando. Two minutes on the beach and I'm shot to buggery.'

'At least you won't get a medal for it like the Yanks.' American troops received the Purple Heart medal for getting wounded, and this was looked upon with derision by members of HM Forces.

'In the last lot they called it getting a Blighty.' Tommy winked at him. In the first war getting a Blighty meant getting a wound that sent you home, got you out of the trenches. 'Your sister got a sort of Blighty last year.'

5

Suzie didn't see the wink; she had turned away, squinting at the little mirror in her handbag held at arm's length, checking out the new lipstick she'd acquired: *Cyclax* Velvet Grape. Also, she'd had her hair done in Sheffield and was persuaded to have her eyebrows plucked. Still couldn't get used to it: wondered if it was too much.

Tommy saw her back stiffen. 'Joke, heart,' he chuckled. Then, to Jim, 'Got herself promoted without taking any exams. Jammy girl, eh?'

'Not funny, Tom,' she snapped.

'Not sitting where I am, heart.'

Suzie didn't bite, wanted to claw his eyes out but knew it wasn't worth it. She was starting to learn about damping down her temper and this was a particularly irritable wound, Tommy nibbling away at last year's still-festering sore.

Last year, '43, there had been a ginormous split when Suzie was moved from the Reserve Squad to an intelligence unit, the War Office Intelligence Liaison Department, on special duties. Tommy had no say in the matter that was seen to be temporary, but Tommy, being the Honourable Tommy Livermore, threw a sort of childish paddy, saw shadows where there were none, and devious moves where none existed. The result was a real divide, an incomprehensible falling-out with Suzie learning more about Tommy than was good

6

for her.

In the end, of course, Tommy had crawled back, pleading for a return to the status quo, but every now and then he gave her a sharp dig just to remind himself of how bad it had been.

Suzie's promotion had come with the move to WOIL and she had been allowed to keep the rank of Woman Detective Inspector after she returned to the Reserve. This still appeared to rankle with old Dandy Tom and she didn't really know why: thought he'd have been proud of her.

They had a scratch lunch. There was always a supply of ham, bacon and eggs, from the home farm at Tommy's parents' estate, Kingscote Grange: 'Where Tommy cut his molars on the old silver spoon,' Suzie told people.

So today they had poached eggs on toast because Suzie hadn't had the patience to do a proper Sunday lunch and her mother had told her not to worry as they planned to take everybody to the Savoy that night for dinner before they drove back to Newbury. If you had money you could still eat in places like the Savoy at almost pre-war standards; and the Galloping Major always seemed to have money. Another thing that puzzled Suzie.

Not that it mattered because as soon as they arrived Ross Gordon-Lowe, full of self-importance, announced that they couldn't stay after all. 'I have a parade tonight.'

'What's he going to parade?' Suzie muttered to her mother. 'Going to march through Newbury with that little moustache— bayonets fixed and drums beating? His moustache got the freedom of Newbury, has it? That what it's about?'

'ARP evening church parade, Suzie. Don't tease him, you know how important it is to him,' and Helen entered the drawing room setting eyes on James in his cast, sling and some sticking plaster on his face. 'Oh, my poor darling, what have they done to you?'

'Slipped in the bath, Mummy.' He gave his most winning smile, the one that seemed almost to slip off his face, wondering why his mum and the major hadn't driven over to Oxford to see him. He'd been there long enough.

They stayed for a cup of tea, Ross Gordon-Lowe constantly taking surreptitious peeps at his watch, which made Suzie angry. Her friend Shirley Cox, woman police sergeant in the Reserve Squad, had recently had an affair with a married man. 'Thing that really narks me is after we've done it he keeps sneaking peeps at his watch,' she said. 'Like he can't wait to get home.'

They stayed for a cup of tea—the Galloping Major only drank half—then both Tommy and Suzie helped get Jim down to the car.

Helen shot her eyes towards Ross and hissed at Suzie, 'Try to understand, darling. He gets petrol for being a warden. Has to keep his end up.'

Suzie thought she'd like to keep his end up, but didn't specify where. She hadn't completely forgiven her mother for marrying him so quickly following the tragedy of her father's death in an unnecessary road accident. Hardly a week went by when she didn't think of that terrible day, even though she now knew the other things, that her dad hadn't left them well provided for which was why Helen had married the artful Gordon-Lowe. The thought of it made her shudder.

They'd just got back into the flat when the telephone started to ring—Tommy's special phone that rang when people asked for, or dialled, his home number in Earls Court.

He spoke for some five minutes and came out to find Suzie making more tea in the kitchen.

'Don't make yourself too comfortable, heart, we're in work.'

'Lift that barge, tote that bail. Where to this time?'

'Odd one. Don't know really. One of those V-1s this morning. Uncovered something, Billy says. Local law wants us over there.' He looked puzzled. 'Brian's picking us up. Told him to bring Ron and your friend Shirley.'

Billy was Billy Mulligan, Tommy's executive sergeant, cooked the books, kept track of time and motion. Brian was Tommy's driver,

9

rumoured to have worked at Kingscote for Tommy before he was even a detective, let alone a detective chief super. Ron was DS Ron Worrall, good at crime scenes and taking the snaps, and Shirley Cox was, well, Shirley Cox, old chum from her days in Camford Hill nick.

'Bet Emma'll insist on coming along for the ride.' She gave him a sideways look and began to perk up her lipstick.

'Shouldn't wonder,' Tommy gave what they called his terrible smile.

Emma was WDS Emma Penticost—their second attempt to replace the irreplaceable Molly Abelard now gone to glory and much missed.

*   *   *

Suzie later maintained that, for her, this was the worst year of the war, eclipsing even the horrors of the Blitz in '40 and '41. D-Day, 6th June 1944, came and went—the largest invasion force in history jumping the English Channel in an attempt to drive the Nazi occupation forces out of Europe. With it there was a sense of euphoria. They had waited since 1940 to return to the Continent, and once the Allied armies gained a toe-hold in Normandy people wrongly imagined that everything would be downhill to victory.

Exactly a week after the D-Day landings came the secret weapons: the V-weapons, the

10

vengeance weapons, which could not, at first sight, be stopped. It was the beginning of a period which to the war-weary inhabitants of southern England was psychologically much worse than the days of the Blitz.

The code word for a flying bomb was *Diver*; for a rocket it was *Big Ben*. They were a major secret in 1944 Britain. The general public didn't have a clue and it was not thought advisable to warn them of the horrible surprise, but word had been dribbling in from occupied Europe since the summer of 1943, and members of the underground resistance in France, together with the slave labour put to work on launch sites, had kept a steady stream of intelligence reaching the secret corridors of the Air Ministry and the War Office in London.

The Royal Observer Corps knew all about *Diver* and *Big Ben*, and on the night of 12th/13th June, just a week after the D-Day landings, Observers Woodland and Wraight at Observer Post Mike Two saw an object with flames spurting from its tail crossing the coast near Dymchurch, a couple of miles west of Folkestone. They later reported that it sounded like a Model T Ford negotiating a steep hill. On spotting it, Woodland lunged for the telephone linking them with their centre in Maidstone. 'Mike Two—Diver, Diver, Diver!' He shouted, then gave the course of this first flying bomb heading for London: the first

Fiesler 103 to give its correct designation.

Observer Post Mike Two was suitably situated on top of a Martello Tower. Martello Towers are dotted along Britain's south coast, originally erected as watch points for another possible invasion—the one planned by Napoleon Bonaparte in the early nineteenth century.

About five minutes later that first flying bomb's engine stopped and it hurtled down to explode in an open field.

The second one to cross the coast that night—torpedo-shaped body with a ton of amatol in the nose, stubby wings and a pulse jet engine mounted at the rear above the tail— landed in a potato field, but the third exploded in Bethnal Green, taking out a railway bridge and two houses, killing six people including nineteen-year-old Ellen Woodcraft and her eight-month-old son, Tom.

So began the sinister and successful V-1 assault on the south of England. The man at the sharp end of the attack was Colonel Max Wachtel, a serious, no-nonsense former artillery officer, now the man in command of Flak Regiment 155(W). Wachtel had supervised the training of the launch crews: a tireless hands-on organiser who at one point was forced to grow a beard to disguise himself in an attempt to mislead the resistance organisations which had spies everywhere.

That first weekend of the V-weapons saw a

steady stream of Fi 103s reaching the capital. St Mary Abbot's hospital in Kensington was badly damaged, and there were incidents in Battersea, Wandsworth, Streatham and Putney.

On the Sunday came a horrific direct hit— at 11.20 a.m. a 103 struck the Guards Chapel of Wellington Barracks, a stone's throw from Buckingham Palace, just as the congregation stood to sing the *Te Deum*. Fifty-eight civilians and sixty-three service personnel died and over seventy more were seriously injured.

Within three days of the first flying bombs 647 landed in the capital. Others were blown to pieces in the sky by the anti-aircraft batteries ringing London, many were destroyed by fighter command aircraft, some were even deflected by pilots using a brave technique which called for fighters to manoeuvre their wingtips under the 103s stubby wings, so tipping the flying bombs onto a course away from their original targets.

The assault continued, night and day until the following year, though in September the V-1s were joined by the equally vicious V-2 rockets which came from the skies with no warning. The people of London and southern England who had been so defiant during the Blitz of the early forties, became nervous and fearful of the new threat: the psychological damage being as bad as the physical destruction.

Some five weeks later, on a Sunday morning, one of the flying bombs—now dubbed 'doodlebugs'—exploded near an Anglican convent in south London, an event inextricably linking the lives of Colonel Max Wachtel and Woman Detective Inspector Suzie Mountford: though it is doubtful if the colonel, commanding officer of Flak Regiment 155(W), ever knew.

CHAPTER TWO

'So, where're we going?' she asked as they hustled down the stairs—couldn't waste time waiting for the lift because Brian already had the car, the black Wolseley, waiting in front of the building.

'Convent. Religious house. Like old times for you, heart.' Tommy breathless, ought to take more exercise. In the car, Brian driving, Suzie in the back crammed between Shirley Cox and Ron Worrall.

Ron asked, 'What's going on, Chief?'— They all called Tommy chief instead of the usual guv.

'Three bodies, one wounded, result of enemy action.' Tommy slewed himself around, looking straight at Ron who sat behind Brian. 'One of this morning's V-1s. Apparently one of them isn't kosher.'

'One of the V-1s?' from Shirley, not paying attention.

'One of the bodies, Shirl. Wake up. I've got no details except a part of the convent's been seriously damaged and there are three fatalities.'

'One of them not kosher,' Suzie said, a bit cheeky.

'Absolutely.' Tommy paused, looked up at the mirror on the passenger side: he liked to have a mirror on the passenger side of his cars as well as the one normally placed for the driver. 'That Emma?' he asked and Brian lifted his hands off the wheel, making a little placating movement.

'Yes, Chief,' he nodded. Yes, it was Emma Penticost. 'Said it was her duty to be with you. Following up in her own car.'

Tommy made a harrumphing noise. 'Lucky to have her *own* car.' Pause. 'Takes it seriously, doesn't she? Being my nanny. Full-time job, eh?'

It certainly is, Suzie thought, glancing back through the rear window to see the nose of Emma's little black MG a few yards behind them, clinging on for dear life.

Brian drove fast, just within the limit, slipping neatly passed other cars as though trying to throw off a tail, giving them an occasional burst of the bell. All unmarked Metropolitan Police cars carried amplified electric bells to warn other drivers to keep

15

their distance. Riding the ringer they called it and Brian was especially fond of using the bell. Sometimes he sang under his breath, 'Ding-dong the witch is dead,' from the Judy Garland film *The Wizard of Oz*. Suzie would sometimes look at Tommy and say, 'Toto, I don't think we're in Kansas anymore.'

It took forty-two minutes to get there. Ten minutes to three on a warm, sunny Sunday afternoon in the middle of August, 1944.

The Anglican convent of St Catherine of Siena lies between Silverhurst Road and Easter Park, taking up a huge slice of ground that once belonged to the Parish Church of St James, on the edge of the invisible frontier where Camberwell drains into Walworth.

Brian pulled over and they stopped, parking before the convent's main entrance in Silverhurst Road, a big, smart signboard next to the door saying, *Convent of St Catherine of Siena, Teacher of the Faith*.

Tommy coughed, 'Here we are then. Holy, Holy, Holy. All the Holies. Let's get cracking.'

'Who's meeting us here from the local nick?' Suzie had spotted a figure stepping towards them out of the shadow of the high grey wall into the blinding sunshine, reaching for the door on Tommy's side.

'According to Billy, their ranking plain-clothes officer. A DS, name of . . .'

'. . . Magnus,' she said, recognising him. 'Philip Magnus. Pip Magnus. Watch him,

16

Chief.'

Tommy nodded and opened his door before Pip Magnus got to it. Suzie slipped out and was on her feet by the time Tommy Livermore exited the car. Behind her Emma Penticost had parked her MG and now stood four paces behind the detective chief super's left shoulder, a stunning athletic figure, prematurely ash-grey hair and that stance that would make even a jaywalker think twice. Emma, Tommy would say, was their secret weapon, their doodlebug, one of the very few police officers allowed to go armed. Certainly the only woman officer with that privilege.

Pip Magnus wore a grey double-breasted suit with fashionably wide lapels, the jacket a touch too tight, straining at the cross button, a grey trilby cocked to one side covering his thatch of straw-coloured hair, everything else in place: the thickset figure running to fat, rubbery lips and slightly bulging eyes, high colour in the cheeks. 'Mr Livermore, sir. Good afternoon, we're honoured, sir.' Hand out, drawn back a little like the handle on a slot machine. 'Detective Sergeant Magnus, sir. Pip Magnus.'

Tommy barely touched the hand, nodded and asked what it was all about and, as he did so, Magnus turned his head and saw Suzie. 'Suzie!' he said, registering a slight shock, and Tommy didn't miss a beat.

'WDI Mountford. You know each other?'

'I'm sorry.' Magnus hadn't heard about her promotion. 'Sorry, ma'am. Yes. *Knew* each other. Camford Hill. Lifetime ago. Met you there as well, sir. When you came over . . .'

'Quite,' Tommy said, 'half a lifetime back.' Suzie didn't even open her mouth. Pip Magnus had been a close crony of DCI Tony 'Big Toe' Harvey, now in Wormwood Scrubs for being bent as a corkscrew. Suzie had served under Harvey and worked with Magnus when he was a detective constable. Slippery as the proverbial eel. 'Might as well use grease instead of soap,' someone had said of him.

'Well?' Tommy took a step past Magnus towards the convent door. 'We going in among the holy ladies or not?'

Magnus put an arm out as though to bar his superior officer's way. 'No, sir. If you don't mind. . . really I'd like to show you where the doodlebug came down. This way, sir,' pointing towards Easter Park.

They could all see activity at the end of the road where it turned into Easter Park, with Easter Road running off to the right. Dust still hung in the air, vehicles were parked close to the wall and there was constant movement around what was obviously the incident.

Suzie glanced at the convent's façade: dirty grey stone; three wide steps up to a solid, four-panelled oak door; three windows reaching away on either side, and three above on the second storey with an extra one above the

18

door, the windows set into pointed arches and barred with grilles let into the stonework. Above the façade there were five stone decorative gables, the middle one containing a statue of St Catherine standing in a tall niche looking down benignly from the roof, a book open in her hand, the other raised in benediction.

Giving us her blessing, Suzie reckoned.

Away to the right a wall swept to the natural end of the road, slightly lower than the façade around the main door, all finished in the same way, big grey blocks of stone now blackened by the soot and dirt of London. You could always smell the soot in London and taste it at the back of your throat. Suzie knew that if she was put down blindfold in a London street she'd know immediately that she was in Britain's capital. Nowadays you often smelt burning, and when it rained the scent of charred wood usually hung in the air, a legacy of the Blitz of 1940/41. As for the dust, there was plenty in London these days, dust laid in former centuries now unsealed by explosions and again brought to light. Dust that had been laid four or five hundred years ago was now the dust and grit of the 1940s.

She followed Tommy, going towards Easter Park, walking the length of the boundary wall.

Another plain-clothes man came moving quickly from the direction of the park with a message for Magnus who excused himself and strode swiftly ahead.

Tommy dropped back. 'Magnus?' he asked.

'One of "Big Toe" Harvey's chums,' Suzie supplied.

Tommy Livermore nodded. A thin grim smile. 'Knew I'd seen him before. Right little darling as I recall.'

'You had an idea he was the one tipped off Lavender. Made sure she got away in time.'

He nodded again.

This was all about Suzie's first big case, the murder of a BBC female announcer in 1940 and the subsequent trail that led them to the psychotic, terrifying killer, Golly Goldfinch. Tommy Livermore had guided her through this frightening period of her life. Lavender was Goldfinch's cousin, a West End tart who had motivated Golly, pushing him into his killing sprees.

*　　　*　　　*

In a way, Suzie thought, it was gratitude that had led her to becoming Tommy Livermore's lover, though a deeper feeling had come with time.

Two open lorries with white ARP insignia on the doors and the hopeful word RESCUE stencilled white along the sides came jolting along the road, overtaking them, the dark blue overalled men in the rear whistling and *chaiaik*ing at Suzie and Shirley Cox.

20

'Nice to be fancied,' Shirley said, echoing many women before and after her.

Magnus returned, hot and bothered. 'We've had the first reports back from the hospital. Confirms what we'd found.' Suzie thought he looked liverish. 'You'll have to go and take a look. It's very odd. Just as we thought.' And Tommy grunted, not committing himself.

They could now see the road ahead was cordoned off, allowing people to turn right into Easter Road, but denying access to the park. There was the constant sound and clatter of heavy manual work, the noise of bombed property being cleared and made safe.

Magnus gestured, suggesting they move to the other side of the road, were they passed two old and discoloured office blocks, a handful of shops, greengrocer, butcher and a haberdasher with practically nothing in its windows except a plethora of pink petticoats and armoured corsets. There should be a medal for any man who could get through that lot, Suzie thought, catching a glimpse of herself in the plate glass, amazingly not shattered by the blast of the explosion. Hardly recognised herself. Bloody hell, she thought, seeing her floral-patterned skirt whipped around her knees and thighs and her short hair looking a tangled mess. She felt hot, sweaty, fat and much older than her twenty-six years, but there she was, the same slender figure, the slim waist, straight back, no sloppiness here.

21

But where was it all going, her youth, her life? Whizzing fast as any doodlebug. When she first moved into CID (the Criminal Investigation Department) in 1940 she had been just twenty-two. Now . . . ? . . . didn't bear thinking about.

Near Easter Park they passed a Church of England school, stamped in the same way as all those Victorian schools, carbon copies of each other, red-brick buildings, big arched windows, the little bell tower for the single bell to summon the weary children to their lessons.

Across the road, the convent wall turned abruptly at right angles, running a good hundred and fifty yards to form the rear boundary of the property. There was the hint of another wall within and in the far corner a short spire ran up from what could only be the chapel.

The flying bomb, the Fiesler 103, had landed some fifty yards inside Easter Park, gouging out a crater in which you could have hidden a couple of London double-decker buses, tearing up trees and the tarmacadam from a path running alongside the grubby grey convent wall.

On the corner the explosion had ripped away the stone blocks of the wall, laying bare three and a half rooms, hurling the stone inwards, bringing down the heavy ceilings. Three cells really. Cells for nuns, each with a simple iron bedstead, a stand chair and a prie-dieu, a crucifix on the wall: spartan little living spaces around ten feet by six, each uniformly whitewashed, grey now and dirty where they'd removed the debris. No sign of life except for the rescue men still busy clearing rock and starting to shore up what was left of the sagging ceilings.

The air smelt as though it was on fire and a curtain of dust appeared to hang permanently over the scene.

The Rescue team they had seen arriving had taken over from a section of ten men now relaxing on the grass, just outside the cordoned area, sipping large mugs of tea and munching on sandwiches provided by a WVS mobile canteen. A fire engine was also in attendance, its crew making the most of the canteen, and there was an ambulance parked nearby.

'We've had to cordon this far back,' Magnus explained. 'Two of the cell doors're damaged and can't be locked,' nodding towards the exposed rooms. 'When the fire service boys and the rescue teams arrived there were nuns coming from the far side, trying to get to the bodies. Had to be told to go back. Bloody dangerous. Have to leave a guard down here all night of course. Some idiot on the piss, bet your pocketbook, will be in there and through into the convent. Raising all kinds of hell.'

'Can't raise hell in a convent. Three nuns, then? In there, three nuns?' Tommy asked.

'Novices, sir. Yes. Four actually, one's in hospital, still alive. We went like the clappers to get them out so the crime scene's ruined.' Magnus hopped nervously from foot to foot, like a child in need of a urinal. 'Three novices, Mr Livermore. Two of them killed by being knocked across their cells by blast and stone. Crushed. The other one was dead already they tell me. Had her throat cut. It wasn't till they got her down the hospital that we were told for sure she wasn't . . .'

'Wasn't a nun . . . ?' Tommy started.

'. . . novice?' Suzie asked.

'No.' Magnus shook his head. 'Wasn't a female. The third one, with her throat cut, wasn't a her. He was a him, and his throat was cut, not by flying detritus but by a good, old-fashioned knife that we've yet to find.'

'Oh, good,' said DCS Tommy Livermore, always heavy on the irony.

CHAPTER THREE

They went down to the hospital to take a shufti at the bodies, not the most pleasant part of the day, getting on for five o'clock and four more V-1s falling not very far off, the sound of their popping, purring engines stopping making everyone clam up until the beast had exploded elsewhere.

24

Magnus was correct; one of the novices was a bloke, meat and two veg, the lot, and with his throat cut, ear to ear like a big extra pink mouth. The two women, both quite young, had been crushed horribly by great hunks of flying stone. Not a pretty sight, one with her neck obviously broken, the other with her chest stove in. Suzie thought of it like that, 'chest stove in' sounded like something from one of her brother's books when he was fifteen or so, full of pirates, swashbuckling, full-blooded adventure and battles galore; people getting their chests and heads stove in.

When they'd marvelled at it all, Tommy talked to Magnus then sent Ron off to take a hard look at the three cells where the deaths had taken place.

'No need to get your magnifying glass out, Ron. Those hairy great ARP Rescue people've been clumping all over the place. Even Sherlock Holmes wouldn't find anything now. Have a good look round just the same. Bring your talents to bear and remember we're still looking for a knife, something sharp that did the damage to the wolf in nun's clothing, if that's what he was. I'll be down later for you to give me the sixpenny guided tour.'

Off he went, happy as Larry, maybe happier. Emma Penticost just stayed in the background, silent, and Tommy turned to Magnus, 'What about the injured one? Sister . . . ?'

25

'Monica.'

Tommy nodded and sent Shirley off to find the missing nun. 'Just get a general picture at this stage.' Then, turning to Magnus, 'You say they've been identified, the bodies?'

'Two of them. Reverend Mother—Mother Ursula—took a gander at them on the grass. She got first look, didn't recognise the bloke, only we didn't know it was a bloke then. Made a good nun, he did, that bloke.'

'You didn't think it was a bit odd?'

'What?'

'Reverend Mother not being able to finger her . . . him?'

'She said something about getting the Hovis Mistress—no, that's not right . . .'

'Novice Mistress,' Suzie supplied.

Magnus gave a leery smirk. 'That's the one. She's pretty old. Old and decrepit, that Mother Ursula.'

'No need to be disrespectful, lad. With any luck we'll all be old and decrepit one of these days.' Tommy drawled, turning his head in Suzie's direction. 'Won't we, heart?'

'Yea, we should live so long,' chuckled Magnus, and Tommy treated him to a withering look. 'She was a bit confused as well, sir. Admitted to it. Said, "I'm a bit confused these days," and there was a younger nun with her who nodded, agreed with her. I don't think her eyesight's up to much either, guv.'

'Yes. Well.' Tommy frowned. 'So really, the

26

three bodies haven't been officially identified?'

'No, guv.'

'You think we ought to go and talk to her, Chief? The Reverend Mother?' Suzie asked.

'Yes. Definitely. We need to talk to her and we need to get the corpses identified. Someone official will have to do it in case the man was a regular visitor to the convent.'

'I don't think nuns have regular male visitors.' It came out before Suzie could close her mouth: thinking aloud.

'I'm aware of all that, heart. I meant, butcher, baker, candlestick . . . Oh, well.'

'You want me in on that, sir, or . . .?' Magnus left it hanging in the air.

'No.' Tommy firm, giving the impression that his dearest wish was to be a long way from Magnus. 'Just remind me, the two women, the novices, which cells were they found in?'

'One of them right at the far end, where the wall turns at the bottom of Easter Park. Then the one that's a bloke, in the next cell. Then the younger nun.'

'The man was kind of sandwiched between the two novices then?'

'In a manner of speaking, guv'nor, yes.'

Wickedly, Suzie thought they really would make a gleesome threesome—then immediately regretted it. Suzie's conscience was easily pricked when it came to religion, the product of being at St Helen's, taught and kept to a rigid discipline by nuns. Even nuns of the

27

Anglican persuasion could hold a special dread and an awesome respect.

They stood outside the main mortuary viewing room in a quiet and nice area for relatives or witnesses to wait until a body was ready for them to have a look-see. There was a table with flowers in a vase, and several chairs, a crucifix on the wall: too bad if you weren't a Christian, but this was a Christian country, right?

'No,' Tommy repeated. 'No, you make sure the crime scene is secure, Magnus.'

'Very good, sir,' obviously relieved. Then a long pause as though he was plucking up courage, standing there opening and closing his mouth like a fish. 'There *was* one other thing, sir.'

'Well?' preparing to leave, giving Suzie the look that said 'we're off'. Glancing at Emma and nodding.

'Delicate matter, sir. Marjorie brought it up.'

'Marjorie?'

'One of the assistants here, sir. Knew something funny had gone on. It's probably nothing but . . .'

'But what?'

'Nuns' underclothing, sir.'

'What about it?'

'Wondered if you knew anything about nuns' underwear, sir.'

'Do I look like somebody who knows

about . . . ? Maybe WDI Mountford . . .'

'What's the problem?' Suzie asked.

'Probably not a problem, but Marjorie disrobed the ladies and . . . well, a bit colourful. She thought it a bit colourful for nuns.'

'Thought what in particular was a bit colourful?'

'The . . . er . . . the drawers.'

'The drawers are a bit colourful?' Tommy almost exploding, looking pop-eyed. Pink. Uncomfortable.

'Well, Directoire, naturally. That's to be expected. Also, both the ladies were wearing them . . .'

'Directoire?' Tommy queried, definitely discomfited now.

'ETBs,' Suzie said with a grin. Don't see why he's embarrassed. Never embarrassed when he's happily removing my drawers.

'ETBs?' Tommy quite out of his depth.

'Elastic-Top-and-Bottom,' Suzie smirked. 'In training we used to call them passion killers; blackouts; the issue ones, woollen in winter, drawers cellular lightweight for the summer. Look, where's this going, Pip?'

'They're made of a silky material. Bright scarlet. Marjorie thought the colour and texture a shade racy for nuns.'

'Not at all. The nuns at my school wore vivid electric blue. Silk. Saucy really . . .'

'How the hell did you know?' Tommy

29

seemed startled. 'I mean, it's not easy to look up a nun's skirt.'

'There was a little walled garden next to the laundry. Our classroom almost overlooked it and on Mondays we'd see the nuns' knickers out on the line like a waving bunch of pennants. Electric blue.'

'You said. Silk.' Tommy fussed about with a cigarette, then headed for the door. Outside he lit up and, as though seeing her for the first time, again nodded to Emma. 'Couldn't miss the excitement, eh, Emma?'

Emma Penticost had a particularly destructive smile which she used now. Sickening, Suzie thought. Could twist Tommy round her thingamy.

'You know why I'm here, Chief,' Emma's smile blasting golden sunshine right into Tommy's eyes.

'Not just for the thrill of it all?'

'No, Chief. Part of my brief, isn't it?'

Tommy grunted, unconvinced.

'Part of my brief is to stick by you, Chief, unless you tell me to get lost. In that case I suppose I have to make my own decision.'

Tommy gave a half-hearted nod and asked Emma to walk with him, indicating Silverhurst Road, back in the direction of St Catherine's Convent main entrance where Brian sat, silent, in the Wolseley. Suzie tucked herself in behind them and they walked slowly back, seemingly in deep conversation.

Emma was what Tommy—using the 1930s gangland description—liked to call the Reserve Squad's 'Muscle'. It was a tradition that had started with Molly Abelard who'd been drafted into the Reserve following a threat on Tommy's life just before the war. Tommy was newsworthy, got written up in the Fleet Street newspapers a lot. They called him Dandy Tom on account of his sharp suits and impeccable turnout. The fact that he was the Honourable Tommy Livermore was also a help and Tom believed that tittle-tattle in the press always boosted his standing among the villainous classes. Dandy Tom, Gentleman Detective. 'Detective, yes,' he would say, 'but I'm not so sure about the Gentleman.'

Molly Abelard had been a splendidly suitable young woman, not simply firearms-trained but also an expert in the field of what came to be called unarmed combat and silent killing, together with more exotic forms of self-defence. She was an all-round human dynamo whom Suzie had disliked on first meeting but had grown to care about in later years. After Molly's death, Suzie was the only one who knew of the serious affair in which Molly had been involved with Tommy's driver, Brian. She had told nobody and thereby formed a special bond with Brian who was the one man, apart from Billy Mulligan, whom Tommy Livermore trusted with his deepest secrets. Lean, bronzed Brian was, for the best part of three years, the only person in the squad who knew of the attachment between Suzie and Tommy.

After Molly, a suitably trained WDC—Cathy Wimereux—had been posted to the Reserve Squad but she had lasted only a few weeks having, Suzie discovered later, made an overt pass at the chief and turned out to be, in Shirley Cox's words, 'Leaky as a buggered alibi.' Shirley was blessed with a colourful turn of phrase mainly from consorting with auxiliary firemen and members of His Majesty's Armed Forces.

They all called Tommy 'chief' but it was Molly who had so christened him and things were still done by Molly's rules, as Emma had quickly determined. As they sauntered back to the convent entrance Suzie listened to Emma laying out her proposals for keeping the chief safe.

'You could still delegate more,' she told him, mentally wagging her finger. 'Your best work's been done when you've used your team as a proper company, marshalling their individual skills, sending them out to cover all the bases.'

Tommy replied with a grunt, knowing that was exactly how he worked anyway, but humouring the girl. 'You really think so,' glancing back over his shoulder and leering at Suzie. 'Then I suppose I should put someone else in charge of this. Someone who knows more about nuns.' Raising his voice, 'Ought to put you in charge, Suzie, eh? I mean you're the one who knows about nuns, aren't you?'

'Schooled by them, yes, Chief.'

'Schooled by them and saw their drawers floating in the breeze, eh, heart?'

'They taught me a great deal, Chief.'

'They teach you fear, heart?'

'Taught me to be God-fearing, yes.'

'I didn't quite mean that.' They had reached the main door and Tommy walked carefully up the three wide and curved steps, placing his hand on the ornate metal ring that was the bell-pull. 'What I mean is that nuns have always been a sign of sheer terror to me, heart. I don't know how they strike you, but they scare the draggies off me.' His slight Scottish accent becoming for a moment more pronounced and, as though providing an exclamation mark at the end of his sentence, Tommy yanked at the pull. From far away they heard the sonorous deep clang of a bell. Even on this hot Sunday afternoon there was eeriness about the sound, a far-away echo from deep within what Tommy viewed as a secret place.

Soon there were other noises from behind the door: first the scrape of a Judas-squint sliding back and the sight of a sharp eye gazing down at them, shining and steady like the eye of a bird. The eye apparently had a voice. 'What can I do for you?'

Tommy's head moved a fraction as he lifted

33

his warrant card so that the eye could take it in. He then recited his rank and name, followed by Suzie's and Emma's credentials. 'We've come to talk with the Reverend Mother,' he said, his voice dry and gritty.

The voice of the eye did not reply, but bolts started to be scraped back. Suzie expected the hoarse barking of dogs, but almost silently the door swung open to reveal a tall, thin nun managing to smile gravely, which was quite a trick.

By this time, Shirley Cox had returned, red in the face and rather puffed. Sister Monica was under sedation and she hadn't been able to talk to her. 'The nurse said we'd be lucky to get anything out of her for some time,' she told Tommy. 'In shock.'

'You'd better talk to her tomorrow, or later in the week,' he told Suzie, who made a note in her pocketbook. Shirley was sent to join Ron in digging around the crime scene.

The habit of the Sisters of St Catherine of Siena was heavy and grey, tied around the waist with a thick rope girdle the end of which hung down the right side, secured with five large knots, representing the five wounds of Christ as they later discovered. A simple black crucifix hung on a grey cord around the sister's neck, her head was encased in a white wimple running just below the neck and covered with a grey veil—the novices, they already knew, wore white veils. They'd seen them down the mortuary.

'Welcome to our Mother House,' the nun said in a young, musical voice, dropping a little curtsey to Tommy which quite threw him. Then she curtsied to Suzie and Emma as they crossed the threshold and entered the cool interior of the convent, into a hall with red tiles underfoot and three great Norman stone arches at the far end.

'Reverend Mother is expecting you.' The nun made a small gesture indicating they were to follow her through the right-hand archway and as they moved Suzie felt the depth of the silence, and caught the sweet smell of polish and incense. The odour of sanctity, she thought.

CHAPTER FOUR

Magnus's assessment of Mother Ursula seemed to be spot on. At first sight she appeared to be shrinking into nothingness, very old, and, if not totally decrepit, at least in the middle stages of physical ruin. Later they discovered that she was in fact almost ninety-seven, having been born in the August of 1847.

She sat on a high, leather-buttoned armchair that made her seem even smaller than she was in reality: an almost doll-like figure swallowed by the height of the chair back and arms.

A young nun, solemn but spry, told the Reverend Mother that the police had come to see her.

'A detective and two women detectives,' Tommy said, introducing himself, shaking her hand.

'Ah.' The old lady had a cultured voice, verging at times on a cackle. 'Another community, the police. Lady officers are not unlike nuns.'

Suzie stepped forward. Mother Ursula's hand felt like a dry leaf and she did not dare put any pressure into the grip. The old hand might crumble away, while the face looked like the face of an aged cat, scored with a criss-cross of lines, the eyes large and slow-blinking, milky, her nose near flattened into her face and below it the mouth thin and small, opening to show tiny, sharp teeth, all her own.

'Thank you for coming to see me,' the old lady said. 'I get few visitors from the world these days.'

Hold hard, thought Suzie, you're the Mother Superior: you should get lots of visitors. 'We have to talk with you, Mother Ursula,' she told her.

'Well, that's nice. That's nice. What are we to talk about?'

She's clueless, Suzie considered. Aged in faith, and with that age comes a broken mental cog, a slip in the brain mechanism. Shouldn't

36

really be in command of even a bunch of nuns.

Tommy said it was about the poor novices who had been killed. 'The flying bomb,' he explained.

'The flying bomb, yes. What a terrible weapon,' shaking her head. 'Sometimes I think this man Hitler is the devil incarnate. We should smite him, hip and thigh as Samson smote the Philistines. But we are, aren't we? In France now, at this moment, young men are dying. In Normandy. Let us reflect on that for a moment and say a prayer for those gallant soldiers.' She clasped her mottled, bony hands together, bowed her head and closed her eyes.

They had no option but to at least go through the motions of prayer, though Suzie did say a silent Our Father and a Hail Mary for the men fighting in and over Normandy.

A minute later, without warning Mother Ursula began speaking again. 'I was so alarmed when that flying bomb fell today, so close. When my dear mother was frightened she used to say, "I nearly jumped out of my skin." Well, I know the feeling for I almost jumped out of mine, what's left of it, when that thing went off. The angelus had just finished and I knew at once it was one of these newfangled bombs; it's not the same as the Blitz which was bad enough, this is different and worse. You hear that little engine and nobody knows when it will stop and send its dreadful cargo down to wipe out people in

37

what appears to be a random way. It's a little like a game we used to play as children: you stood in a circle and put a bottle in the middle and you'd spin it. When it stopped the neck would be pointing to someone who was deemed "out". You follow? But I was most concerned because the bomb was so close. You see there are more of us here at the moment . . .'

'Really?' Tommy was about to continue but Mother Ursula went steaming on.

'. . . It's holiday time, the summer, so sisters who spend term times at work in schools all over the country come back to this, the Mother House, for the summer. By the middle of August we're quite full up with few spaces left for visitors. We are a teaching order you see, Mr . . . ?'

'Livermore,' Tommy started again, 'and I . . .'

'Mr Livermore.' Mother Ursula did not hesitate for a second. 'Dear Canon Brooking who founded our Community of St Catherine of Siena in 1871 saw it as a way of fulfilling two requirements: first to make provision for a religious order for women who also had a vocation to teach; second, to provide a phalanx of devoted Christian teachers in a profession that was gradually being filled by men and women with no formal religious beliefs or inclinations. Oh, we were very much part of the Church Militant when we first marched

38

forth to do battle in the schools.'

'Yes, Reverend Mother, I . . .' But Tommy didn't stand a chance. Mother Ursula was giving them a little lecture and she wasn't about to curtail it.

'We have sisters serving in schools all over the country, you know. All over. Some become helpers in small parishes and so assist, part time, in local schools, others are resident in schools, and of course we have our own school, St Catherine's, Winsley, near Bath. Fully staffed by members of the community, with its own chaplain. Everything. And, of course, there is also our Mission in Africa—sixty sisters doing three years duty there all the time.'

At last she paused to take a breath and Tommy stepped in. 'Mother Ursula, the novices who were killed?'

'Yes?' vague, as though only dimly recalled.

'You saw the bodies, I understand. And you identified two of them.'

There was a long silence which, Suzie thought, you could hear it was so tangible, and somehow she didn't see the conflict between silence and sound. She was conscious of the room, the crucifix on the wall, the small bookcase with its rows of religious works. Above the books hung the sentimental Holman Hunt Victorian print *The Light of the World* that always jogged Suzie into thinking of the King's broadcast at the first Christmas of

39

the war, when he had quoted the words of the poet Minnie Haskins:

And I said to the man who stood at the gate of the year: 'Give me a light that I may tread safely into the unknown.'

And he replied:

'Go out into the darkness and put your hand into the hand of God. That shall be to you better than light and safer than a known way.'

Like so many people at that time, in the closing days of 1939, standing above the abyss of war, the words had given Suzie hope and a little courage.

The young nun stood behind Mother Ursula's chair and looked about to speak, lips parted. She had a lovely open face and Suzie wondered if sometimes being a nun was simply a retreat from the hardship of the world. She knew this wasn't always so, and a wise old priest had once explained to her the drive and devotion that was needed in a woman who put herself under discipline to a religious order, the firm grip of a life lived in prayer and to the glory of God. There was certainly no escape from reality in that.

'I saw the bodies, yes. And I recognised two of them, yes,' Mother Ursula finally said.

'Then could you name them for us, Mother?'

Again a silence stretching into the next world.

'No, my good man. No, I couldn't. I

40

recognised them. Two of them, but I could not tell you their names. They were novices. I really don't keep the names of all my sisters in my head. Sister Eunice, the Novice Mistress, will tell you who they are. I simply recognised them as novices preparing to enter the Community of St Catherine.'

Tommy seemed taken aback. 'But you are the Mother Superior.' He sounded lost and in need of help.

'No,' she smiled. 'No, I am the Mother Superior General which is something completely different.'

At last the younger sister spoke. 'In our order,' she began, 'the Mother Superior General is a titular position, usually given when a Mother Superior retires or becomes too old to carry the burden of leadership. The Reverend Mother Superior, Mother Rachel, is visiting our sister house in Farnborough today, with Sister Eunice. They should be back soon and they'll certainly do as you require. Make a formal identification.'

'And give us some details, Sister . . .?' Suzie began.

'My name is Sister Eve. Details of what?'

'Of who these dead sisters are; their background; their families.'

'As far as they are able, yes. Mother Superior'll provide all that.'

'I didn't recognise one of them,' Mother Ursula piped up. 'She seemed a tall girl, big

41

boned, but I don't recall seeing her before.'

'There has been a recent arrival,' Sister Eve told them. 'Three or four postulants came up from our little house in Farnborough. Postulants stay there for six months, or a year, before they go out into the world, or come here to serve the three year novitiate.' Her eyes flicked away as though she was reluctant to meet anyone else's eyes. Sliding away shyly, Suzie reckoned.

'Three and a half years before they enter the Order?' Tommy asked.

'Sometimes that doesn't prove to be enough time, Mr Livermore. Those who arrived today were to be Professed shortly: take their final vows. It's not all beer and skittles being a nun, you know.'

The remark took them by surprise. Tommy and Suzie spluttered, Emma coughed and Mother Ursula gave a low, growling laugh. 'Certainly it's not all beer and skittles,' she said. 'It's not living in a rose garden either. People find it difficult to understand how regulated our lives can be, especially when for part of the time we live in and out of the world: out there teaching, and keeping to our somewhat rigid lives of restraint.' She seemed to have thrown off her more uncertain, age-ridden persona. 'And people find it difficult to understand that we can have a sense of humour about the world and our faith.' Again a small laugh. 'Beer and skittles.'

Once more a pause, during which Tommy seemed lost for words; Suzie didn't want to jump the gun, and Emma remained silent because she was merely observing, holding a kind of watching brief—a change for her.

At last Tommy said, 'You say they'll return soon, Sister Rachel—Mother Rachel—and Sister Eunice?'

'Actually they're usually back by now.'

'Talking about laughter and faith,' Mother Ursula was off on her own again, 'I remember when some people were shocked at Father Brooking's changes at St James's: the use of vestments, incense, the ritual and practice of the services and sacraments. When I was in my teens I was a regular member of St James's congregation with my parents and brother and sisters. I went in one afternoon in summer, I recall. Just popped in to say a prayer, bit of peace and quiet. It was a still afternoon, and the coolness of the building struck me on entering. I remember that most vividly, going from the hot street into the cool calm of St James's. In those days there was an unpleasant little verger, name of Chickit. I shouldn't speak ill of him I know, but, well . . . he came up behind me and whispered, "You want to see something?" and pointed up towards the nave, under the tower. Father Brooking was seated by one of the big pillars on the south side of the transept, and a figure, I don't know if it was a man or woman, knelt beside him. The

43

awful Chickit whispered, "You see that? That's Confession." ' She gave another of her growling laughs. 'He was shocked and I think wanted to frighten me, because he said—and this is the amusing part—"It's getting more like the Roaming Catholics every day." The Roaming Catholics.' She repeated the line, diminishing the humour. They laughed politely and Tommy started to tell an off-colour ecclesiastical story concerning a canon and an actress. Suzie prepared to faint or do something equally extreme to cut off the punchline of the story, which had something to do with cannonballs, when the door swung open and a tall imposing nun carrying all before her strode in.

'Mother Rachel,' she announced. 'You are the police?' Her face round and florid, the voice crisp with drawling vowels, hand outstretched towards Tommy who said later that he felt as though he was being asked if he were the entire Metropolitan Police Force.

Mother Rachel's grip was so strong that Emma later declared she'd almost started to do the moves for an arm lock, and Suzie felt unsteady for a good thirty seconds, some of it due to the almost hypnotic quality of the nun's piercing brown eyes. Mother Rachel, they agreed, was a character with a capital K: every word and move larger than life, her voice a bellow, and her actions wide and overstated.

Behind her trailed a thin, sharp-featured

44

and unsmiling Sister Eunice, the Novice Mistress. For no particular reason she reminded Suzie of a hornet, and later Tommy consistently spoke of her as Sister Eunuch.

Both ladies were angry. Suzie, who had met angry nuns before, during her schooldays, reflected that she'd never seen nuns quite as angry as this pair. She physically flinched at their arrival.

CHAPTER FIVE

Mother Rachel made a sweeping gesture, indicating the police officers should follow her, sharply telling Mother Ursula and Sister Eve that she would see them later. That there was threat in the words and the promise of dire punishment was in no doubt. Sister Eunice strode after the police trio like a sheep dog herding lambs into a pen. Suzie felt distinctly uncomfortable.

Mother Rachel led them along the corridor, walking not with the gliding manner of a nun on wheels but with firm long strides, her heavy sandals clicking against the russet, polished tiles with a noise almost identical to those of the jackboots of Nazi officers you heard on the BBC, or as depicted in British Lion films.

At last she opened a door to her left leading into a large, comfortable room, dominated by a pinewood desk littered with documents, and positioned in front of two long, mullioned windows looking out onto a stretch of neatly mowed lawn. Cypresses flanked a path below them, leading to the ornate-looking chapel, gargoyles above the single door and a small spire—the one they had glimpsed from the other side of the wall, where the V-1 had landed.

The windows inside the Mother Superior's office were diamond leaded lights and they could see that the windows of the chapel, below, were intricate stained glass, high, reaching from almost the ground to the sloping roof. After the close blast of the V-1 explosion it was a wonder that the windows had remained intact.

Mother Rachel stood behind her desk, leaning forward, hands flat supporting her heaving body as she muttered and fought to control her breathing. Behind them Sister Eunice clucked, growled and also worked on her breath.

'Are you all right, Reverend Mother?' Suzie asked.

'No . . . No!' She said, taking gulps of air between the words. 'No! No! No! No I am *not* all right!'

Sister Eunice took a step towards the desk.

'I am sorry,' Mother Rachel was gradually gaining control. 'I do apologise. Anger is my besetting sin, and I fear good Sister Eunice feeds her anger on mine. I shall pay for this, it is sure, but I really can't understand the workings of my sisters' minds. Mother Ursula is an old lady now and Sister Eve is not the sharpest of young knives—in fact there are times when I think she is a total moron. But there are forty-five other sisters here in the convent at the moment. Nobody had the wit to telephone our house in Farnborough, our house of the Holy Family, to inform us of this tragedy. Saints alive, where are their heads?' she shouted. 'Where is their common sense? Sister Faith who, like Rhoda at the house of Mary the mother of John, is our gatekeeper, has even less intelligence. I could give up. They should all be scourged.' She brought the flat of her hand down upon the desktop making even Tommy wince.

'Calm yourself, Rachel,' Sister Eunice said in a voice as sharp as her nose and with a slight Northumberland inflection. Suzie heard, in her head, the good sister saying, 'why aye', the Geordie catchphrase, or 'calm yourself, hinnie'.

'You'll have one of your turns unless you calm down. Recite the rabbit song.' She didn't actually say 'pet' but it was implied. Mother Rachel began quietly and rhythmically to chant:
'Run rabbit, run rabbit, run, run, run.
Don't give the farmer his fun, fun, fun.
He'll get by, without his rabbit pie,

So run rabbit, run rabbit, run, run, run.'

As she spoke, so she started to relax, the flush left her face, her breathing became normal and she gently subsided into her chair.

When she next looked up at them, Mother Rachel was smiling broadly.

'Never fails,' she beamed. 'The old rabbit song does it every time. Thank you, Sister,' to Eunice who now sat in another chair as Rachel bade the police officers sit.

'We spent a good day today with the novices in Farnborough,' she began, 'and we came back here singing, merry as grigs on a mountain. We sang, "Immortal, Invisible, God Only Wise", then "Underneath the Arches"—another Flanagan and Allen song like the rabbit song—and the umbrella song. We're partial to Flanagan and Allen, Eunice and I. At the little party we have on Christmas afternoon we do a turn which includes Flanagan and Allen . . .'

'Yes,' Sister Eunice piped up, 'and we do a little skit as well: two Germans in a shelter in Berlin.' She coughed. 'Vot vos dot?'

'Dot vos a bomp,' Mother Rachel replied, and they both laughed.

'I shouldn't say it but we're the best on Christmas afternoons. Sister Agnes does her impression of an aged canon reciting "The Charge of the Light Brigade" '—she spoke in a sonorous, studied voice:

'Cannon to the right of them,

48

Cannon to the left of them,
Cannon in front of them
Volleyed and thunderéd.'

Then a little laugh, 'And Sister Cleo does her conjuring tricks. Sometimes the good fathers from St James's drop in and give us a few choruses of "Widdecombe Fair", and Sister Anne does a monologue after the style of that nice Joyce Grenfell, not as polished of course but she shows spirit, does a Sunday School teacher trying to explain the miracle of the loaves and fishes.' She chuckled, 'No, William it wasn't whale meat. There was no whale meat in those days. Yes, yes, Harriet, I know about Jonah in the whale. What I said was there was *no* whale meat.' And Eunice joined in the laughter.

Tommy tried to whip things back into order, 'Reverend Mother, you got back here, and . . . ?'

'Yes.' The Reverend Mother composed herself. 'We arrived back here to discover there had been a tragedy, with novices killed and in hospital. Sister Faith was in a terrible state. She hardly made sense. Pray, please tell us the facts, Inspector. I must now have the facts.'

'Detective Chief Superintendent,' Tommy corrected, jealous of his rank, and Mother Rachel spread her hands in apology. Then Tommy broke the news that two of her novices were dead, killed by a flying bomb, one was in

49

hospital, and there was another body. 'A male, dressed as a novice, with his throat cut.'

'A man? Dressed as a . . .? As a novice? A man? And his throat cut? That's very unusual in a religious house.'

'I'm afraid so, Mother, yes.'

'Right,' thought Suzie, 'dead unusual in a religious house.'

'Someone dressed in drag, eh?' Mother Rachel said in her loudest voice, again taking them by surprise. 'Oh my dear Superintendent, we know all the words, and that's what they are, only words—though perish the thought if people ever become so degraded to use the worst of them in ordinary speech.'

'Amen to that,' Sister Eunice said solemnly, making the sign of the cross.

'What do you wish us to do?' Mother Rachel, serious now.

'We would like you to formally identify the bodies,' Tommy dropped his voice. 'Also I'd like you to look at the male corpse and tell us if you recognise him. Are any men allowed into the convent?'

'Oh, yes. Father Sheldon, the vicar of St James's, and his three curates, Fathers Carefull, Judge and Evans. Good priests all of them. In the constitution the good Canon Brooking laid down for us all those years ago, he made it the specific job of the priests of St James's, to minister to us. This saves much trouble.'

50

'Anybody else, apart from the clergy?'

'We have a gardener, Mr Cobbs, and he usually has two young men to assist him. They don't stay long these days as they are quickly called up to serve in the Forces, so we have had a member of the Land Army—a nice cheery girl called Topsy—posted to us . . . a land girl. I am told she spends a lot of her spare time at the palais de danse and in the Grove public house, but what is one to do? Mr Cobbs made a remark about her giving a new meaning to back to the land.' She paused, sighing. 'I expect all our lay staff to come to the sung mass on Sunday and they mostly do.'

'We grow all our own vegetables, and keep chickens also,' Sister Eunice told them, apparently harking back to Mr Cobb and his team.

'We also have a general odd-job man, Mr Taylor, who gets in specialists if we need help.'

'Like in that terrible winter of 1939/40,' Eunice added. 'We had an awful time with the water pipes and cisterns being frozen. Dear Mr Taylor, he worked positive miracles.'

'Of course you'd recognise any of these gentlemen?'

'But of course. We know them well.'

'Then I think we should take both of you down to the hospital, and the mortuary, so you can view the bodies. Then, perhaps, we could come back here and you may be able to give us some details. Parents, addresses, that kind of thing.'

'Yes.' A cloud seemed to cross Mother Rachel's face. 'We shall, of course, have to inform the unfortunate victims' families. I do so hate that kind of thing.'

'I think you can probably leave that to us,' Tommy told her, and the Mother Superior nodded, looking relieved.

As she stood up Tommy asked, 'And they are the only men who come into the convent: Mr Cobb, Mr Taylor, and the clergy?'

Mother Rachel sat down again. 'No, there are odd priests of course. Some of them very odd. We have people who come to take retreats—times of devotion and meditation. And once a month we have a different preacher of a Sunday. Some good . . . some . . . well, last month we had an RAF padre. He was not a success; announced that his sermon was "Shooting a line for God". Not the best of starts.' She swallowed hard. 'Alas, he continued to talk about a Christian death being a wizard prang for God. I really cannot stand slangy people. The way that one talked we'd be using slang in the responses—"The Lord be with you."—"Wizard,"' she intoned.

It quickly became clear that Tommy was in no hurry to move the good sisters down to the hospital to identify the bodies. Here he was, relaxed, leaning back in his chair, one hand hanging loosely to the side as though dangling

52

in river water from a punt: his head lazy against the chair back, eyes fixed benignly on Mother Rachel almost willing her to go on talking.

Suzie knew that look: it was Tommy's listening and watching pose in which he dragged information from interviewees by force of charm and a ready ear. She remained still and quiet, noting that Emma Penticost had stationed herself by the door, standing like a statue apart from her eyes which flicked constantly from the two nuns to the window and beyond.

Mother Rachel talked about the Community of St Catherine of Siena, in particular the daily routine of those nuns who remained in the Mother House here in Silverhurst Road: the rising bell at five-thirty each morning; mass at six then the day studded with those little services known as the divine office—matins, terce, sext, nones, lauds and compline—serving as a discipline of prayer, sung at their appointed hours in the chapel or, for the nuns 'in the field' as Mother Rachel put it, recited in a convenient church or quiet place. 'We think of it as a great wheel of prayer,' she said. 'And to us nothing is more important than worshipping God in a strict and regular manner. It is our duty as a religious order. Difficult for men and women out in the world to understand. So often people regard prayer as a parroting of words learnt in childhood.'

To Suzie's surprise Tommy asked if Shakespeare hadn't had something to say about that in *Hamlet*. And Mother Rachel told him, yes, Claudius at prayer when Hamlet wanted to kill him. She even quoted it:

' "My words fly up, my thoughts remain below: Words without thoughts never to heaven go." '

'You know your Shakespeare, Reverend Mother.'

'I know why Hamlet didn't kill Claudius when he was at his prayers.'

'Why?'

She laughed, gruff and throaty. 'Because Shakespeare was a good playwright and killing Claudius would've cost him the rest of the play. Ended it all too soon.'

Tommy asked Mother Rachel if it was usual for the novices to be in their cells at that time of day. 'Noon, couple of minutes either way when the V-1 struck?'

Suzie remembered looking at her watch. Three minutes past twelve noon exactly. This must have been the one they heard in Upper St Martin's Lane.

'Absolutely normal. All the sisters return to their cells at noon when they're here in the convent. They say the Angelus and then spend half an hour in quiet prayer and contemplation, before going to the refectory for what you would call lunch at half past

54

twelve. We have a strict routine of work and prayer: the singing of the daily office, which I've told you is a set of punctuation marks in our days. In the morning sisters usually work on their special subjects. Those who teach must also learn. It is part of our duty. In the afternoon we carry out set tasks, helping Mr Cobbs and his team in the gardens, cleaning individual cells, keeping the passages and corridors clean, tidy and polished. Four sisters are detailed each week as sacristans, and of course there is much to do in the way of mending, keeping the vestments in good order. And naturally there is cooking. We have many good cooks here. It is sometimes difficult to avoid the sin of gluttony. Even now, with the rationing.' She laughed. 'You and your people must eat with us sometime, some evening perhaps,' she said, and Tommy Livermore blanched at the thought of the Reserve Squad sitting down to eat with platoons of nuns.

After about an hour's conversation a bell began to toll deep within the building.

'A call to prayer?' Tommy asked.

'Rather a call to the inner woman,' Mother Rachel smiled. 'That is the call to the refectory. We have our evening meal at seven.'

'Then you must go, Reverend Mother, and we'll wait until you've eaten, then go with you to identify the bodies.'

'Speak for yourself,' Suzie thought, 'I'm bloody famished,' and was immediately aware of a twinge of guilt at having thought a swear word, so ingrained was her school training. In the presence of nuns, Suzie was returned to near child-like innocence and discipline.

'I shall do without my evening meal,' Mother Rachel said. 'It is a good punishment for my earlier unbridled loss of temper. Sister Eunice must follow her conscience, for . . .'

'I ate a hearty midday meal at our Farnborough house, Mother,' the Novice Mistress muttered, and Suzie recalled the passing-out parade at Hendon when the day's visiting bigwig had told her unit to stand easy and carry on smoking. From the rear Sergeant Mullet, their course sergeant, had murmured, 'That doesn't apply to you.'

'Then, shall we now go down and you can identify the bodies?' Tommy got to his feet again and gave the nod to Emma who opened the door to reveal Ron Worrall and Shirley Cox waiting outside.

Mother Rachel said something about her convent crawling with police officers and Tommy introduced Ron and Shirley.

Ron carried a thick cellophane bag containing a knife: blood smearing the inside of the bag. 'Success?' Tommy raised his eyebrows.

'It was in the cell where the body was found,' Ron Worrall told him.

It was a sharp, nine-inch, straight blade with a bone handle. 'Possibly a kitchen implement,'

56

Tommy said and asked if the kitchens could be checked for a missing knife.

Mother Rachel assured him that it would be a priority, then together they left for the hospital.

CHAPTER SIX

Suzie and Tommy did not get back to Upper St Martin's Lane until after eleven that night. Brian drove the two nuns to the hospital, together with Suzie and Emma, leaving Ron and Shirley to talk to a pair of frightened-looking novices in the kitchen, and rake through the knives. Tommy stood watching, not taking part, legs astride and hands clasped behind his back: an invigilator. Nothing was missing and Tommy said they would have to check with ironmongers and places where knives were sold locally.

The nuns were restrained and calm when they viewed the bodies. Suzie was impressed by their total faith in the two novices now being at peace with God. She had even asked them about their conception of the afterlife. 'Just "being",' Sister Eunice said. 'Just being in a sea of warmth and love, surrounded by those you have known and loved during your time here.'

Mother Rachel was more vivid. 'Oh, I think

it will be an eternal funfair,' she grinned. 'Without the vulgarity, of course.' Then she went solemn and said, 'I shall have to speak to the sisters tonight. Possibly later, before Compline. They'll need to be told. That's only fair.'

'Won't they know already?' Suzie asked.

'You mean from the other novices who were in their cells when the flying bomb came down?'

'Yes.'

'Possibly. They do chatter so. Yes, it'll be round the convent like wildfire.'

'Or holy fire,' Tommy, almost smirking. Then, 'But they won't know about the male? The murdered male.'

'The male in sheep's clothing? No. No, of course they won't know. Unless one of them did it and makes a deliberate mistake. That Inspector Hornleigh in *Monday Night at Eight* seems to think they *all* make mistakes.'

For a moment they were again surprised by Mother Rachel's knowledge of BBC wireless entertainment programmes. *Inspector Hornleigh Investigates* was a regular feature in the *Monday Night at Eight* programme in which the fictional detective challenged listeners to spot the error made by the criminal.

'Ah,' the Reverend Mother explained, 'we sometimes listen to *Monday Night at Eight* during our weekly period of general association and leisure which usually falls on a

Monday evening.'

Tommy nodded and she added, 'Between eight and nine. You must consider us very worldly but some of the sisters, out in the world, teaching in schools, have to listen to that dreadful Tommy Handley.'

'Have to?'

'They wouldn't know what the children are talking about if they didn't. Tommy Handley is pretty much obligatory.'

Back in the Reverend Mother's office, Sister Eunice came in with two slim files. 'Here we are. Novice Bridget Mary and Novice Mary Theresa. Both would have taken their vows—be Professed, as we say—in a couple of weeks. Good, intelligent women. I had high hopes for them. They both came to us in 1940, that dreadful summer. They've only just come here from our house of the Holy Family, in Farnborough. In fact Mother Rachel and I were there to see them leave, this morning.'

Man knoweth not the day, nor the hour, or something like that, Suzie thought. It all seemed most poignant.

'Their families?' Tommy asked.

'Bridget Mary is easy. Her father's vicar of St Martin's near Bedford Park. Her name in the world was Joan May Harding. Father Harding was a true friend of our community, came over every couple of years or so to take a Lent retreat for the sisters who were here in the convent for Lent and Easter.'

59

Eunice took a deep breath, as if to prepare herself. 'Novice Theresa is a different matter. More difficult. She came from the village of Churchbridge, on the Severn River, six miles or so from Gloucester, out towards Tewksbury. In the world her name was Winifred Audrey Lees-Duncan. Only daughter of John Lees-Duncan, landowner, so-called gentleman farmer, though he spends more time in big country houses and gambling in his London club, I'm told—or was when I last heard. Held an honorary rank of colonel with some half-baked military outfit during the '14–'18 show.' She stopped with a guilty look over her spectacles and cleared her throat.

'Home is The Manor, Churchbridge, Gloucestershire. Her mother is Maude Lees-Duncan whose occupation appears to be riding and doing good works locally. Winnie—Novice Theresa—had two brothers, one of whom lives abroad, somewhere. In Mexico I think, Michael Lees-Duncan. The other—Gerald—last heard of somewhere in Scotland. That's how things stood in 1940 anyway.'

'Ages?' Tommy asked.

'The brothers?'

He nodded.

'Both in their mid- to late twenties.'

'Not serving King and country, then?'

'Not when I last heard, but that was four years ago.' Sister Eunice's tone turned cold, distant. 'Novice Theresa came to us against

60

the wishes of her parents. In a very real sense she has been cut off from her family who are against all forms of organised religion. Proselytising atheists, I believe. Very difficult people. When Theresa came to us she brought a legal letter of instruction forbidding us or her to be in touch with them ever again.' She flourished the letter, handing it over to Tommy who quickly read it and asked if he could hang on to it. 'Don't worry.' He gave them his terrible smile. 'WDI Mountford has a broad back. She'll take care of matters in Gloucestershire. We're the police so this bit of legal shenanigans doesn't apply to us.'

Suzie's heart sank.

They went through the question of the man who had been dressed as a novice, but neither of the nuns could add anything.

'Never seen him before.' The Novice Mistress shook her head. 'And I think I would have remembered that face if he had come into the convent disguised as a novice. It's true that we had three new novices who only arrived here today, but both Mother Rachel and I have known them for a long time as postulants at Farnborough: at our House of the Holy Family. In fact, they only came here, to the Mother House, yesterday. We saw them leave our Farnborough House after breakfast this very morning.'

'So you can't possibly say how he got into the convent, this man?'

They shook their heads, sadly it seemed, and Tommy said that this meant they, the police, would have to spend a lot of time here in Silverhurst Road. 'We're going to be forced to question every lady who was here this morning. Every sister and every novice, plus whatever other staff were around—your gardening people for instance.'

'They're seldom here on a Sunday,' Mother Rachel told them. 'But we'll ask, of course. Is there anything else we should do?'

Tommy said they should try to stay within the bounds of the convent for a few days. 'We'll probably be back on Tuesday or Wednesday. You'll also want the bodies for burial, so we'll let you know when they are released from the coroner.'

They tied up some loose ends and Mother Rachel said it was time for her to be in chapel. 'Compline,' she explained, 'during which I shall make these tragic events known to my sisters.'

Tommy told her they'd rather she didn't mention the male novice, and she said there were bound to be questions.

'Then you must be like the three wise monkeys,' Tommy said.

Mother Rachel moved her hands over her ears, then her eyes and finally her mouth, ending by giving him a beatific smile.

'Perky lot, those nuns,' Tommy said as they drove back into central London.

Suzie grunted. In her schooldays she'd had a lot of truck with nuns. 'Personally,' she told him, 'I think they're very tough birds. Tough, sneaky and willing to mislead the police if it's a question of defending their community against scandal.'

'And who can blame them?' Tommy once more smiled his terrible smile.

*   *   *

Since D-Day and the invasion of Europe, railway travel had become a little easier. A huge amount of materiel and thousands of men had moved from England onto the Continent and, while there were still large numbers of troops stationed in the south and around the major airfields occupied by the RAF and US 8th Army Air Force, the major railway companies were not under the stress that had weighed on them earlier in the war.

Suzie travelled towards Gloucester from Paddington, sitting back in a first-class carriage that was her right as an officer. Two WAAF officers and a male civilian shared the carriage and Suzie, who felt depressed and nervous at the job she was called to do, stared blankly at the passing scenery.

The sun shone and the countryside looked its summer best as they whistled and chugged on their way, stopping at Reading and Kemble, Stroud and Stonehouse, heading towards

Gloucester. The views were so peaceful that it was hard to imagine the hell going on across the Channel as the military pushed their way inland from Normandy.

She watched a group of children clustered round the gate of a field giving V-signs at the train, the wrong way, enjoying every minute of the vulgarity. Tommy had once told her that when the Prime Minister first used his trademark sign they'd had to explain to him that he would have to make sure his palm faced outwards. Apparently he'd laughed his head off when the crudity of the two-fingered movement became clear to him.

Suzie remembered what a naval officer had told her about sailing through the Suez Canal: about the groups of little Egyptian boys who clustered around exposing themselves to the ships. 'Flashing us like cheerio, both front and rear,' he had said. 'Didn't know whether you liked bananas or peaches by the time they'd finished.' Suzie had been revolted by the thought. And by the young officer. 'You're a bit of a prude,' he had said, so she went silent on him, thinking, yes, she probably was a bit prudish and what was wrong with that?

At Gloucester there was a police car with a sergeant driver waiting for her, arranged by Tommy, and she was whisked out of the city along pleasant roads, through cathedral arches of trees in full leaf and a countryside that seemed unbelievably placid.

64

The driver was a detective sergeant who introduced himself in a less than jovial manner. 'Mills,' he told her in a flat mournful voice. 'DS Mills.' Yes, Suzie thought, Dark Satanic Mills, then was worried, wondering if she had said it out loud.

Three times she tried to engage DS Mills in conversation, but he remained silent, knew nothing of the Lees-Duncans or the village of Churchbridge. 'I came from Berkshire originally,' he said in a sudden shower of words. 'Ask me about Berkshire and I can tell you anything.' But he clammed up once more when Suzie greeted this information with delight, saying that she came from Berkshire also. Newbury.

'Never had cause to visit Newbury,' the driver said as they turned into a drive on the outskirts of Churchbridge village and glimpsed a magnificent Queen Anne house, large, imposing, complete with outbuildings and stables.

Even the gravel under the tyres was deep, the crunch sounding expensive, while the house was impressive, the frontage thick with Virginia creeper. Look wonderful in the autumn, she thought, her imagination seeing the layers of creeper turning into flaming blood red.

Like a jigsaw puzzle picture or the top of a box of pre-war chocolates: the house itself huge, done in a weathered red brick with east

65

and west wings leading off from the main house and some forty-odd windows visible along the front elevation, a row of dormers sprouting from the roof.

A tail-coated elderly butler opened the door to her—it was that kind of house—and was unimpressed when Suzie showed him her warrant card. He would, he said, see if Mr Lees-Duncan was at home, and left her in the large hall that smelt of money, dog and leather. After a few minutes the butler returned (Suzie thought of him as 'Old Scrotum, the wrinkled retainer', one of Tommy's favourite terms for faithful servants) and showed her into a large and quite lovely drawing room. A bay window looked out onto a striped lawn that had been manicured to within an inch of its life, and a rose garden where a young woman worked, in the uniform of her class, a long wide-skirted dress, floppy hat, gloves and a trug. The furnishings of the room were slightly turn of the century, big and plushy; oil paintings of ancestors and horses hung on the walls, there were flowers in large cut-glass vases, and a big blue and white jug full of gladioli stood in a deep fireplace.

John Lees-Duncan was a tall man oozing charm and dressed in worn tailored tweeds. He was fine-looking, in his sixties, sixty-five-ish she reckoned, his face tanned, fit, and with twinkling, mocking grey eyes.

'Well?' he smiled, sticking out a hand.

'You're not from the Gloucester constabulary are you? See your warrant card?' She held up the card, making sure he didn't reach out for it. 'You auxiliary?' he asked, pleasant yet conscious of his own commanding presence. His handshake was dry and firm and Suzie thought how well he'd get on with Tommy.

'I think, sir, you'd best sit down,' she said, lowering her voice.

'Don't think I'll have people telling me to sit down in me own house.' Still pleasant, the smile almost bewitching, but the eyes hard as rock and bleak as a winter sea. 'Look, whatever you've come to say, out with it. Don't suppose you've got all day any more than I have.'

If you're going to be like that, she thought, then here goes. 'You are John Lees-Duncan?'

'Absolutely.'

'Father of Winifred Audrey Lees-Duncan?'

'Yes,' count of four, 'I suppose.'

'Then I have some unpleasant news for you, sir. Your daughter was killed during a flying bomb attack in London yesterday, sir. I'm very sorry.' That's what they always advised you to say. That you were sorry.

For a moment, John Lees-Duncan stood with his mouth open. Then his face crinkled and he began to laugh.

'Winnie's dead, is she?'

'She is, sir. The Convent of St Catherine of Siena received a direct hit.'

'And she was in this convent, was she?'

'She was, sir. A novice.'

He lifted a hand, his forefinger pointing out of the window. 'Then who the hell's that, out there cutting me roses?' he asked.

CHAPTER SEVEN

She was tall and slender with short, unassisted, old gold hair in a pageboy bob, no fringe, Winifred Lees-Duncan. Suzie thought Tommy would certainly like her if only for the thighs which moved almost salaciously against the thin material of her long, predominantly blue dress. Maybe he'd like the accent as well. Very county: yah, yah.

'You'd have adored her,' she told him on the telephone. 'Kind of subservient blonde fizzer with, I suspect, a delayed timer and a quick-release mechanism. You'd be over the moon for her. She's a WAAF Flight Officer, or whatever they call them. You'd be shot down in flames as the Brylcreem boys have it.'

'Nonsense,' he said. 'You do talk a lot of twaddle, heart,' rather liking the idea of her thinking he was no end of a dog with women.

'She has a pet name as well. Nobody calls her Winifred or Winnie . . .'

'I bet they call her Wonky. Wonky Lees-Duncan . . .' School thing. Old Wonky

68

Lees-Duncan of the Upper Fourth. Good on the lax field, eh.'

'As a child she couldn't say Winnie. She called herself Wiltow—you know kids—in time it became Willow. That's what everyone calls her—Willow.'

'As in "a willow grows aslant a brook"?' Tommy asked.

Suzie tried to think of something cheeky to top the Shakespeare. Perhaps, 'On a tree by a river a little Tom-Tit sang Willow, tit-willow, tit-willow,'—Gilbert and Sullivan. Decided against it: Tommy would only get vulgar.

She had been talking to Tommy on the telephone, a trunk call from Sheffield— murder of Mrs Doris Butler—because when she got back to Upper St Martin's Lane there was a note:

Sorry, heart, the Sheffield case blew up again and they need the brains there, on the spot, so I'm taking Ron and Laura. It appears that the late Mrs Butler is lamented by three, possibly five, swains. A situation that poses a problem or four. So, you're in charge of the Convent Mystery, as Fleet Street will undoubtedly call it—male nun who never was, kind of thing. Ring me. Love for ever and a day, Tommy. Then a little row of Xs indicating kisses: uncharacteristic for Tommy Livermore. Then a PS: *Emma, like the poor, is of course still with me and Sheffield, so important to our war effort as the steel capital of Great Britain, is just as it was—dirty, smoky and*

69

dingy from the factory chimneys and the steel works.

*   *   *

So she rang Sheffield nick and was told that Detective Chief Superintendent Livermore was having dinner with Detective Chief Superintendent Berry, Sheffield CID. Emma Penticost was there, though, said the chief was staying at The Royal Victoria, where they'd all stayed at the start of the Doris Butler murder case a few weeks ago. 'He's OK, ma'am, and I'll see that he stays OK,' she told Suzie who grunted and put down the phone.

She remembered the Blitz humour of that stay at The Royal Victoria—'Glad you didn't try Marples Hotel,' the porter said. 'They've got no rooms at all.' Later they found that Marples—in the city centre—had received a direct hit in December 1940, killing over sixty people: Sheffield's worst air raid incident so far.

She rang The Royal Victoria and left a message asking Tommy to telephone as soon as he got in. She suspected the receptionist she left the message with was the snooty one with the snub nose and superior manner: the one who had been unpleasant and condescending when Suzie and the rest of the Reserve Squad stayed there: the one Tommy seemed to like: all over her with, 'Oh, Miss Hunter this, and

70

Miss Hunter that.' Her name was Christine Hunter and Tommy started calling her 'Our Chrissie' which hadn't gone down well with Suzie.

While she waited for Tommy to phone she wandered around the flat, hated being there alone, loathed it ever since the psychotic, murderous Golly Goldfinch had jumped her in the bathroom during that terrible time at the end of 1940. She hated being alone there now, just not used to it: twitchy, moving through the rooms, mind teeming with the horrid memories, touching things to calm her, the locks on the doors, Tommy's Harris tweed jacket with the big leather buttons—she buried her face in it and inhaled, getting the scent of him, the soap and his tobacco—picked up his ties one by one, old school, police college, a blue with white polka dots, red with the same and a splendid silk creation by Sulka; then the pistol they kept, illegally, in the drawer of the bedside table, checking the mechanism, letting the magazine drop out of the butt, then slamming it home again, making certain there was one up the spout.

In the largest room, at the front, looking over the street, Tommy had hung a painting over the fireplace. He'd brought it up from Kingscote: a copy, Canaletto, *Venice, The Grand Canal*, a big canvas that she'd have sworn was an original, but he'd never have let on, any more than he'd ever call the artist by

71

his proper name. 'Ah, old Cannelloni,' he'd say, 'good enough to eat.' That was Tommy: sound, tough copper and schoolboy. She smiled, getting his measure again. Getting it at last.

She was in the front room—the drawing room as her mother called it—looking down on Upper St Martin's Lane, when the telephone rang and she lunged for it, almost tripping over. But it was James asking if she'd do him a favour. 'Not today, Suze, but sometime next week.'

She told him to hurry up because she was expecting Tommy to ring.

'Thing is Suze, that Maren. Emily. One that drove me up.'

'Oh, yes?' Well done, Jim. Hormones raging, I'll bet.

'Well, we've got a kind of tentative date. Been talking to her on the blower.'

'She's an OR.' Meaning other rank, meaning officers keep your hands off.

'Commandos don't bother about things like that.' A bit lofty and full of himself. 'I want you to cover for me if necessary: back me up with the ma if I say I'm in London for a medical appointment or something. Actually I do have to go back to the hospital soon so it might not be needed.'

She told him of course she would back him up, tickled that her little brother was showing interest in young women. In truth she found it amusing: 'Old Jim,' she thought. 'You can't get into much trouble, seeing as how you're a cripple.' Then she asked how their mother was.

'Picking fruit. Bottling it. Jams and pickles. All that.'

'Enjoying having you home?'

'Think I'm a buffer between her and the GM.' GM for Galloping Major.

'And the children?' Her sister's kids, Charlotte's children, Lucy and Ben. Ben, who could not speak and could not hear, locked into his own world, in his head.

'They're great. Ben can do a lot of signing now. Seems to know who I am.'

As they said goodbye, Suzie told him, 'Watch your back, Jim.' One of Tommy's favourite warnings.

'Not my back I'm worried about. Not with Maren Emily Styles,' Jim closed the connection, Suzie put down the receiver and the phone rang immediately, Tommy breathing in her ear. 'Who you been talking to, heart?' Smile in his voice.

'My brother. Getting the hots for that Maren who drove him over on Sunday.' She started to tell him about the goings on at Churchbridge, Winifred Lees-Duncan not being the body.

'You're absolutely certain, heart?'

'That Winnie Lees-Duncan's alive? One hundred and fifty per cent. Absolutely pukka

73

gen. There's no doubt.'

'Then who's the nun, heart?'

'Someone who knows the Lees-Duncan family that's for sure, though I don't trust the father: John Lees-Duncan, gentleman farmer.'

'OK. Sum him up, heart.'

'Cold, uncompromising, arrogant. You're made for one another.'

'Well, tough 'cos I ain't coming back.'

'Tommy,' just this side of pleading.

'No can do, heart. They need me here, we're up to five runners now and I fancy myself as an interrogator. You can do the job. I mean you're so good with nuns. Know 'em like the back of your whatsit. Brought up with 'em and all that. Sat at their feet, what?' Tommy the bluff, pleasant cove who got on with everybody.

'How's Chrissie?' Suzie asked.

'Chrissie?' Tommy pondered, as though trying to match the name with a face.

'Yes, Tom. Chrissie Hunter, receptionist, long legs, snub nose, "Coming, Mr Livermore."' Doing a passable imitation of Jack Benny's rasp-voiced retainer, Rochester: now a favourite of the Jack Benny radio show, a hit on the BBC since the US troops had arrived in the UK. Rochester's favourite cry was, 'Comin', Mr Benny.'

'Oh, yes. Chrissie,' kind of savouring the name. 'Yes, I remember. I think she's left here. Haven't seen her, heart. Now, the nuns . . .'

'Tell me what to do, Tom.'

'See the nuns, that Mother Rachel's a good un. See her and make sure they've got a pretty picture of La Winnie in the flesh as it were. Then go back to the gallant John Lees-Duncan and give him a look-see. Find out if he recognises her. Show it around a bit.'

'You ring him first, Tommy? Please. I need him brought down a peg or three before I see him again. Lean on him and tell him he's got to cooperate.'

'I'll get the Assistant Deputy Commissioner to do it . . .'

'Super.' And perhaps, she asked, he could get someone in Gloucester to mark Lees-Duncan's card as well.

'If he's so unpleasant . . .'

'It's probably me.'

'Check him out with CRO, and ask the Branch just to be on the safe side. Talk to Woolly.' Woolly was Woolly Bear, Superintendent Basil Bear, the 2i/c of Special Branch, an old chum of Tommy's. ('School together, heart. Used to share a study back in the dark ages.')

'And don't forget you've got to see the parson, whatname, Harding, father of Joan, Novice Bridget, isn't it? Mother Rachel's done the dirty work—broken the news—but we'll have to follow up.'

'OK. But what if they haven't got a photo of Winnie, or the one purporting to be Winnie?'

75

'Nip down the mortuary and take a photo. Nothing difficult about that. We do it all the time. Open the corpse's eyes and put a lot of shine on the face to light the eyes, give them some life. Does the trick. Get it nice and grainy. Nobody'll know the difference.'

'I can't do all this by myself, Tommy. I need some help.'

'Stop whining, woman. Take Dennis, he's free.' He chortled at his watery joke. Dennis Free was free. 'Just do it, old heart. You're always grumbling about not being trusted with a case of your own. Well, now you've got a case of your own. Go to. Take Dennis and Shirley and do it. Dennis knows how to take pretty pics: he'll do it.' Pause, count of three. 'And while he's at it he can take a picture of the other corpse, the bloke. Give them a flash of that an' all.'

Silence for a moment, then—'Second thoughts, heart, have your pal Magnus get his tame photographer to do it. Owes you a favour, eh?'

'Piece of cake,' she said, up to her knees in the irony, and hung up on him wondering if he was making a fuss of Christine Hunter and fuming at the idea of Magnus being an old pal.

She rang Pip Magnus at the Silverhurst Road nick and got the runaround so she used Tommy's name and rank so the CID Department finally patched her through. Yes, of course he'd do that. With the girls—his word—the damage was all off the faces and they could hide the vivid extra mouth the bloke had developed where his throat had been cut. 'Nothing to it at all, guv. When d'you want the prints?'

'Yesterday but first thing tomorrow'll do.'

'You want them delivered to the Yard?'

'I'll send one of my boys in for them. Coming down your way tomorrow anyway, Pip,' pause, 'and Pip?'

'Yes, guv.'

'Don't publish in the local gossip column or I might just reciprocate with some jolly stories of your time at Camford with that old lag Harvey.'

'Right, guv.' No shame.

Tony Harvey, one-time detective inspector, now doing an unpleasant stretch in the Scrubs. A copper who was bent as a bradawl, and had been caught bang to rights, in spades.

*   *   *

In room thirty-six of The Royal Victoria Hotel, hard by Sheffield's Victoria Railway Station, Tommy Livermore stretched and thought, for a second, how nice it would be to get out of his clothes and settle down in bed. No chance of that. His old acquaintance 'Razzy' Berry, head of Sheffield's CID—amazing how the old-boy network oiled everything official—waited for him downstairs. Over at the nick they had two men helping with their inquiries into Doris Butler's death: Kenneth Craig and Pete Hill, both close friends of the late Mrs Butler. Close friends and possible murderers. Could be either of them.

For a moment, Tommy had a picture, vivid in his head, of Doris Butler lying spreadeagled in her little kitchen with her straw-coloured hair matted dark red and brown, and her head twisted at an unnatural angle. On the small dresser there was an apple with one bite taken from it, the flesh in the bite starting to brown, a packet of Bisto and another of powdered egg nearby.

Tommy Livermore had a golden rule with murder investigations: always get close to the victim and try to forget his or her faults. Doris Butler (née Haynes) had been silly: silly to have got herself married in 1938 at barely seventeen years of age; silly to allow her instincts to remain out of control; silly to encourage her men friends to disregard her marital status; silly to continue seeing other men in 1940 when her husband, Roger Butler—later Corporal Butler of 1st Hampshires (only in the Army could a lad from Sheffield find himself in the 1st Hampshires)—went off to war to be killed four years later on D+2 when his head was neatly removed by a passing shell fired from a German tank. Doris by then was already dead, battered to death in her kitchen by, Tommy

78

was certain, one of her many other lovers. She was, as Ron Worrall succinctly put it, 'cock happy' a term with which Tommy wholeheartedly agreed.

It had been Ron who had first alerted Tommy to the area of half a dozen beech trees and undergrowth just outside the Butler's little garden, on the edge of the scrubby meadow— Blue Fields as it was erroneously called. The trees afforded an excellent view of the house, and in its early June foliage the tiny oasis provided good cover that had obviously been used well by some watcher. The ground was trampled and scuffed, there was a selection of cigarette butts trodden into the earth (they counted fifteen in all) and the bark of one of the beeches had been picked off like somebody nervously picking a scab from a grazed knee. When he stood in this natural hide, Tommy saw that the bark would have been almost level with an average man's waist. He pictured a faceless person standing, silent and unmoving with murder in his heart, fingers scratching at the crusty bark.

Doris would have told this shadowy lover, 'Don't be silly. He never touches me. Might not even be married.' And the man would watch as Doris and Roger chased each other round the house and, maybe in this warmer weather, even leave the bedroom window open at night so that the observer could hear the sounds of the marital sport and so be driven into a frenzy of jealousy. Frenzy was the right word. Tommy had seen the results of sexual jealousy many times. Sex was a mainspring of murder. Many a nice young man or woman had been led fatally astray by sex which had the power to drop a bomb of madness into the brain.

On their first visit to the little semi-detached house in Bluefields Road, number 65, Suzie had done the door to door with Dennis Free and Shirley Cox, turning up a file full of rumours, hints and innuendoes: 'No better than she ought to have been,' was the common thread. 'Had a number of men friends—mind you I'm not accusing her of anything wrong,' cropped up a lot, and everyone said they, 'didn't really know her, Doris. Not really. Kept herself to herself.' She never went down the Star and Garter, the pub at the end of Bluefields Road where the Butlers had lived since their marriage in '38: the fields almost devoid of grass, wasted, like a burnt piece of desert, blackened and ravaged by the railway that passed by on its way to London, and on some days slick with the smoke from the steel works.

Even the next-door neighbour, Phyllis Carter, said she hardly ever saw Doris, but she had once successfully borrowed two chairs from her, the night her husband, Martin—a wopag with the Fleet Air Arm, currently in HMS *Formidable*—had been home on leave

80

and they'd had a bit of a knees-up. 'I arsked her to come and join us, but she never took no notice.' When Suzie had looked puzzled she told her that a wopag (pronounced Wop. A.G.) was a Wireless Operator Air Gunner. 'Brave buggers them wopags.'

Tommy, in room thirty-six of The Royal Victoria Hotel, glanced in the mirror, straightened his tie and put on what Suzie called his charming face. He was ready to go out to work in the interrogation rooms down the nick. Charm he considered was half the battle. Charm beat badgering, hectoring and brutality hands down. Mind you, Tommy believed that in every charming man there was an intransigent bastard crying to get out. No wonder the newspapers of Fleet Street called him Dandy Tom.

Yet all in all, at that moment, tired and about to face a possible killer, Tommy would have given a great deal to be with Suzie Mountford, though he'd never let her know.

*   *   *

In the nick, Pete Hill was what they called medium height, late thirties, running to fat with a sulky face and shifty eyes. Ron and Laura Cotter were already with him in an interview room reeking of uneasy silence. Big elegant Ron Worrall with his Roman coin cufflinks and the highly polished brogues

81

which he wore like a badge of office, and little Laura, perfectly built with a penchant for the poems of A E Housman, her thoughts shaped to Housman's thoughts—

Mine were of trouble,
And mine were steady,
So I was ready
When trouble came.

*   *   *

'Hallo, Pete.' Tommy smiled at him. 'Sorry to have bothered you, but we think you may be able to help us.' The direct approach, using Pete's Christian name like an old friend. People didn't do that on first meeting, even in a holding cell or, as in this case, an interrogation room, and it threw Pete a couple of degrees.

'Aye.' A shade to the left of taciturn.

For the first twenty minutes or so it felt almost like a casual conversation in a bar: Tommy relaxed and pleasant: Pete anxious to assist. Starting off with the whens and wheres.

'We're inquiring into the death of Doris Butler.'

'Aye. Tha wants me to help wi' inquiries. Sarn't said,' nodding towards Ron Worrall.

'Good.' Tommy sat himself down facing Pete. 'You were, I believe acquainted with Doris Butler?'

82

'Aye, 'course I knew her. She were—'

'A close friend?' Tommy cut him off.

'My younger brother was at school wi' her. That's how I met her. I were two classes ahead of her.'

'Then you were at school with her as well.'

'Aye, a'were.'

'When did you last see her?'

'Wha', our Doris?'

'When did you last see Doris, yes.'

'Saturday night the end of week before D-Day. Before invasion.' He really said, t'invasion, but the t' was silent.

'And where would that have been?'

'St Giles' Hall. Dance. Dance there most Saturdays. I said to Alf Binns that there weren't so many military people about. Not so many uniforms.' Touch of a vulpine grin that was not very attractive. 'Now we know, don't we? They'd all gone south, ready for t'invasion. Bloody marvellous.'

'And you saw Doris Butler at the dance?'

'She's there most Saturdays.'

Ten minutes on Doris and the dancing, then Tommy slewed onto another subject:

'Why aren't *you* in uniform, Pete?'

'Me?'

Tommy nodded. 'I'm not talking to anyone else.'

'On account o' me leg.'

'What about your leg?'

'Broke it. A fracture t'doctor said. Fractured

83

me leg in 1937 and it wasn't set proper. Mum said stay in bed and it'll be all right: I mean, we wasn't paid up on panel then. But it never set proper.'

And on to hammer in on Pete's present employment.

'Where do you work? What profession?' This last a bit of a stretch. Tommy was half convinced that Pete Hill was involved in something dodgy. Wrong, Tommy.

'I'm a qualified electrician wi' me own business. Hill and Ashworth. Electrical maintenance. No job too small.'

'And you go out and about?'

'Aye.'

'You climb ladders; you wriggle through attics; you adapt to difficult and different exigencies?'

'Aye, I do, if that means what I think it means.'

'And you manage to dance?'

'After a fashion, aye. Can't run, though. Can't run and can't march. Have difficulty climbing. Have to do a lot of marching in t'armed forces.'

'So I've been told, yes.'

'Very keen on marching they are. Never understood t'reason mesen'. I mean you're there to fight, en't you? Not to march, unless you're on ceremonial stuff, like in front of Buckingham Palace.'

'When you're out on a job, wiring say, don't

you have to climb?'

'I'm gaffer. I get others to climb if I can't.'

'You danced with Doris on that Saturday night, Pete? A week before the invasion?'

'No.'

'Had your own girlfriend, did you?'

'Danced wi' a girl called Eileen Shanty. We been seeing each other regular. Fat Eileen they call her, but she pleases me. I favour girls you can get hold of.'

Tommy Livermore muttered, 'Let me have girls about me that are fat,' then appeared to be lost in thought, trying to make up his mind about some profound problem.

Finally Ron Worrall leant forward and spoke for the first time, 'Pete, would you be willing to have an X-ray?'

'X-ray? X-ray where?'

'See if you've got a bone in your leg, Petey.' Tommy's face in a hideous grin.

Pete Hill looked as though his nose had been poked into a skunk's tail. 'Look, now. Wha' . . . ?'

'We want to make sure you've got a bone in your leg, Pete.' Laura almost giggled.

'Now wait a minute. I came along to help. Tha's what the' wanted, and . . . You can't think I . . . Oh no.'

'Oh no what, Pete?' Tommy's face wasn't even creased.

'Wha's this about? Tell me that.'

'What d'you think it's about, Pete?'

'Well, obviously, Doris. I mean you said so.'

'Yes. And . . . ?'

'And she's been done in. Murdered. Some bugger stopped her clock.'

'Yes, and we know you were a regular visitor to her house, Pete. You went to see her at least every third night when her husband was away. That's what we wanted to talk to you about.'

'By heck. You think I—'

'Want to eliminate you as they say, Petey,' Ron explained. 'Eliminate you from our inquiries.'

'But I was looking out for her. You must know that. I'm poor Roger's cousin after all. He bloody asked me to look after her. If he was still alive I couldn't bloody face him.'

'His cousin,' Tommy stated flatly. Not that it made any real difference of course, but it would have been nice if someone had said something. Some ninety-five per cent of murders were committed by a member of the family.

'Aye. Roger's mother and my mother. Sisters. So we're first cousins.'

'You didn't think to mention this sooner?'

'Well, everybody knows, just like they know Doris was a bit of a tart. Shouldn't speak ill of the dead, but it's true. Never was close to her, not until Roger went off, got hisself called up. I tried to tell you, but you shut me up.'

'You simply said you knew her.'

'That's what you asked. Did I know her?

And what's all this about X-rays?'

'My sergeant's sense of fun,' said Tommy already forming a few sentences in his head: what he'd say to old 'Razz' Berry's CID. Relationship of one of the suspects. Aloud he asked Pete Hill where he was on the night of 5th/6th June.

'I were in London.'

'Really?'

'Aye, really.'

'Anyone see you there?'

'Three American officers and three or so other representatives from electrical firms. I were appearing in front of a board wi' Cherry Ashworth my business partner.'

'She's not in HM Forces either?'

'It's a he and no, seeing he's in his late sixties, near seventy. Was a sleeping partner until war started up. We shared a room in this American place out towards Rutland Gate: answering questions and showing off our knowledge to t'Americans,' soft *t* again, unheard. 'So's they would use us as civilian contractors in their military hospitals and places. We applied for it; all official. We do it anyway for t'Army, Navy and RAF, but the bloody Yanks seem to have to test us out first. Make sure we're fit enough to do it for them. Yes, I were with them having me breakfast on t'Monday when news of t'landings came out.'

Tommy thought a small vulgar expletive. Am I wasting my time? he wondered, then told

87

Hill that he was free to go.

'But stay in Sheffield; we'll need to talk again.'

'I can't promise. The work I'll be doing for them Yanks'll be down south. In t'badlands.'

'You've got a car and a special petrol allowance, no doubt?'

'Aye.'

'I whistle and you'll come running back. Understand?'

'Aye.'

Tommy had developed a blinding headache, so he sought out Detective Chief Superintendent Berry and asked if he would make Kenneth Craig, their other suspect, comfortable for the night.

'Oh, and perhaps you'd get your brilliant officers to check up on his background. I've just discovered Pete Hill is Roger Butler's cousin.'

'Didn't you know?' 'Razz' Berry sounded as though the entire world knew of Pete Hill's relationship to the late Roger Butler. In fact he made Tommy feel positively ignorant.

'On second thoughts let Craig go home, then get your lads to make certain he's not related to the victim,' he added. 'I'll talk to him tomorrow. Tell him to come back about nine o'clock and have one of your lads keep obbo on him so we can be sure he won't take flight. And Hill as well. I'll want a word with him again. If only for the experience.'

Tommy reflected that this was all very English, the way they went about the investigation: asking questions, staying polite for most of the time. Very English and vaguely amateur night. What irked Tommy was that he thought of himself as totally professional. A dedicated copper.

When he got back to the hotel, Christine Hunter was on duty at reception.

'Mr Livermore, how lovely to see you back again. I'm on all night so if there's anything you need—anything—just give me a tinkle.'

Tommy heard Suzie's voice, 'Coming, Mr Livermore.'

'Yes, Christine. Thank you,' he said with a controlled smile. Walking towards the lift he thought, 'Not even to help with the seven armies in Normandy.' Christine Hunter was a lot of woman. Far too much woman for one man, and he already had one of those back in London.

CHAPTER EIGHT

At dawn's early crack Suzie rang the Reserve Squad offices on the fourth floor of New Scotland Yard. Billy Mulligan picked up and said, 'You're ringing me at the crack of dawn, Suz—ma'am,' correcting himself. 'Let me guess.'

'I want to use the Railton. Got to go to Gloucester.'

The Railton was the saloon car they had half-inched from the Flying Squad. Dull red and a bit flash.

'And you want Dennis to drive it over to St Martin's Lane with Shirley Cox. Sort of any time now.'

'You are conversant with all things, Billy.'

' 'Course I am. Know a lot an' all, 'cos I've already talked to the chief.'

'Who is also the great, wise and omnipotent . . .'

'Take it as read.' Billy, it was said, had known Tommy in another, earlier life, like Brian. For Suzie he was the nearest thing to perfection as far as the job was concerned: even appearing to have a private line into the future.

'I don't suppose we'll need them but you'd better tell Shirley and Dennis to bring overnight bags.'

'Just in case.' Even at a distance, over the telephone, Billy was able to be silent and deadpan at the dreadful pun. 'I already told them.' There was a rustling of paper at his end. 'This John Lees-Duncan,' he said with great care, reading it off a flimsy. 'The ADC (Crime) is having a word with him it seems; and Mr Livermore says someone in the stratosphere at Gloucester nick is going to talk to him as well. Make sure he's not going to be obstructive.'

'Great. Tell Dennis and Shirley we're going up Silverhurst Road—the convent—first.' Suzie thanked him, closed the line and dialled the number for the Branch, as they called Special Branch, asking for DCS Bear. Just as Tommy had told her—*Talk to Woolly Bear.*

'Bear,' said Bear.

Suzie introduced herself and mentioned Tommy's name.

'Ears,' said DCS Bear which Suzie translated as the way some educated people said, 'Yes'. 'Ears. Mr Livermore said you might telephone.'

'About a joker called John Lees-Duncan, sir.'

'Ears. John Reginald Palmer Lees-Duncan, born February 1894.'

Ten years out, Suzie thought, doing the mental arithmetic. She had put him down as sixty plus. He was barely fifty.

'Mr Livermore says you're above average and can keep things to yourself so I'll send a file over.'

Above average: keep things to yourself. Patronising sod. 'So you have something, sir?'

'Not a great deal. Straws in the wind sort of thing.'

'I'd be interested in anything, sir.'

' 'Course you would, but not on an open line, Mountford.'

Tommy said that people in the Branch were

91

paranoid 'because they're always listening in to people they imagine people're always listening in to them'.

'Got a couple of pages. Not Charles Dickens, but it has a little flavour. Prefer you keep it to yourself. Mind you do,' Bear said. 'I'll send it right up.' Pause, little cough. 'You're the Montford got in all the papers a few years back, aren't you?'

Suzie loathed being called Montford. 'Ears,' she said, about to close the line, but Detective Chief Superintendent Bear cleared his throat and asked if Mr Livermore was there.

'On a case, sir.'

'Where?'

'Sheffield.'

'What case?'

Suzie didn't imagine it; Woolly Bear's tone altered, subtly, nothing dramatic but the words were snapped with an edge, something clouding his query. She told him, Sheffield, murder and Doris Butler, beaten to death in her little kitchen.

His reaction—she thought of it later—was as though he had gone off the boil. 'Oh, yes. Right. Right.' Not with her, taking a couple of steps back from the conversation. Then he again said, 'Right,' and wished her good day.

She dialled Billy to tell him something would be coming up from the Branch and would he send it over with Dennis, presuming that Dennis and Shirley hadn't yet left.

92

'You been talking to the Branch, ma'am? Better watch yourself. Chief says the Branch gets in your head and meddles with it: drives you nuts then spits you out piecemeal.'

'The chief thinks that of a lot of things, Billy.' She sat back and found anger sweeping around her head, touching the nerve ends.

Mr Livermore says you're above average and can keep things to yourself. Then she thought it was funny, Bear's reaction to Tommy being in Sheffield. Not funny ha-ha, but funny peculiar.

Really? She thought again, then reflected on how lucky she was. Only in the Reserve Squad, only under Tommy Livermore would she, and the other girls, get any proper respect. They certainly wouldn't in Mr Bear's Special Branch. Tea girls and typists, that's all they'd be there.

When Suzie first joined the Met she realised double quick that her job would probably not be tracking down criminals or keeping order on the streets. In training they were acclimatised to obeying orders.

Usually without a second thought.

Someone of higher rank gave you an order on the parade ground and you conformed to the instruction without considering the outcome. It was the way of conditioning the mind and body. Through bullying hot afternoons drill sergeants screamed at them. At the time much of this had seemed facile to Suzie, who recalled the near hysterical tantrum

an unpolished button had caused—
'Reprehensible!' the parade inspector had screeched, almost levitating. 'Absolutely reprehensible and unforgivable.' A tarnished button. But she never had dirty buttons again.

On another occasion the drill sergeant shouted at her, 'What's the matter with you, girl? You, Mountford? What's the matter? Got itchy-coo?'

It had taken much detection to discover that 'Itchy-Coo' had been the title of some popular song from a previous generation.

The shouting, screaming and bullying did the trick and her class of policewomen went off to their first postings safe in the knowledge that as long as you obeyed an order nothing much could go wrong. Obey orders to the letter and you were as safe as a mouse in a cheese shop.

This was in the late 1930s, when Suzie first joined the Met, and even then the public perception of women policing the capital was mixed and strange: clergymen agonised over whether to give up their seats on the underground to allow uniformed policewomen to sit down; magistrates pondered the question of men feeling emasculated if arrested by a woman.

One magistrate said, 'It must hurt a man's feelings, to be arrested by a woman.'

It *should* hurt his feelings, Suzie thought with a touch of bite and bile. Quite rightly so.

But it was a long time before Suzie even had the opportunity of arresting a male. In many ways she grew to feel that she was not in the job to fight crime; she was there to serve the male police officers—do the typing and filing, even the occasional bit of shopping, make the tea, do the odd spot of cooking, making sandwiches or knocking up fried sausages while nipping out to get a few penn'orth of chips so that the blokes went to bed with full stomachs.

When not doing office or household chores the policewomen as often as not were nurses, looked after children, comforted the bereaved, dealt with people in shock and guarded women prisoners. Sometimes reports came in of women police officers working in plain clothes to trap drug dealers selling cocaine in the underground lavatories of Piccadilly Circus. Suzie even knew one of them when she was on the beat working out of Vine Street Police Station in the West End, but that kind of excitement did not seem to come her way: until 1940 when she was working in the Criminal Records Office at Scotland Yard itself.

By 1940 times were changing something chronic: women manning anti-aircraft guns in city parks, women riding motorbikes through bomb blasts to get messages to other units, brave women driving ambulances through the horror that was the nightly bombing. Women starting to do a hundred and one other things.

At the time, Suzie was vaguely aware of the idea that a lot of women were unlikely to be happy when their lives returned to the old normality of peacetime; When it was all over, when they sounded the last all clear, when the bluebirds circled the white cliffs of Dover and when the lights went on again all over the world, as Vera Lynn, Anne Shelton and a dozen others sang. Having tasted a kind of freedom and a terrifying excitement, many women would feel unsettled living their lives as housewives.

Working in CRO—the Criminal Records Office in Scotland Yard—meant she was again back on secretarial duties, typing information onto 5" x 2" filing cards, filling up daunting forms, answering telephones, finding files when they were requested, sitting for hours on end in front of an Underwood typewriter in that long room ruled over by a male sergeant of the old school.

She was there every day in CRO at the beginning of the Blitz when her life changed for ever, without warning.

The night before it all happened she hadn't gone 'down the shelter' in the basement of the building in Upper St Martin's Lane. Instead, she stayed in her bed, awake for a time as the bombs exploded nearby, frightened like everybody else because it was bloody frightening; but stoicism was often good

96

camouflage for courage and you didn't let on that you were terrified when your friends were around: bravado really. On that night there were no friends about but she still lay shivering in her bed, her head under the clothes, her mind searching for something to calm her nerves.

In the morning she was late for duty, blaming last night's raid for her tardiness, trying to sound perky and cheeky. The CRO sergeant, Rex Fulbright, wasn't having any of it, said he was in the raid as well and he wasn't late, was he? His voice leaping to a rising screech; told her there were orders for her and she'd be up the creek with no paddles if she didn't shape up. Hardly knowing what was going on she found herself in front of the woman police superintendent in charge of A4, the policewomen's branch of the Met, a leathery lady, hands the colour of kippers and with an irritating drawl and the faint scent of horse.

Naturally she thought she was in trouble, but it was quite the reverse. She couldn't take it in, what the super was telling her. Since the fall of France, since Dunkirk, in spite of police duties being mainly reserved occupations, the Met was haemorrhaging manpower. More than ever women were now required to take on jobs that were previously only the preserve of men, that's what the female super told her. She, Susannah Mary Mountford, was to be promoted and as from today would be an acting, temporary, unpaid woman detective sergeant, posted to the Camford Hill nick where, eventually, because of air raid injuries and shortages of manpower, she found herself the ranking officer in an unpleasant headline murder. Learn on the job, they told her, and learn she had to.

The victim was already notorious, a BBC announcer, a new breed because she too was a woman: Jo Benton, a girl who had been criticised for paying no attention to the BBC's official guidebook regarding vulgar language, the one that was later known as the infamous Green Book.

The British Broadcasting Company seemed terrified of comedians, newsreaders, narrators and commentators using smutty expressions, and good old Jo Benton had plunged in following a freezing weather forecast with the deathless line, 'Well, winter draws on, eh?' which every schoolboy knows is interpreted as 'winter drawers on', a phrase specifically alluded to as forbidden in the BBC's guidelines on coarse speech. This goes to show how touchy the BBC was and how relatively innocent the listening public: but then it had to contend with people like Max Miller and George Formby who sang about Mr Wu who 'had a funny eye that flickers, you ought to see it wobble when he's ironing ladies blouses'.

Anyway, Jo Benton ended up being

garrotted with piano wire in her smart house in Camford and Suzie Mountford became the CID plain-clothes sergeant in charge of the investigation causing Fleet Street newspapers to tell everyone it was shocking that one of the fair sex could be leading male detectives as the head of such an unsavoury case. The fact that the Blitz was in full swing and the manpower shortage was acute didn't appear to enter the minds of correspondents who complained to the papers about the unsuitability of young women getting their hands dirty with murder, signing their letters 'Concerned of Banbury', and the like.

At this point they had no idea that WDS Mountford was receiving assistance from a senior police officer, DCS Livermore, known to the more colourful journalists as Dandy Tom on account of his stylish clothes made for him by one of the more flamboyant tailors of Savile Row.

Suzie had not come across Tommy Livermore before she was told to look to him as her adviser and mentor. Listening to him on the telephone she conjured up a middle-aged man of conservative outlook and dress, so when she finally got to meet him the shock was more than considerable.

He strode into the foyer of Devonshire Mansions, off Marylebone High Street, where Suzie was investigating a lead in the Benton case. He marched in with his retinue around him. 'Orchestra, dancing girls and a male voice choir,' as Suzie said to Shirley Cox, Tommy wearing his tailored, double-breasted dark overcoat, the Homburg tilted at a rakish angle. Like a souped-up Anthony Eden, she thought. Her mother, like so many middle-class English women at the time, adored Anthony Eden and thought him 'the most gorgeous man ever'. But to Suzie it was Tommy Livermore with his raffish smile, lifting one side of his mouth, the glint in his eye and the self-deprecating humour that won her within seconds.

Later, she realised that a spark had leapt between them in the vastness of the old art deco foyer of Devonshire Mansions: the well-known static crackle that can pass between a male and female who recognise each other as probable lovers. The flash of revelation remained with her, though, after that first introduction, she had second thoughts, wondering if she was mistaken about the almost tangible charge moving both ways: after all, he was a senior officer with a lot of clout. She had grown up in the Thirties and now, in 1940, the class distinctions were still at their peak, and the old middle-class pigeon-holes were after all set in stone.

But when the chief super asked her out to dinner her heart leapt and for a moment she thought the unthinkable.

The lightning between them had been there again when he picked her up from the flat and drove her to the Ritz, but any flirtation was quashed once they had taken their seats in the grand Louis Quinze dining room and Tommy became all business, explaining to her that she had, in many ways, been working directly for him since she'd been promoted, and would she like to officially work for him and with him—in the Reserve Squad—from now on?

It appeared that Tommy, with a few others—a very few—had been thinking in terms of a different world, and a different time, when the war was over. Unbelievably they had concluded that when this happened many of the women who had served in the armed forces, the police, even the fire service, would not be best pleased to be scuttling back into the role of housewives and mothers: subservient partners of 'breadwinners'. Large numbers of women, they felt, would be ready to go on living and working in key jobs, not least of all in the police forces.

'If we can start to form the nucleus of what will eventually be powerful groups of senior women within the Met, then we can at best have a foundation upon which we can build.' He paused, eyeing her up across the starched napery, glittering silverware and shining smooth glasses.

'It'll take decades,' he added. 'Men don't like change and will prefer to think of women in the home. In the bed. In the kitchen.'

Once more the little sparkle passed between

them, and she gave a silent gasp, felt something tighten within, move up, coil around her heart and squeeze.

'And you're suggesting that I'm one of the Class of 1940,' she said.

Tommy gave her a smirk. 'Oh, heart, you *are* the class of 1940. We picked six of you, pulled you in from the typewriters, the tea makers, the duty cells, the kiddie patrol, the whore minding, the nursing and doing the inspector's shopping of a Wednesday afternoon. We shoved half a dozen of you out into a whole rack of divisions, under some of the hardest cases in the Met. Then we sat back and watched. We're doing the same thing in January with a new half-dozen. God help them.'

Silently, Suzie wondered about how she had done in this test that she had no idea she was taking.

As if hearing her he said, 'As for your lot, four of the girls folded in a month, the fifth is about to crumble any minute. Couldn't take it, didn't like the atmosphere, felt they couldn't slap a detective inspector's face when he stuck a hand up their drawers, didn't like it when the men tweaked their titties, or patted their soft little behinds. You name it, they couldn't deal with it: couldn't take the responsibility; couldn't do the job.'

She remembered that she felt the flush rise from her neck and sluice across her face.

'On the other hand, you, heart, got a break.' Pause, big smile. 'I think you've done wonderfully.' Smile again, this time for the cameras.

She recalled that at the time his praise was like pouring a stiff brandy down her throat, a warm flush spreading through her body and a quick sense of lightness, the whirl of intoxication.

As they left the Ritz Tommy said, 'But, like I said, heart, it's going to take coppers decades before they'll accept women as police officers.'

He was right, they hadn't come near to accepting women, even now in 1944, and she couldn't see it happening in the foreseeable future.

Now, in the present, Shirley arrived in Upper St Martin's Lane, with Dennis Free driving the crimson Railton and enjoying it, feeling no end of a lad. Meanwhile, Suzie was warm and comfortable, the sensation induced by the memory of that dinner at the Ritz. Nothing had happened until much later, after the horrific Christmas when he'd been down to Kingscote, 'Flogging peasants,' as she had cheekily named it. After that his trips to Kingscote Grange were always to flog peasants. But that year, 1940 he had come steaming back from the family seat on Christmas Day to deal with the dreadful events that surrounded Suzie's family.

It was only later she discovered the electric

charge had gone both ways, and some weeks later Tommy Livermore made a woman of her—sooner rather than later. But that was after Christmas, near to the time he made her a stalking horse, a tethered goat to catch the revolting schizoid who had corrupted their lives at the time: the one he had called the bottled spider.

But Tommy really wooed me, she thought. Wooed me properly, and rightly. We should be married.

Dennis had the envelope from the Branch with Woolly Bear's *Strictly Confidential* neat in the top left-hand corner above the address to Suzie at the Reserve Squad.

She read it in the car going over to Silverhurst Road and the convent.

Now it was essential for her to ring Tommy in Sheffield.

At the convent, she told Dennis and Shirley to nip over to the nick and get the pix from Magnus. 'And if he tries to play silly buggers threaten to telephone the ADC (Crime) and ring me here, at the convent.'

Dennis grinned. 'My pleasure,' he said, not meaning it, a lowly DC phoning the ADC and telling tales about a DI. Horsefeathers.

Sister Eunice told her yes, they had a photo of Sister Theresa. A snap of Winifred Audrey Lees-Duncan. 'We take a picture for our records on the day an individual is accepted as a novice. Keep them. Interesting to look back and see what some of the older sisters looked like when they were bright young sparks.' She dropped her voice to almost a whisper. 'Mother Rachel was a real bobby dazzler when she arrived. No end of a bright young thing.'

And yes, of course they could have it. Take it. She'd get a brown utility envelope.

Then the good Sister Eunice left Suzie, in her room here with the sit-up-and-beg telephone, the tall crucifix on the wall next to a holy picture, left alone, so she could put a trunk call through to Sheffield and her boss, master and lover Tommy Livermore.

CHAPTER NINE

In Sheffield, Tommy wasn't much concerned now with Pete Hill, the first suspect. Ron and Laura, with the aid of local officers, had followed up on the man's weekend cover and, yes, he had been in London, just as he'd said, 'With that Mr Ashworth, the one they called Cherry,' being interviewed by Americans to assess their suitability for doing electrical work in the US hospitals in southern England: a job for which he had applied on behalf of his small company.

In spite of this supposed cast-iron alibi Tommy still wasn't happy, wanted to dig deeper, wondered why the Yanks would allow men from the north to travel down to their hospitals: why they'd employ civilian electricians anyway? They seemed to have enough specialists of their own. Built their own bloody hospitals, had better equipment than our people; did every blasted thing and cleaned up after themselves and all. Bloody Yanks. Oversexed, overpaid and over here.

He saw Hill anyway, only for a few minutes, asking one last question as he left the interview room.

'Got any smokes on you, Pete?' patting his pockets, looking as though he'd lost sixpence and found a button: twitchy at not having a fag.

'Don't use them.' Pete Hill pulled out a pipe, and grinned, tapping his teeth with the stem.

In the hidey-hole among the trees and bushes behind Doris Butler's house, the watcher had smoked Gold Flake cigarettes. Tommy thought if he found a possible whose preference was Gold Flake he'd have something to go on. You couldn't pick and choose though. A bloke who smoked Gold Flake might really prefer Players or De Reske. You bought what you could get these days. Some were even reduced to Abdullah. Horrible. Turkish.

So, now it was Kenneth Craig's turn. Ken Craig: short, thin with a washed-out face and eyes the colour of a clouded summer's day:

dark ringed eyes, deep and furtive. To Tommy it was as though the intelligence in the man's eyes had withdrawn, lurking somewhere inside his brain, behind a boulder of frontal lobe, peering round, listening not to the questions but what was behind the questions.

Ken Craig had no form, nothing known: but what had that to do with anything?

Tommy gave him a smile and asked why he was not in HM Forces. Craig beamed back, slyly, the fingers of his right hand indicating the circular silver badge in the left lapel of his sports coat, telling he had done his military duty. 'Dunkirk,' the man said, his voice touching on husky so that he paused clearing his throat.

'Dunkirk,' he repeated. 'Those bloody Stukas got to me.'

'You were injured, wounded?'

Craig leant forward, cupping his right ear. 'That dive bombing made me a gibbering wreck. Damaged me hearing, knocked the stuffing out of me. Give me the shakes.' He swallowed, eyes even more shifty. The Stukas were Junkers 87s, the ones with the strange, crooked wings, the long, wide slats on the trailing edges, and the sirens attached to their big fixed undercarriages so they could make a dreadful shriek as they plunged towards their targets.

'Pretty tough on the beaches, yes?' Tommy prepared to hear the whole story, but not

107

holding with men who went soft because of a few bombs. Tommy wasn't a naturally sympathetic man. Got to keep your end up, he'd say, got to rise above it, be a man.

'Tough? Tough en't the word . . . Mister . . .? Mister . . .?' Clawing for the name they'd told him.

'Livermore,' Tommy supplied flatly, almost with disinterest.

'Mr Livermore.' Giving the impression that he was trying to be very polite and helpful. 'Tough? It were bloody murder. It were living on the edge of death, close to the pit, wi' old Satan leerin' out on you. Hell. That's what it was.'

What is Hell?
Hell is oneself.
Hell is alone,

*   *   *

Tommy thought the bit about Satan was over the top, and he didn't believe that Craig had to scratch around for his name because he was always in the papers—the Hon. Tommy Livermore, the copper most often on the front page. *Dandy Tom Does It Again* they would write.

'Most unpleasant,' he said aloud, as though he didn't believe a word of the Dunkirk story. 'How long were you there? On the beaches?'

'Four days. And the sergeant major kept

108

sayin' things like, "Men who 'ave not brought their buckets and spades will not be allowed to paddle", daft things like that. Didn't make it any easier.'

'I don't suppose it did. I know a lot of officers who were there: said the noise and the people were difficult. What do you do with yourself now, Ken?'

'Nay,' said Kenneth Craig raising his cold blue eyes to look straight at Tommy. 'Nay, I can only do part-time work. Doctor has me on pills, supposed to make me less worried, but what does doctor know? Bloody pills and a bottle of some muck. I take 'em and they only give me constipation. I'm anxious all the time. Can't keep me mind still. Me thoughts like a bloody merry-go-round jangling about.'

*   *   *

Eventually he asked Craig where he lived, knowing full well that the man lived with his mother, his father dead ten years ago in an accident.

'And how do you manage? Financially, I mean.'

'I have my Army pension. We manage.'

'No work at all?'

'A bit here, a bit there.' Pause. 'Like I said, can't do much. Bit of delivering.'

'Delivering what, Ken?'

'Things. Letters an' that; for council.

Council runner they calls me, make it sound military. Rent collector an' all.'

'Ever go up Bluefields Road?'

'Come on, Mr Livermore.' The sly look and thin smile again. 'You know I been up Bluefields. That meddlesome busybody Phyll Meecham as was, her that married Martin Carter, in the Navy. Number 63. She's told you I been up at 65, Doris Butler's house. You know it. Very bad with payin' the rent, Mrs Carter. Very bad. Offered me a bargain once.'

'I know it,' Livermore agreed, then paused. He didn't know it, but could guess. 'Up to no good, Ken. Got a fag?'

'Yes, sure,' diving into his pocket, coming out with a packet of Gold Flake, giving a momentary jerk as he realised he had walked into something, wasn't sure what, but there was something just over the horizon.

Tommy leant over, helped himself to a cigarette, took out his lighter—a Zippo he'd had off an American serviceman he'd interviewed in some nick, West End Central probably, off Regent Street—and lit his first, as was his right, then stretched out and lit Ken Craig's smoke.

'Used to watch her, did you, Ken? From the trees at the edge of her little garden?' The cigarette butts stubbed into the earth were all Gold Flake. 'One day,' Tommy had said when they were collecting the fag ends, 'One day,

110

we'll be able to put the smoker to the fag from his saliva on the tip. Save a lot of time that will and one day the boffins'll be able to do that.'

Ken Craig shifted uncomfortably and wouldn't meet Tommy's eye. 'Come on, Kenneth, you can tell me. In the long summer evenings you'd creep up there and hide. And you'd watch through the trees.' He didn't say anything else then, but he thought a lot. Couldn't prove a bloody thing, but . . . then Craig broke off, raised his eyes and finally gave Tommy a cold, blue, hard look.

'She used to leave the windows open sometimes, and she'd undress in front of them.' He gave a low rumble of childish giggle, his hands going to his waist as though recalling her taking her undies off, mimicking it. Thumbs running around her waist under the elastic.

Tommy nodded. 'And you let yourself in through the kitchen door, right?'

'Bloody 'ell, no. No, I never been inside there, not ever in her house. No.' Much too quick.

'You sure, Ken?'

'Sure as eggs, Mr . . . Livermore?'

Tommy nodded. So.

'I never did,' Craig said, his voice moving up the scale. 'I never went in, not even when I took up stuff from the council, saying her rent was overdue. Knocked at the door always, see if she were in and have a word with her, but I

111

never put a foot over the doorstep.'

'All right,' Tommy nodded, speaking quietly. 'All right, Ken, but you saw other people inside with her.'

'Oh yeah. 'Course. Saw a lot of them and she used to take off her clothes with them. Go Humpty Dumpty with them.'

'You saw that?'

'Yes. Not half.'

'You're telling me the truth, Kenneth? Not telling porkies? You just watched her from that little den? Didn't leave it: didn't go into the house? Didn't go higgledy-piggledy with her?'

'Never, sir. No. Never did.' Long pause as though thinking about it. 'No. I did not.'

Tommy wondered again, inclined to believe the man, smelt right, sounded right. But . . . No. No, of course not.

'You recognise any of them? Any of them you saw with her?'

'I know all of 'em.'

'Really?'

'There's two I seen here today. Here in the station. In the nick.'

'Tell me, Kenneth.'

'Well, there's the other bloke you been seeing. Old Pete Hill.'

'You saw Pete with her?'

'Clear as day, doing the business.'

'And who else, Ken?'

'That sergeant. Sergeant Dave Mungo. Seen
112

him there with her in the buff, going at it hammer and tongs: going like a steam engine and she went off like a train whistle at the end. "Whooooo, oooooh Dave, David, ooooooh!" Saw and heard the whole thing. "Wheeeeooowww," she went, like the Flying Scotsman.'

DS Dave Mungo, to whom Tommy had been introduced on the previous evening. 'My right hand: my fighting arm, even though he's only here on attachment,' DCS Berry had said, and Tommy had shaken the man's hand. Now, he unconsciously wiped that same hand on the back of his trousers.

Mungo had what journalists called rugged good looks, bit craggy, bright and tall, bronzed, outdoor lifeish, hey ho, the wind and the rain, bit of sun thrown in. Mungo had moved, stepped forward, a smidgeon too close to Tommy. 'We should speak, sir.' The smile a touch too ingratiating. 'Sometime. Yes,' Tommy had said, knowing of old the CID coppers who tried to butter him up, get close and transferred to the Reserve Squad, thought it was glamorous, full of action, place to be.

'Stop there, I think,' flashing his eyes at Kenneth Craig, then at Ron. 'Almost lunchtime. You've been a good lad, Ken.' Craig nodding, grinning, bouncing up and down, like a bloody monkey on a stick. As he reached the door Craig said, 'Oh, and there was little Roddy Holbrooke. Surprised at that.

113

I was really surprised, cos I always thought little Roddy was a poof. Minced a lot, you know, poofy walk, like he was swaying along on wheels, arm out from his side an' the hand poofed out like a bloody manichean.'

For manichean read mannequin, Tommy thought. The Manichean heresy, he smiled to himself. That's what Roddy Holbrooke had got: bloody Manichean Heresy.

One of the DCs was just outside the door. 'There's a WDI Mountford on the blower, sir, wanting to talk to you urgently.'

*   *   *

'Tommy, darling,' she said, breathy, the words used to signal she was alone, sitting in the Novice Mistress's office.

'Suzie, heart,' he said, matter-of-fact, to signal Lord knew what.

'How's it going, Tom?'

'Just got another taker, heart. Bloody copper in this nick. I could scream. Really upset.' Calm as a summer pond.

'Tommy, I need help.'

'Oh, God.'

'Well, not help exactly. More advice.'

'About what?'

'Our friend Lees-Duncan. John Reginald Palmer Lees-Duncan.'

'I told you, talk to Woolly.'

'I talked to Woolly. He sent me a little

114

billet-doux.'

'You want to watch that, heart. Billets-doux from a Special Branch super. Dodgy. Marked SWALK was it, or NORWICH?'

'Norwich?'

'Heart, Knickers Off Ready When I Come Home. Norwich.'

'Tommy,' mock exasperation, slap-on-the-wrist. 'It was a précis of information on Lees-Duncan, the billet-doux. I just need one or two things clarified.'

'Go ahead.'

'BUF?' She gave the initials slowly.

'What about them?'

'Well, British Union of Fascists? That's right, isn't it?'

'Mosley's lot, yes. Finally closed down in '40.'

Sir Oswald Mosley, founder and leader of the British Fascist movement, the man who saw himself as the future Führer of Great Britain, mocked by some, cheered by others and feared by quite a few. With his serious, self-interested mien, his small army of quasi-military 'blackshirts' and his ranting, tub-thumping, Hitler-like speeches he had been arrested under an amendment to the Emergency Powers (Defence) Act in May 1940, locked up in Brixton but later moved to be with his wife—one of the eccentric society Mitfords—in Holloway.

'They let him out last year,' Tommy

115

muttered. 'Mosley. Illness. Lees-Duncan part of his lot?'

'Woolly's little dossier says that in the Thirties they had Lees-Duncan under what they called "loose surveillance", and he seemed to turn up at a lot of house parties where Mosley was a guest.'

'Why does that not surprise me?' Tommy asked of nobody in particular. 'I've told you before. Study German for your School Certificate and the Branch immediately has you tagged as a spy. Old Mosley appealed to some of the upper classes. Went to lots of country houses, told them what a good fella Hitler was.' He trailed off and there was silence on the line. Then, 'Bloody spy mania, that's what the Branch has.'

'Well, Lees-Duncan apparently was one—a spy; only they called him an informer.'

'Mmmm.'

'He was a spy for someone whose name I know, but I can't place . . .'

'Tell me . . .'

'Vansittart.'

'Robert Vansittart?'

'Who *is* he?'

'He's *Sir* Robert Vansittart, Chief Diplomatic Adviser to the Foreign Office.'

'Ah. Knew I'd heard the name. He would have agents then?'

'Don't know about that.'

'Well, they refer to them as informers.'

116

'Probably, yes.'

'Friend Lees-Duncan claimed to be one.'

'Did he now?'

'Early in 1940 the Branch pulled him, Lees-Duncan, felt his collar, gave him a rough interrogation. Had a member of the security service there as well.'

'Thumbscrews?'

'Oh, the lot I should imagine, and when they got to asking about Germany and his many friends in the enemy camp, John Reginald Palmer Lees-Duncan said he was one of Vansittart's informants. Didn't deny he'd had contacts within the Nazi Diplomatic Corps, their Army and the Luftwaffe. He said it was all in a day's work, clean as soap powder, Lux, Rinso, whatever you want.'

'And?'

'And they checked with—I suppose—the Foreign Office. The notes said they followed it up and Vansittart was a bit cagey. Didn't want to say anything. Faffed around then finally said that Lees-Duncan *had* been one of their informants.'

'*Had* been?'

'Yes. Close as they'd come to it. There's a long note saying that Lees-Duncan possibly still had channels open to the Nazi military. Not in so many words but they were saying they suspected him of being a double. A double agent.

'Since '39 he's apparently disappeared a

117

couple of times, gone off without warning. They're unhappy about his sons as well— Michael and Gerald. Michael in Mexico, and Gerald living almost silently on the east coast of Scotland: very handy for the Firth of Forth, watching the naval traffic in and out.'

'So what d'you think, heart? Bearing in mind the fact that you couldn't stand the man?'

'I think there's something to be suspicious about, Tommy, but what do I know? I've no real experience of these things. Woolly Bear must know his job, surely, and he's obviously dubious about the man. I mean . . .'

'Woolly's dubious about everyone, except possibly Old Etonians, and he can be cagey about them.' Tommy Livermore chuckled. 'Yes, it's obvious Lees-Duncan isn't one hundred per cent clean,' he laughed again, 'and the swine speaks German. You're the fella at the sharp end, heart. You're the one who'll have to take a good long look at him. By the way he's been given a white-hot poker astern; been told not to play the squire with you. They've as good as told him he'll be shot at dawn if he doesn't cooperate. On the Tower of London rifle range, quarter to dawn, on a particularly cold morning.'

'That's a bit strong.'

' 'Tis isn't it?' She could hear the laughter in his voice.

'Before you go, heart,' he began.

118

'Yes . . . ?'

'Tell you something, heart. Just the two of us, right?'

She waited because Tommy had his serious voice on.

'Fella I know in MI5, in the security service. Guy Liddell actually. Told me once that the German informers run by the Foreign Office's Diplomatic Adviser were pretty unreliable. Porous actually.'

He meant porous piss which was a saying of the time. Suzie thought people said it about her, 'That Suzie Mountford's porous.' They didn't, but she sometimes put herself down with fantasies like that.

'Not very good then?' she said.

'Duff, heart. Old Guy Liddell said he wouldn't use any of them, not even for practice.'

There was a silence, as though neither of them had anything more to say. Eventually Suzie told him that Woolly Bear didn't seem too happy about him dealing with the Butler case in Sheffield. 'I mentioned it, and he kind of withdrew,' she said. 'Almost disappeared on the telephone.'

'Like the Cheshire cat?'

'More or less. Just left a great big question mark.'

'That's what Woolly is.'

'A Cheshire cat?'

'No, a big question mark.'

119

Another strangled silence.

'Right, how's the hotel?' she asked.

'Wizard,' Tommy said with his smiling voice. 'You were right, that girl *is* here, that Chrissie.'

'Really. Watch how you go then, Tommy.' She dropped an icicle into the words, just rubbed it along to let him know. 'All of you'd better watch out.'

'All of us?'

'Yes, you and Peter Rabbit, and Mrs Tiggy-Winkle and Jeremy Fisher.'

'Needn't bother yourself about Chrissie, heart. Tries too hard. Not for me. Like Guy with those informants, not even for practice.'

At last Suzie put down the telephone and went in search of Sister Eunice and the photo of Novice Theresa when she was still Winifred Audrey Lees-Duncan, or at least was supposed to be Winifred Audrey.

CHAPTER TEN

A few weeks before the Reserve Squad got the call to the Convent of St Catherine of Siena in Silverhurst Road, there had been momentous news from Germany: a serious attempt on Hitler's life at his headquarters near Rastenburg, in East Prussia. It had been in all the papers and on every radio news bulletin.

People were agog.

Now, far away in the Baltic, on the same day that Suzie came to collect the photograph from Sister Eunice, an unexpected visitor arrived on Usedom Island to take a look at what progress was being made by the men working on the Army rocket; the A-4; the Vengeance Weapon Two; the V-2.

SS-Gruppenführer Max Voltsenvogel arrived by motor launch. He came over the Peene River through the muddy narrows and marshes up to the artificial docks dredged out and constructed on the island near what had once been the village of Peenemünde.

Colonel Voltsenvogel was known even to his friends in the SS as 'Death's Head' Voltsenvogel; it was something of a joke—but only occasionally when things were relaxed. For most of the time the 'Death's Head' appellation was far from funny. Indeed, there was something deeply scary about Voltsenvogel, whose reputation was guaranteed to send a shiver down the spines of even the most innocent men; for it was said that Max Voltsenvogel could obtain a guilty confession of original sin from a newborn child—extracting it by simply looking at the victim.

Gruppenführer Max Voltsenvogel was head of Intelligence Projects, a department mainly of his own devising, on Adolf Hitler's personal staff. A highly trusted officer, he could plan and execute operations of his own, for, as well

121

as other attributes, he was possessed of a silver tongue.

Voltsenvogel was short and stocky with a bullet head and memorable face: flat ears against the large cranium, deep-seated eyes, big cavernous nostrils and large teeth, square, like small tombstones. His skin was unnaturally tight across his face so that the thin lips were pulled back displaying the teeth in two uneven rows. Indeed as some said he could easily have played the part of Yorick in Shakespeare's *Hamlet*. Yorick appears only as a skull dug from a grave by an amusing gravedigger in that play so this was, they said, typecasting for the colonel—except for the amusing part.

In spite of his physical appearance, Voltsenvogel was a dandy, liked wearing riding breeches and highly polished boots with lifts in the heels giving him an extra inch of height. In his mind, however, the lifts gave him an extra five inches. Like many small men he was sensitive about his height and overcompensated, a blusterer and a vicious bully. Short men are often given extreme power at times of change and crisis. Those who promote them should have care.

As if to supplement his grotesque features the colonel carried a swagger cane made of treated bone—some, naturally, claimed it to be human bone—one end of which was carved in the representation of a skull. This memento

122

mori was in fact the haft of a thin, tempered steel blade, around eight inches long, that nestled within its bone sheath. Voltsenvogel's reputation was such that people assumed the blade had been used in murderous diversions.

He came unannounced to Peenemünde bringing with him a technical sergeant and a corporal called Schmidt who doubled as his personal servant. They were not out of place, for SS uniforms abounded on the island: the SS had long since hijacked the *Vergeltungswaffe* programmes. In particular they were in control of the A-4 weapon. In the tangled web of the Third Reich it was always as well to be implicated in any project with special significance for the Führer. From the beginning, Hitler had been totally involved with both of the so-called vengeance weapons, seeing each of them almost as sacraments of war that would unlock the gates of victory no matter how the world was marshalled against him.

Voltsenvogel wondered how the local officers would take to his arrival in their mess. After all, his special relationship with the Führer was well known, and the events of 20th July were not ten days old. An officer from the Führer's inner circle arriving so soon after the assassination attempt was bound to cause at least a small twitch of concern. So when he walked into the mess that evening he could not fail to notice how people gave him shifty, anxious glances, and be aware of the undoubted lull in conversation: a general *froideur* descended among those gathered in the ante-room.

The attempt on the Führer's life had taken place at the melodramatically named *Wolfsschanze* (Wolf's Lair) near Rastenburg, in the mosquito-laden forests of East Prussia.

Colonel Count Claus von Stauffenberg had flown down for a strategic meeting with senior officers, and the Führer. He entered the conference room with three pounds of explosive in his briefcase wired to a percussion cap and a simple timing device. The officers were ranged around a large wooden table covered with maps and papers, so von Stauffenberg armed the bomb, placed the briefcase on the floor under the table, sliding it towards the Führer with his foot. He then made an excuse to leave the room, waiting outside until the device exploded with a mighty roar, leaving a dark pall of smoke hanging over the wooden building.

Surely the Führer could not have survived such destruction, he reasoned.

The dead and wounded were carried out and von Stauffenberg stayed until a body was removed covered by Hitler's cloak. At that point he could be forgiven for thinking his part in the plot had succeeded.

So he left, returning to his aircraft and flying back to Berlin.

By a miracle, it seemed, the Führer survived; another officer had kicked the loaded briefcase away from Hitler's end of the table, so when it exploded many were injured and four died. But Hitler lived. Von Stauffenberg flew back to Berlin and prepared to take part in the second phase of the plot: the takeover of the military and the nullification of the National Socialist Party in order to bring the war to a quick conclusion.

It was not to be. By the following afternoon von Stauffenberg was court-martialled and summarily shot, in the courtyard of the War Ministry. More suspects were being rounded up, already there had been many arrests, some, it appeared, at random. It was said that if you looked at somebody in an inappropriate manner you could be accused. It was all reminiscent of the days of finding witches by seeing who sank and who floated.

Hence the circumspect manner in which Voltsenvogel was greeted.

'How nice to see you, Gruppenführer,' lied the adjutant of the A-4 Programme, SS-Obersturmbannführer Erich Lottle. 'We had no notification of your impending arrival. Is there anything I can do . . .?' Lottle had a good line in frozen smiles.

'Just a short visit. An overnight stay.' Voltsenvogel smiled his foxy smile, lifted his chin and looked Erich Lottle in the eyes. 'The Führer is anxious to find out how the

Vergeltungswaffe Zwei is progressing: he simply asked me to come down and get the information myself. I am a direct conduit to the Führer.' Adolf Hitler had asked no such thing, though naturally he would be pleased to hear, for the Allied armies were fighting hard to push themselves away from the vicinity of the Normandy beaches around Caen and the Cotentin peninsula. 'If the Americans and British continue to move south we're going to need the A-4. We can't leave it all to the Fiesler 103.'

The A-4 was the great 8,800 pound long-range rocket, 46 feet high, powered by a propulsion engine burning a mixture of alcohol, liquid oxygen, T-Stoff (hydrogen peroxide) and Z-Stoff (sodium permanganate) carrying a warhead of around one ton of high-explosive, and guided by a sophisticated gyroscopic system.

Erich Lottle told him the A-4 programme had made great strides. 'Who would you like to speak with to get the details? General Dornberger? Von Braun?' Dornberger, a founding father of the rocket project, held the rank of Lieutenant General while Werhner von Braun held only a courtesy SS rank.

Voltsenvogel gave him the foxy smile again, perhaps a shade broader this time. 'I think I should go to the top. To Hans Kammler.'

'But, Gruppenführer . . . ?'

'I think I should speak with General

126

Kammler.' Voltsenvogel left no doubt that he meant exactly what he said, but of course he knew what nobody else knew that Kammler would be promoted in a few weeks, elevated to Major-General, vaulting in one bound over Walter Dornberger who had spent years clawing his way to the top of the A-4 programme.

By this time Max Voltsenvogel was seated and had ordered a large schnapps, totally at ease among the engineers and fellow SS officers. Lottle signified that he would like permission to sit next to the colonel, and Voltsenvogel inclined his head, answering in the most cavalier fashion.

'I fear you will have to wait a few days to speak with General Kammler.' SS-Obersturmbannführer Erich Lottle lowered his head so that his lips were only a few inches from the colonel's ear before he spoke. 'At the moment the general is at the far end of the island conducting a test launch of one of the testbed A-4s. There have been problems.'

'Then *you* tell me about them. I've yet to meet an adjutant who doesn't know the ins and outs of his command. Some, I find, know a great deal more than their commanding officers.'

Lottle, a tall man, thin, a beanpole with a face tarnished by worry, long sagging cheeks, dull, pouched eyes and a mouth turned irrevocably down at each corner gave a huge shrug as though accepting the colonel's judgement with some misgivings. Then he explained the rocket programme was still irretrievably running behind schedule—nobody's particular fault, simply an unfortunate fact of military life. 'There have been problems, Colonel,' ticking them off on his fingers. 'They have only just solved the difficulties regarding mobile launching sites.'

Voltsenvogel nodded.

'Then there were the fuelling difficulties allied to the launching. We also have the unfortunate problems with the turbo steam pumps.'

Voltsenvogel raised a hand as if accepting fate.

'And latterly there has been a more serious malfunction.' Lottle squared his shoulders as though preparing to give Voltsenvogel the worst possible news. 'The rocket is breaking up from its warhead above its impact point.'

Voltsenvogel listened almost as gloomily as the adjutant. Finally he asked how long it was estimated before they expected to have dealt with the faults. 'My dear Lottle, we need to get the A-4 into action. The Führer depends on it now the Allies have arrived.'

'Four, five, six weeks,' Lottle told him as though this was some minor hiccough in the works. Also as if they had eternity to get the A-4 into operation. 'Everything has been overcome except for the new, breakup disasters. The warhead is detaching itself from the main rocket as it reaches its apogee and starts the downward journey. These are naturally stabilisation difficulties. They are working on modifications of the tail fins.'

'And your four, five, six weeks is realistic?'

'I would say no later than September.'

It had better be early September, Voltsenvogel thought to himself. The rocket was essential now they were under such pressure along the northern coast of Fortress Europe. The Fi-103s had proved to be a huge success. The Allies back in England were stumbling and petrified by the new danger, for they had written off any further assault from the skies now that the Luftwaffe had been defeated. He had heard the Führer say they were running around like chickens with their heads cut off. 'Tell Himmler that,' and he had laughed. Himmler, of course, had once been a chicken farmer.

Voltsenvogel remained sanguine regarding the future. The Allies may well have their foot inside Fortress Europe but he was convinced they would never defeat Germany. It was unthinkable and he played his own part in the great struggle. Even now he was involved in an operation that remained uniquely his and profoundly secret: a plan that would rock the Allies back on their heels and make them slacken their tenuous grip on Normandy. The A-4 rocket would play its part in what would be the greatest psychological defeat of the war.

The key components for the operation were already in place in England. All but the launching of the V-2 rockets were in position for Operation *Löwenzahn*. Operation Lion's Teeth.

Tomorrow, Voltsenvogel would return to his headquarters in Holland and continue the battle from there.

CHAPTER ELEVEN

Laura Cotter stooged up Bluefields Road feeling less than happy with her lot. The air was suffused with filthy, sooty factory smoke: the red brick of the semi-detached houses grimed almost black by the pollution. In these days you didn't produce the country's steel without making smoke and dirt.

Tommy Livermore said he wanted Emma Penticost and Ron Worrall with him in the interview room. Laura was to do what the initial investigating officers had omitted—go back into the victim's life, and sort out the small print of her existence.

The Sheffield CID had only scraped the surface of Doris Butler's twenty-six years. They had dug out the basic information: the wedding in 1936 against her parents' wishes— they had finally relented and given their reluctant blessing ('So as not to spoil Doris's day.'). Before that there were the jobs she had done: the Pitman's shorthand/typing course, then the work, first in the council offices, one of two secretaries to the town clerk, later for a solicitor, Mr Fullalove. Friends said it was a good name for Doris to be associated with, Fullalove. Lastly, almost as an afterthought, in a footnote to the original murder reports, was the information that Doris had worked four days a week as a civilian clerk to the RTO at Sheffield's Victoria Railway Station, through which the main London North Eastern Railway ran the most important of its trains. The RTO was a military appointment, usually Army—the officer who was law to all military persons travelling on the railways.

Eventually Sheffield CID woke up to the fact that they couldn't interview the parents because Mr and Mrs Haynes—Doris had been a Haynes up to the wedding—had died together in the same air raid that destroyed the Marples Hotel in the city centre: December 1940.

Tommy saw Laura's face when he gave her the instructions. 'Just get on with it,' he said. 'Follow up. Do it,' in that hurtful way he sometimes turned on when things went awry. 'You know how to sort out the details of a victim. Go backwards and forwards; up and down; you never know what you'll turn up.'

She pulled herself together and said, 'Yes,

131

Chief,' even managing a limpid smile.

'Fine-tooth comb time, Laura,' he nodded, giving her his terrible smile.

She even heard him say, 'Keep her out of trouble,' as she was leaving, closing the door.

He didn't even let her use a car, or take someone with her. It was all bus and Shanks's pony—as her mum used to say when she had to walk anywhere.

There was some kind of flap on about the case; you didn't have to get even a pass or credit in instinct to know that; also to be aware that it was something internal, in the Sheffield nick. Tommy had said he wanted Emma and Ron with him in case he lost his temper. Never a pretty sight, he said with an awful rasp. Laura thought she was best out of it. So she plodded on, her mind brimming with Detective Sergeant Dennis Free of the Reserve Squad who was off working with DI Mountford in Gloucestershire, far away. Smiling as she trudged, thinking of Dennis and his lovely, open smile, his nice, strong arms, hard body and the unruly hair that would fall in front of his eyes—'Lau, I'm blinded by my hair,' he'd say in a strangulated voice. 'I can't see. Help me, Lau, help.' And she'd help him and that would be nice. Crumbs how she loved Sergeant Free. Laugh through the tears, Woman Detective Constable Cotter.

Now she was doing her job, schlepping around witnesses, digging the dirt, sorting wheat from chaff, doing a recce in depth. First off was Mrs Carter—Phyllis—neighbour of the late Mrs Butler, the one whose husband, Martin, was Fleet Air Arm: a Wopag. Wireless Operator Air Gunner.

'Get in close and then work outwards,' Tommy always counselled. 'Talk to them. Waffle with confidence.' Which meant pretend you know more than you do. 'Needle them. Get under their skin, up their fundaments, wiggle about a bit.'

Phyllis Carter's house was, to use Laura's mum's favourite expression, 'prick neat', which she presumed had something to do with 'clean as a new pin', though she'd never heard anyone else use the term, 'prick neat'. Her dad always said, 'neat as a bee's foot', but he'd had Irish connections so anything he said could probably be traced to the banks of the Liffey. Anyway, Mrs Carter's little semi looked as though she ran the Ewbank cleaner over the carpet every hour and polished the stair rods after that, then spent the afternoon with a duster stuck to her hand.

In the front room there was a big print of cows drinking from a mountain valley stream right over the fireplace, hanging from a cord reaching up to a moveable hook over the picture rail. There was red tissue among the coal in the fireplace, and a picture of roses in a glass bowl on the wall directly opposite the Highland cattle guzzling in the foothills. The three-piece suite was obviously kept for special occasions: it had matching cushions rarely dinted and beige antimacassars over the back of the chairs, two for the settee, and a large pouffe covered in matching floral material— cabbage roses and greenery—pushed into a corner near the French windows. There was a set of nesting tables but no sign of a cup of tea with a Nice biscuit to beat back the pangs until lunchtime.

Phyllis Carter was thin, all angles and sharp features, with light brown hair, bronze really, pulled back from her face, tied in a bun at the nape of her neck, severe, held in place with hairpins. She sat opposite Laura, but on the edge of her chair, as if the possibility of fully relaxing and putting her whole bottom on the seat was anathema to her.

'I've told all I know,' she said, whining a shade defensively. Frightened eyes, Laura considered.

'I just came to see if you were all right.' Laura tried her trusting smile, holding her hands wide apart, as if inviting Phyllis in for a cuddle.

'I'm fine. The newspapers've stopped bothering me, oh, six or seven days ago.'

'They'll start again once we've made an arrest.'

'You got someone in mind?' Phyllis obviously lacked social skills, her eyes darted around the room as though searching for neglected dust, not sure if the room was fit for visitors.

'We're working on it.' Laura sounded confident, like a poker player with a full house, aces on kings. 'Just don't want you worried, that's all.'

This triggered a response. Phyllis seemed to draw back a little and her eyes became more wary. 'Should I be worried?' A mite out of breath.

'Well, just thought you might be. Doris Butler had some unpleasant visitors, we hear.'

'She had some pleasant ones as well.' For the first time, Phyllis Carter gave a hint of humour, a tiny smile crossing her lips like a neon sign lighting up. Just for a second Laura saw it, then it was gone.

'You saw some fanciable ones then?'

Phyllis gave a swift shake of the head. 'I'm a happily married woman, Miss Cotter.'

'Possibly, but you can still think, can't you?'

No reply.

'Particularly when your hubby's away at sea in these dangerous days.'

'I suppose so.' Not an unqualified agreement, in fact not an agreement at all.

'You've told us some names already . . .'

'Two names, and one of them uncertain.'

'Had any more thoughts?'

'No. None. I seen quite a few blokes but never recognised them.'

'And Mrs Butler . . . ? You say you borrowed

135

some chairs from her when your hubby was on leave. Did she stay friendly?'

'Not really. A nod sometimes in passing. Doris was a strange girl; I doubt she'd even own to being at school with me.'

'At school with you?' That hadn't come up before.

'Oh, only at mixed infants. We were mixed infants, then still together at the C. of E. School for Girls.' She stopped as if somehow she had said too much. Then she took an audible breath as though about to continue but nothing came of it.

'You were friends as children?' Laura asked.

She didn't reply immediately, then didn't answer the question when she spoke, going off on a riff of her own (Laura thought in riffs, jazz-lover that she was, listening to Django Reinhardt on *Jazz Club*, old records from Le Hot Club de Paris; BBC Home & Forces Programme). 'Doris was kind of a snob. Went on to Sheffield High, out at Broomhill, them wi' the brown uniforms: got a scholarship.' Another pause. Wait. 'Problem with Doris, she married beneath herself.' Looked up under her eyelashes. Count of around ten. 'Rog Butler was a bit of an oik really. I reckon she only married him because her mum and dad didn't want her to. She was just man mad, Doris. Didn't matter who they were really as long as they'd got the equipment.' She thought better of the last remark. 'No, no, I shouldn't

136

say that, but she did have the reputation of being a little tart. No shortage of money though, her dad being a chemist. Had a shop in the centre. Her mum had been wi' him in the shop that day, when the bombs began to fall.'

Laura asked if she saw much of Doris after she went on to the grammar—Sheffield High School for Girls.

'Used to see her on the bus sometimes. And out on a Saturday, buying war paint, powder and lipstick. Liked to tart herself up on the weekends.'

'Special friends?'

'She had a gang she used to go round with— Milly Hadrill—Millicent—Betty Cummin, didn't know if she were coming or going, they used to say. Julia Archard, Georgina Howith, stuck up that one. That were Doris's special friend, Georgie Howith. Went around like they were joined at the hip, never out of each other's pockets.' She smiled to herself and Laura had the feeling that Phyllis Carter didn't have many people to talk to. Spent a lot of time with herself. 'Look how they ended up, Doris in a three up, three down, with Roger Butler; and Georgie Howith now Georgina French. French, Summers and Landis, estate agents with a big place up Ecclesall. Could fit Doris's house half a dozen times inside the French mansion, The Towers they call it. Showplace. I bet she didn't give Doris a second thought once she got off wi' Alistair French, though I'd like to know why he isn't in the Forces: looks fit enough to me and that's not a reserved occupation, estate agent.'

'She still live there? Up Ecclesall?'

Phyllis nodded. 'Wi' all the steel owners, yes. You won't catch Georgie round Woolworths make-up counter of a Saturday afternoon these days, oh no.'

'The Towers?'

Phyllis gave a giggle, not particularly mirthful. 'No, some people's idea of a joke. No, I think it's called Beeches, or Birches. Might as well be called Britches. That's what Doris and Georgie were after most weekends.'

'And you say she was clever, Doris?'

'Oh, yes. But never really used it, except, perhaps, when she worked for the Army. The RTO at Victoria.' The smile again.

'Clever? How?'

'I heard languages. They said she was good with foreign languages, but I wouldn't know. Doris wouldn't give me time of day even when she was still at school in her brown uniform.'

The conversation went on for another ten minutes. Laura knew about girls like Doris, boys as well. She'd been at school with a brilliant boy, well, he'd been at King Arthur's Grammar and she'd been at St Anne's. Danny Timson, got the best results ever in his School Cert, all credits and distinctions. Went into the Navy and invalided out in '43. Could've taken

138

his pick of jobs, gone to Oxford or Cambridge or both. Went on the buses. Conductor. 'No ambition,' her father said. 'No will to succeed. Head stuffed full of facts, nothing to back them up.' She wondered if that was true or whether he was a fish out of water, uncomfortable out of his own class, because class mattered whatever people said.

She untangled herself from Phyllis, told her to telephone the station if she had any problems, said she'd been a great help.

Next on the list was Eileen Shanty: Fat Eileen, Pete Hill's girl—Pete the electrician who favoured girls you could get hold of; Pete Hill, Roger Butler's cousin looking out for Doris.

And Eileen was certainly plump. You could have made three of Doris out of Fat Eileen.

'Saw her at the St Giles' dance that Saturday, Doris,' Eileen told her, pleasing and smiling in spite of the excess flesh—had to be some thyroid disorder, Laura thought. But she was light on her feet and laughed a lot. 'Yes, yes, Doris was often at the St Giles' dance of a Saturday. Never brought Roger with her when he was home.' Giggle. 'Might've met too many boyfriends if she'd brought him. Bit leery, Doris. Though she did bring that lodger she had stayin' wi' her a few weeks before. Weren't shy about *him*. No.'

'What lodger?' Laura asked. First time they'd heard of a lodger far as she knew,

139

though the chief didn't tell them all the good secrets.

'He were wi' the Poles, I think. Polish pilot or something, they said. Big bloke, always grinning and speaking fifteen to the dozen. Maybe not a pilot but definitely a Pole. Polish.'

Well I never, Laura thought to herself, and went off to pin down Georgina French, Georgina Howith as was. But there was nobody home at The Laurals—as it turned out to be—except a crisp woman in a starched pinny who told her that Mrs French was out for the afternoon and wouldn't be back until six or later.

So Laura took herself back to the nick where Tommy had been in a high old temper that afternoon.

*   *   *

In the bundle of documents passed to Tommy Livermore under the heading 'Doris Butler: Sheffield Murder Investigation' were a series of reports by an eccentric detective constable named Horace Betteridge, known to his mates as Harry Betters.

Betteridge spent many of his duty hours on obbo, skulking around likely places such as Sheffield's Victoria Railway Station, St Giles' Hall and other interesting locations near the centre of the city, dodging trams and keeping an eye out for the shady side of the local

140

populace: people concerned with thieving, dealing in illicit food or clothes coupons, food itself and people involved in matters illegal running from homicide to whoring.

He was a thin man, thirty years of age, five-eleven in his stocking feet, with a strange walk giving the impression that he was always negotiating steep stairs, even when he was on the flat. He also possessed a livid scar running straight across his forehead, the remnant of a collision with a large brick during an air raid in 1941. The brick had not survived; Betteridge had. Some said that his oddities dated from the impact of the brick. Sergeant Percival, one of the desk sergeants, had been heard to mutter in the vicinity of Harry Betteridge, 'And some fell on stony ground.'

Many of this young DC's reports bordered on paranoia or fantasy, but there were times when he managed to drag interesting facts into the light of day. The three reports in the Butler file had been made during the weeks leading up to her demise.

'I have known Doris Butler since she was Doris Haynes,' he began the first report. 'On the face of it she is a well-brought-up girl, but she appears to me to be a young woman of somewhat loose moral behaviour and it strikes me that when loose morals show themselves a life of near-criminal folly cannot be far behind. I was, therefore, not wholly surprised to see her, from time to time, in the company of men

141

who were neither her husband, nor male relatives.'

If Tommy had not known better he would have put Horace Betteridge down as a lay preacher attached to one of the nonconformist churches, or maybe a small extreme and strict religious sect. He was none of these things but, as Superintendent Berry often remarked, 'Betteridge is a man who likes the sound of his own voice, particularly when he is making comments in writing.' Mr Berry was not averse to mixing metaphors and, on this occasion, seemed to have done the mixing with a patent kitchen whisk.

Now here was Betteridge standing in front of Tommy Livermore, wraith-thin, head in the clouds and a strange expression on his pasty face. Turn sideways and he'd disappear.

'Detective Constable Betteridge,' Tommy started, formally and not unkindly because Ron Worrall was adamant that the man was an anomaly. 'Odd, Harpic, right round the bend,' he'd said. 'Good at the straightforward stuff, but put him in a complex situation and he's off with the fairies.'

'Detective Constable Betteridge, I want to talk to you about these reports you made about men seen with Doris Butler during the three weeks or so before her murder.'

'Oh, yes, sir?' He had a high, not unpleasant, voice stuffed full of inflections that always seemed to be asking questions.

'What drew your attention to these men?'
Smile, grin, switch off.

'As strangers, sir, they were a matter for
consideration.'

'Strangers?'

'I was brought up in a village, sir. Any
strangers walking into our village were
considered suspicious until they was proved
otherwise.'

Tommy thought the man had finished and
was about to frame another question. Wrong;
Betteridge was off again. 'My first DI
understood. Like me he was always suspicious
of foreigners. "Harry," he used to say, "Harry,
always remember that wogs begin at Calais." I
am even more suspicious these days, sir.
Always suspicious of Johnnie Foreigner.'

Tommy Livermore stifled another smile.
Jee-rusalem. Here we are heading towards the
middle of the twentieth century and we've got
idiot policemen talking about 'Johnnie
Foreigner'.

'You suspected these men because they
were foreign?'

'Well, two of them was, guv.'

'Just because they were foreign?'

'They seemed very chummy with Doris, sir.'

'And what was suspicious about that?'

'Sheffield was all Doris knew, Mr
Livermore. She'd never been out of the
country as far as I knew—except maybe a day
trip to Boulogne.'

'And what difference did that make?'

'She was on intimate terms with these men, soon as she met them. Well, intimate talking terms that is. Possibly the other as well.'

'She was an attractive girl, wasn't she?'

'Very attractive, sir. But she was married an' all.'

'Tell me about the first man.'

'Yes, sir. I finally approached them—him and Mrs Butler—and he identified hisself as a Frog called Maisondel. Henri Jacques Maisondel. Said he was staying at the Butler house—that semi they had up Bluefields Road. Doris chipped in and said he was an old family friend and was staying there all above board. All proper. Said he was just down from the north and going to report to Free French Forces HQ, in Duke Street, London.'

'And you still felt suspicious.'

'About Maisondel? Yes, sir.'

'Why?'

'I just felt there was something not quite right, sir. Something wrong. They seemed very close, him and Doris Butler.'

'You've agreed that Mrs Butler was a most attractive woman.'

'Indeed she was, Mr Livermore. Oh yes, price above rubies. Married woman, though. Wasn't right the way she was carrying on.'

'How *was* she carrying on?'

'All lovie-dovie like, sir. Wasn't seemly. And in French also. Good at languages, Doris.'

'So what did you do about it?'

'Passed it on to the MPs at the RTO, Victoria Station. And made the report that you have there, sir.' He leant forward pushing a finger towards the papers in front of Tommy.

'That was the sum total of it?'

'Sum total, guv. Yes. Oh, there was one thing. The day I first saw Maisondel with Mrs Butler?'

'Yes?'

'That was the first day I became aware of Sergeant Mungo.'

'Really, this was . . .' Tommy turned to the top of the report. 'This was 19th May?'

'Then about a week later, round about 25th May, I seen Doris again. This time with the Pole. That is the Polish officer, Korob. They was also a bit close to one another which wasn't right because in the intervening period her husband had been home on leave. Fact he'd only just gone back and there she was arm in arm with this Pole. Stefan Korob. So I stopped them again and she got quite snooty. "Major Korob is attached to General Maczek's staff," she tells me, all la-de-da and says something to him in Pole and he laughs.'

You bet, Tommy thought, detecting a case of the green-eyed monster here. Old Betteridge had the hots for Doris back in the mixed infants, he reckoned. 'So you followed the same course. Checked it with the MPs, wrote a report, then clocked Mungo for the

145

second time. Looked like Mungo was carrying out his own bit of observation.'

'Quite right, sir. Second time I noticed Mr Mungo, though I still didn't know who he was. No idea he was in the job.' Which was the way coppers talked about other coppers: 'he's in the job,' they'd say meaning he's a copper just like me. 'And it was decidedly iffy, sir. I approached him . . .'

'Mungo? You approached Mungo?'

Betteridge nodded. 'But he didn't call hisself Mungo. I'd seen him lurking about and I'd had enough so I approached him.'

'And?'

'I identified myself. DC Betteridge, number, station, all that. Asked him who he was and what he was doing. Reluctant.'

'Mungo was reluctant?'

'Showed me his identity card, said his name was Short. Anthony James Short. Lived here in Sheffield. Said he was down the railway station waiting for a friend who had said he would be arriving soon.'

'And his identity card?'

'Bore it out. Anthony James Short. Address checked out an' all. Next time I saw him he was Mungo. David Charles, on attachment to Sheffield CID. Mr Berry dead proud of him. Mystery, guv.'

'You're absolutely sure this Short was Mungo?'

'Stake me life on it, sir.'

146

Everybody carried an identity card or a military paybook. Blue oblong card folded over. Gave you a number: your name and address. You carried your identity card everywhere you went—coppers carried warrant cards of course, but if you weren't in His Majesty's Armed Forces you carried your card and had to show it if asked. Tommy thought about it for a moment. Strange bloke, Betteridge. Could have made a mistake.

'Then there was a third newcomer wasn't there?' he asked.

'There was, sir. Three days before Doris went missing, then was discovered bereft of life.'

Bereft of life? Tommy thought. Crikey. 'What kind of books you read, Betteridge? Poetry of Patience Strong?'

'I don't have the patience for poetry, guv.' And Tommy wondered if the detective constable was taking the mickey.

'And this third foreigner?'

'Wasn't a foreigner, guv. British through and through.'

'To the core, as you might say.'

'Indeed. Gittins, guv. Stanley Gittins, corporal. 1st Battalion, Suffolk Regiment. Returning to his unit from leave.'

'Another old friend.'

'Old and intimate friend of Doris Butler's by the look of things, guv.'

'Sergeant Mungo still in evidence?'

147

'Skulking, sir. Secreting himself behind piles of luggage and in doorways.'

'Secreting himself?' Tommy wondered how that went. 'I shall speak to Sergeant Mungo now, Ron.' He looked up at his sergeant. 'And we will talk again, DC Betteridge.'

'Very good, sir.'

The DC shambled out and Tommy waited for Mungo to be brought in.

Kenny Craig had said it all, was willing to testify in court if need be.

That sergeant. Sergeant Dave Mungo. Seen him there with her in the buff, going at it hammer and tongs: going like a steam engine and she went off like a train whistle at the end.

Now, Tommy thought it was time to deal with it, bring it out into the open, kick it around, thump it, spit on it. He told Ron they should be casual about it, tell Dave Mungo that Mr Livermore wanted to see him, not make a song and dance. So that's what they did while Tommy waited and fumed at the thought of a DS here on attachment doing the business with Doris Butler in full view of an open window so that Ken Craig could finger him, if for no other reason than Ken Craig was a dirty little bugger.

And what of Betteridge saying Mungo claimed to be a civilian: Short, Anthony James?

And only a couple of nights ago, DS David Mungo had said to Tommy, 'We should speak,

148

sir.' Yes, Tommy thought now. Yes, we're going to bloody speak; and Ron brought Mungo in, Ron just behind his right shoulder, Emma Penticost on his left, a pace behind Ron, all expectant, precise, giving off the static of readiness, face eager, eyes bright.

'Sit down, Mungo.' Tommy took no notice of the sergeant's hand coming up, reaching forward trying to be chummy. 'Just sit down and answer my questions.' Looked at him for the first time: looked and bored through him, po-faced, not a flicker. Mungo, light-haired, muscular, bronzed, quick deliberate movements, gave the impression that he was straight as a die.

Straight, Tommy thought and said, 'I'm going to put things to you straight, Sar'nt Mungo, no messing.' Deep breath, hold it for a count of twenty. Smile. 'I've a witness says he saw you with the late Doris Butler doing the horizontal tango. Saw you in her bedroom, through an open window, a week or so before she died. Lovely summer evening, he says, and you banging at the deceased like a piston engine. He'll stand up in court and identify you. Delighted to do so, because I detect that he doesn't much like the police. Man name of Kenneth Craig.'

'Never heard of him.' Mungo shook his head.

If Tommy had expected a big reaction he wasn't going to get it. Mungo didn't flicker, didn't wince as if socked on the jaw. Tommy had more or less expected the invisible bullet trick. This man, Mungo, so damned full of self-confidence, shook his head again. 'Couldn't have happened, sir.' All suave and how's your father.

'That all you've got to say for yourself?'

Mungo nodded.

'What?' Tommy yapped.

'Sir, I can't make any other comment. He couldn't have seen me because I wasn't posted here on attachment to Mr Berry's CID until the day after Doris Butler was murdered. Well, the day after her body was found.'

'And DC Betteridge claims you identified yourself as an Anthony James Short living here in Sheffield. What of that?'

'No comment, sir.'

'What are you, Mungo?'

'Detective Sergeant David Mungo, Special Branch, on attachment to Sheffield CID to assist on the Doris Butler murder, sir.'

'Ahhh.' And the scales fell from his eyes, Tommy thought. Mungo of the Branch, one of Woolly Bear's merry men.

'So I suppose you know nothing about having identified yourself to DC Betteridge as one Anthony James Short?'

'I've heard the story, sir.'

'And you deny it?'

'Don't recall it, sir. Before being moved down here I was working a case concerning

150

flashing lights off the Welsh coast.'

'Not those lighted arrows the more insular Taffies pointed towards Liverpool to assist the Luftwaffe?'

'That was a few years ago, sir. These were different lights.'

'So you don't know anything about a Free French soldier, a Polish officer or a man called Gittins, corporal from 1st Battalion, Suffolk Regiment? All friends of the late Mrs Doris Butler? Ever heard of them at all?'

'Yes, I've read Betteridge's reports.'

'Any comment you'd like to make?'

'None I *can* make, sir. Except you'd best talk to Chief Superintendent Bear.'

'I'll do that, Mungo. Did you follow up on Betteridge's reports?'

'I did, sir. Yes.'

'And?'

'And I can't talk about it, sir. But I followed it up with the MPs at the Railway Transport Officer's department at Sheffield Victoria.'

'They were forthcoming?'

'To some extent, sir, but I'd prefer it if you talked to Mr Bear.'

'I'll do that, but I'd suggest you hold yourself ready to return with me to the RTO tomorrow morning. Say at 9 a.m. ?'

'Suits me, sir.'

Tommy seldom swore—not what you'd call real swearing—but he broke the rule when he finally got through to Detective Chief

151

Superintendent Bear of Special Branch. 'Woolly, it's Tommy Livermore. I've just been talking to young Dave Mungo. What the fuck's going on with him here?'

'Can't talk about it on the telephone, Tommy,' not a hair out of place. 'Come down here and I'll tell you all. But not on the telephone. No can do. Not on an open line.'

CHAPTER TWELVE

The journey to Gloucester was arduous: Dennis Free driving, Shirley Cox in the back and Suzie sitting up front chattering to Dennis, talking about the nuns—'Fancy giving up your identity,' Dennis said. 'Wasted lives, I reckon.' Suzie didn't respond, knew what it meant to be a nun from her school days, just nodded, and glad she had not been called to that kind of life. These nuns taught, she said, so their lives were not wasted.

'Well,' Dennis smiled to himself. 'Well, I don't know. I don't think I believe in God. Not a God that allows things like this bloody war to go on, people like Hitler and his terrible . . .'

Suzie grunted, said the war was the fault of men and women. 'There's such a thing as free will,' quite snappy. 'God doesn't intervene when man goes astray. Like now. Like this war. We've got to find our own way back.'

152

'You mean, will we ever learn?' Shirley Cox said from the back seat.

'Something like that, but we shouldn't talk about religion or politics. Very few people can agree on both scores.' She half turned and saw her little attaché case on the shelf behind the rear seat. She had packed it carefully: pyjamas, spare undies, schoolgirl sponge bag, and a copy of the book she was reading—Lloyd C Douglas's *The Robe*, the epic inspirational novel about the effect of Christ's robe on the Roman soldier who wins it in a dice game at the foot of the cross. She was enjoying *The Robe*, getting towards the end, thinking what she'd read next. Suzie was lost if she didn't have a book on the go.

The little case had belonged to her dad who used to carry his Masonic gear around in it. Her mum, Helen, had sold the Masonic stuff and Suzie had purloined the case.

She had the photos in her briefcase, the one that could easily double as a school music case: had done in its time. They were all black and white of course: a glossy of Novice Mary Theresa as she was on entering the convent— fair hair falling to the collar of a white blouse, a short stylish jacket over the blouse— probably from a good suit, Suzie thought— plaid skirt, heavy and pleated with her feet in what looked like sensible brogues. The girl's eyes seemed wide and bright, her head tilted upwards, almost arrogantly, so that the eyes

153

seemed to be focused on you—a demanding gaze—lips parted though not in a smile. She seemed to be saying, 'Yes it's me and you can do what you like about it because I'm going to do what I think is best for me.' A woman who knew her own mind: had to if she planned to be a nun, subject herself to obedience and discipline. Bride of Christ.

On the back of the print was a typewritten slip that read: Winifred Audrey Lees-Duncan. Entered Novitiate 5/6/40 d.o.b. 6/8/13.

Under that photograph were three others: the two novices in death, though the pictures were so cunning, you wouldn't know. They looked to be sleeping while the man passed as being alive: a dark, unruly thatch of hair ruffled above his unlined forehead, eyes open, glinting from the light the police photographer had skilfully used; a straight, almost Roman, nose above a full mouth, closed and stilled now for ever. Square jaw, no dimple, and below it the gown they had pulled up to cover what Suzie thought of as a second smile—the cloven throat where the knife had sliced. Good, but wouldn't fool everybody.

After the first few miles they didn't talk much, certainly Suzie made it plain that she wasn't going to argue about religion, and once out into open country she found herself thinking about how nice it would be to settle somewhere near her old childhood haunts, in the countryside near Newbury. Her mind

154

began to revolve around idealised pictures of meadows, corn fields, brooks and streams, woods and, in particular, the copse they had called the Dingle abutting onto her family's property, Larksbrook, where she had been so happy growing up, until her father was killed less than a hundred yards from their drive. Sometimes, living in the dirty, dusty, crowded, tired city of London, her heart longed for what she recalled as clean air, the fresh country smells and the freedom of her old home. She knew this was very much an idyllic memory, not one hundred per cent accurate, but she drew courage from the knowledge it was there, that she could, if absolutely necessary, run to it if the need arose. Lord, she had been lucky growing up with a loving mother and father, and few concerns in her safe middle-class family. Even the books she could recall from the early days featured a boy, a girl and safe-looking parents. She had been surrounded with love, her elder sister and younger brother, her daddy and mummy. Sister and father gone now. She swallowed and pulled her mind away from the unpleasant things, back to the positive memories.

There was a small stream that widened into a pool in the Dingle and they spent hours as children playing around the water, making a raft and braving a rope swing on which she and Charlotte could traverse the pond. The rope was an odd, orange colour and there had been a terrible row which ended in painful spankings—quite right, she now thought—after they had goaded the much younger James onto the swing. Terrified, he had slipped and hurtled into the water from which her father had splashed in to rescue him, though it was Helen who had administered the punishment, much to the two sisters' shame and chagrin at the time. Charlotte must have been twelve but that didn't save her from her mother's hard-backed hairbrush. But they didn't take risks around the water again.

They reached Oxford just before half past three and stopped for tea, fish paste sandwiches and rock cakes in a café in the Turl. On their way again by four they reached Gloucester at a little before six and took the road straight out to Churchbridge. The gravel crunched under the tyres of the crimson Railton around twenty minutes later when they turned into the drive of The Manor with its red-brick front and the wonderful cloak of Virginia creeper waterfalling down between the windows.

'Storing up terrible trouble for his brickwork, that creeper,' Dennis muttered.

Shirley Cox said he probably had minions to deal with it, and Suzie gave a little bleat as she thought of the butler, up a ladder with shears, while the fiery Lees-Duncan shouted orders from the ground.

Inside it became immediately apparent that

156

John Lees-Duncan had been advised and cautioned by somebody; a changed man, more contained, not trying to charm or bluster, and in command of his temper. He was also taking no chances for his solicitor was with him, a plump, middle-aged man introduced casually. 'Howard Baldwin,' Lees-Duncan said. He pronounced it Hard Baldwin. 'Had a meeting this afternoon so Howard's stayed on. Thought it best.' They had rung from Gloucester: a courtesy call even though the Lees-Duncans had been informed this morning that they were on their way.

Suzie wondered why he *thought it best*. Feeling guilty about their last meeting? Or conscience pricking about his previous snide behaviour? She still didn't like him. His attitude was that of someone who considered himself vastly superior to other men, no matter how he tried to hide it.

Mrs Lees-Duncan didn't put in an appearance, but the blonde Flight Officer Willow Lees-Duncan was still in attendance. 'Got an extra few days on the strength of this mix-up,' she said to Suzie with a winning smile, and Suzie so wished that Tommy could be here. She was certain he would preen and flatter.

'I have a photograph of the lady who claimed to be you, Miss Lees-Duncan,' delving into the briefcase and bringing out the picture of the late Novice Mary Theresa. Shirley Cox watched the girl and Dennis only had eyes for John Lees-Duncan. Dennis was good at detecting reactions.

'The one killed by the flying bomb,' she added.

'Good Lord!' Lees-Duncan looking over his daughter's shoulder.

'It's Dulcie,' said Willow, a crack in her voice, roughness in her larynx. 'Dulcie Tovey. So that's where she went. No wonder we've never seen her again.'

'Good Lord,' Lees-Duncan repeated, and again, 'Good Lord!'

'You recognise this person, then?' Suzie took a step forward.

'Yes, yes.' Willow spoke first. 'Of course.'

'Daughter of me head gardener,' Lees-Duncan frowned. 'Me only gardener nowadays.' Then, 'Good Lord!' he said yet again.

'And you had no idea . . . ?' Suzie began.

'Thought she'd gone away, joined the ATS or something. They didn't get on, Bob Tovey and his daughter.'

'That's an understatement,' Willow said with a near jokey laugh. 'She looked after him when her mother, Katie Tovey, left. Came back. Didn't want to come back but she did. Fought like cat and dog.'

'Eventually up and left. Must've gone from here to this nunnery. She'd have been better in the Forces or as a Land Girl.'

158

'She was always religious,' Willow said, a sad, yearning in the words. The WAAF officer was upset.

'Where did this Mr Tovey go?' Dennis asked.

'Still here. Still in my service. You'll have to talk to him, I suppose.'

Suzie told him, yes she would have to see the man.

'Cottage other side of the kitchen garden.'

They were in the same drawing room where Suzie had first interviewed him and Lees-Duncan started towards the small pair of french doors in the wall to the left of the big bay window. 'Take you over there myself,' he said but Suzie reached out, touching his arm with her hand.

'Just one other thing, sir,' she said, the idea coming into her head. 'While we're all together here, just on the off chance.'

She returned the photograph of Novice Mary Theresa to her briefcase and extracted the one of the man. She thought, this one's rising from the dead, but didn't say anything. 'On the off chance,' she repeated. 'Off chance you might know this man.'

They craned forward and Willow gave a horrible little strangled cry, as though the breath was being pummelled out of her by a shock. 'Daddy,' she cried. 'Oh God . . . Daddy! Daddy! It's Michael . . . Daddy! . . . Michael!'

'Dear heaven, what has that stupid boy

159

done?' As he inhaled, John Lees-Duncan gave a sob. 'Dead, isn't he? The boy's dead.'

Suzie nodded and both Dennis and Shirley stepped closer.

'My brother, Michael,' said Willow. She had gone white and looked stricken.

The lawyer just stood there opening and closing his mouth, like a fish. 'Oh, my,' he said wrapping his meaty hand around John Lees-Duncan's forearm. 'John. Courage. Oh my,' like some clergyman in an Aldwych farce.

CHAPTER THIRTEEN

Later, Suzie was pleased with herself; pleased about the way she dealt with it all: decisively, intuitively; didn't have to stop and think about the what and how of matters: asking Lees-Duncan if she could use the telephone ('If you must,' he responded, returning to the imperious manner she had found so distasteful on their first meeting); then telling him that if the photograph was indeed that of his elder son, Michael, they would have to talk at length, by which she meant an interrogation, though she didn't say it aloud. Her first duty, she added, would be to see the gardener, Tovey, and break the news of his daughter's death.

Lees-Duncan simply shrugged. 'If that's

160

what you've got to do,' he grunted.

'Perhaps you should tell Mrs Lees-Duncan about your son as well, sir,' she began, but he waved her away saying his wife was unwell. He would talk to her later and, yes, that was certainly his eldest son.

Willow sobbed quietly, eyes brimming as she explained that Dulcie Tovey was her age, that they had been close, 'like sisters,' she said and Suzie asked about her brother, Michael, and Willow told her that Dulcie and Michael had also been close, which was not what she was asking. Though it was interesting anyway. Her father made some remark about it being an unhealthy relationship, and Suzie was not certain if she meant Michael with Dulcie or Willow with Dulcie.

It was clear that Dulcie's death made more of an impact on Willow than her brother's demise. John Lees-Duncan said nothing, but his hands trembled like those of a man naked in a blizzard. Then he began talking to Willow, chivvying her, Suzie thought, until they were having a full-blown, inaudible argument, each speaking in a low mutter that rose and fell to some tempo of their own choosing.

Unaccountably, Suzie thought of the jacket Novice Mary Theresa wore in the photograph, wondering if it was a hand-me-down of Willow's. They had been close and it was so obviously a tailored item. Had she passed it on to the gardener's daughter?

She took Shirley Cox to one side and quietly pointed out that it was now necessary to separate the Lees-Duncans and probably the gardener, Tovey. 'I'll need to talk to each one of them without the other. I'll try and get Gloucester nick to send up some extra bodies,' which she reckoned would be like getting hens to lay square eggs. 'You find somewhere to take Willow where I can talk to her. I'll look after the father first after I've seen the gardener.' She turned away then, as an afterthought, 'Oh and drop that useless legal sparrow Baldwin down the nearest well.'

'Of course, guv. Anything you say, guv.' Shirley gave her a raised eyebrow, right corner of her mouth turned up in an exaggerated smirk indicating this last would be as easy as making dentures for hens.

'The telephone?' Suzie asked Lees-Duncan who inclined his head towards the hall.

'And Mrs Lees-Duncan?'

'Poor Isabel,' he said, shaking his head. 'She's not available. Unwell.'

Suzie nodded to Dennis and Shirley, closed the door on her way out, and picked up the telephone in the hall.

When the operator came on she asked to be put through to Gloucester nick, repeating the number straight from the notation in her pocketbook. She was given a bit of a run around at the other end but finally found herself speaking to the duty officer, an

Inspector Gaimes, Cyril Gaimes, known to the staff of Gloucester central police station as 'Waiting' Gaimes because of the unconscionable time he took to make up his mind on anything: whether he wanted sugar in his tea, or how many officers he should dispatch to an incident.

She explained the situation: her need for at least one uniformed constable and a WPC to keep things legally secure. The inspector hummed and hawed, said he couldn't possibly spare anybody, so she reminded him that Churchbridge was in his manor, and the situation was serious: two deaths, one possible murder. No, she thought, definite murder but didn't say so. Finally the inspector said he would point the local village 'bobby' in the direction of the Manor House, and he'd also have another officer sent out with a WPC in tow.

As she replaced the receiver she glimpsed the butler standing at the foot of the stairs, stock still; had no idea how long he had been standing there, vaguely aware that she had first seen him out of the corner of her eye as she finished the conversation. She turned and he diplomatically cleared his throat, his hand coming up and head bobbing in a little bow. Old Scrotum, she thought, smiling to herself and thinking fondly of Tommy. The wrinkled retainer.

'Is there anything, madam? Anything I can

do?' A precise voice, pitched low. They also serve, she thought, who only stand and wait, or just creep around earwigging.

'You heard what I said on the phone?'

'Yes, madam.' He was tallish, well built, broad shouldered, muscular, though past retirement age, which didn't count these days when people were staying in jobs for the duration. Suzie thought there was something military about him; maybe the steel in his light grey eyes or the way he carried himself.

'Your name?' keeping her voice down, not wanting to be heard on the other side of the door.

'Sturgis, madam. Alfred Sturgis.'

'They just call you by your surname? Sturgis, right?'

'Yes, madam.'

'I've brought sad news, bad news. You know that?'

He nodded.

'Which, in turn has revealed more tragic . . .'

'Young Mr Michael . . . ?'

She nodded, 'And the gardener's daughter, Dulcimer.'

'Yes, I am sorry to hear it, madam.'

'You've been with the Lees-Duncans for how long, Sturgis?'

'A little over twenty-five years, madam.'

She almost expected him to say, 'man and boy,' but he stood there waiting. Not a flicker.

'I believe Mrs Lees-Duncan is unwell.'

164

'Mrs Lees-Duncan is unwell most afternoons.' He cupped his right hand and made a drinking movement, then a tiny shrug as if to say it was ever thus. He looked sad, as a clown will look sad at the circus. Suzie had always found clowns sinister. Sturgis was sinister, the way he stood, subservient; the manner in which he had appeared, suddenly and silently at the foot of the stairs.

'That been going on long?' she asked.

'A good few years, madam, yes.'

Twenty-five years, she considered. Quarter of a century, a long time to remain in service to one family. Take care, she thought. He may have been willing to tip her off about Mrs Lees-Duncan, but he could well be tied to her husband with bands of steel and reinforced padlocks. Bide your time. 'Sturgis, I have more police officers on their way now. Could you alert me when they arrive?'

'Certainly, madam.' Couple of seconds pause. 'Certainly.'

She did not care for Sturgis. Not at all. As she walked back to the door, Suzie could feel his eyes on her back. Dear Lord, she thought, this should have started when the novices were killed by the V-1, but it's really only starting now. It's starting here. She had no idea why this thought struck her so forcibly.

Now it begins.

The narrow French windows in the left wall, to the side of the great bay window, were still open and the group remained almost as she had left them, seated at the end of the long green settee, a luxurious piece covered in some kind of velvet, dark green like the bottom of a pond. John Lees-Duncan leaning forward, right hand to his chin, elbow braced against his knee, eyes down staring at the carpet, seeing nothing, the face full of pain. Willow sat to his left, far back in her seat, cheeks damp, eyes opening again as Suzie came into the room. Shirley Cox sat on Willow's left and Dennis stood behind John Lees-Duncan.

Outside, the sun was going down, shadows long across the flat-clipped lawn; a sense of the day winding down, birds heading back to their nests; far away an animal call and, coming in from the east, visible now, two aircraft, Lancasters, thrumming their way to wherever they were headed, eight Merlin engines throaty and regular, pulsing through the still air. She knew that in the future the sound of aircraft would be a signal memory of this time of war—aeroplane engines always sounding over the busy skies day and night.

'I want to see Mr Tovey, now,' Suzie said, standing directly in front of John Lees-Duncan. 'Dennis, with me. Shirley look after the young lady while we're away. Other officers should be here shortly. Send one after us. Mr Lees-Duncan, I'd be obliged if you would come with us, show us the way.'

Lees-Duncan raised his head, 'I can show you the way quickly enough.' Back to his surly self. 'I don't need to come with you.'

'I think you do, sir.' All calm, but firm: the concrete hand in the steel glove. 'Come along now.'

Dennis encouraged him, moving closer. Dennis had a threatening quality about him when he wanted to use it: a kind of movement of the shoulders, a swagger, part of a strutting walk. Dead encouraging to anyone who wanted to drag his heels.

Lees-Duncan shook his head. 'I'm in me own house. I don't have to do anything . . .'

'Sir, I realise this may seem strange to you.' Suzie spoke quietly and with a smile she hoped would convey charm. 'But I'm the officer in charge of this investigation and you really do have to cooperate.'

'I'm in me own house.' Lees-Duncan's accent was what you might call educated, apart from the somewhat old-fashioned application of the occasional me instead of my: pronounced sort of meh.

Then who the hell's that, out there cutting me roses?

'We'll see about that. Howard!' As though he was calling a dog to heel rather than his lawyer.

Suzie turned towards the chubby little man, 'Yes, Mr Baldwin, please tell your client.'

'Well, I must protest, Sergeant . . .'

167

'Detective Inspector,' knowing what Tommy meant when he talked of the iron entering his soul. 'And what have you got to protest about, sir? There is a question of identification. His son, Michael, who has died in suspicious circumstances . . .'

The caution appeared to have gone from John Lees-Duncan; in its place was the bluster with a hint of bully. 'Suspicious? You said it was a bloody doodlebug.'

'The man was found dressed as a novice of the order of St Catherine of Siena.'

'Wha—'

'Found in a cell that had been demolished following a V-1 flying bomb exploding in the vicinity . . .'

'There! Enemy action.'

'The man was not killed by the explosion, sir. His throat had been cut.'

This brought Lees-Duncan to a halt, as though brakes had been applied. 'You mean . . .?'

'I mean, sir, that this is a murder inquiry and in all likelihood we'll have to take you back to London with us so you can identify your son's body. Then we'll have to talk to you at length, find out what you know about your son's movements . . .' She stopped, remembering words he had spoken earlier. 'You said just now, Mr Lees-Duncan, something about an unhealthy relationship. I wondered what you meant.'

Lees-Duncan frowned, smiled but said nothing.

'I wondered who you were talking about: your son? your daughter? Dulcimer Tovey?'

'Most likely all three,' he said, leaving them none the wiser.

Suzie looked at him wishing she understood, then said they had better go and see Mr Tovey. So off they went, Lees-Duncan leading the way, followed by Dennis with herself just behind and the lawyer, Howard Baldwin flapping around at the rear.

As they crossed into the garden she asked, 'Mr Lees-Duncan, when did you last hear from your son, Michael?'

'Nineteen thirty-nine, when he walked out of here with his brother. May of that year.'

'You haven't heard from your two sons since '39?'

'What did I just say? Difference of opinion with the pair of them. May, '39. Walked out, both of them.'

'And you had no idea where they'd gone?'

'Friend of mine saw Michael in New York later that year. I caught sight of Gerald in the Troc in '42. He didn't see me. Or didn't want to see me. Ask Willow if you don't believe me.'

A wide gravel path ran along the side of the lawn, within half a dozen paces of the narrow French windows. In front of them, at the far end of the lawn, lay the rose garden, formally laid out, the roses past their best, the place where Suzie had first glimpsed Willow in her flowing dress, big hat and trug, cutting roses, the wide-brimmed hat reminding Suzie of the lady who appeared as a kind of moving colophon for Gainsborough Pictures. She had seen a Gainsborough production only a few weeks ago—*Millions Like Us*, Patricia Roc, Anne Crawford, Eric Portman and Gordon Jackson, the message of which, she reckoned, was that everyone—from those in the front line to those making tiny components for aircraft, ships or guns—were winning the war. Millions of little people fought for victory each in his or her own way.

To their left was a long flowerbed—good old staples, lupins and delphiniums and poppies at the back, antirrhinums, snapdragons, with neatly spaced pansies at the front, flowers looking a shade rough as summer took its toll. The flowerbed was backed by a weathered red-brick wall. Halfway down the bed there was a break to allow access to a door in the wall, green paint, blistered and cracked but secure, with an iron thumb-latch. The door led into a long, blossoming kitchen garden, a greenhouse to the left, sticks for peas and beans, lettuce, a broad potato patch, carrots, some fading large cabbages, tomatoes and cucumbers jungling the greenhouse. Everything neat and ordered, a cinder path running straight through to a small orchard behind which Suzie glimpsed a solid grey stone

170

cottage.

The path took them straight into the little orchard—no more than a stand of trees, apples, plum and a few raspberry bushes protected with netting to the right—up a slight grassy rise to the rear of the cottage. Lees-Duncan stopped, gestured with his hand. 'You'll find him up there, Tovey.'

'You come and introduce us.' Suzie thought she didn't have to be a psychiatric wizard to see that Lees-Duncan was reluctant to talk to his gardener.

Baldwin, the lawyer, stayed back as though he wanted nothing to do with what was going on.

The cottage's back door was open leading, it seemed, straight into a kitchen where a short, wiry man—a grey man, Suzie thought—was slicing up carrots on a chopping board by the sink, while a stew simmered on the gas hob, smelling like something Mum used to make.

Suzie rapped on the door and the man looked up. He wore old working trousers, an open-necked shirt with a waistcoat. His grizzled hair was cut short and he had a droopy growth of grey bristles on his upper lip, below a small nose. You couldn't tell if the bristles meant he was growing a moustache or if he had simply not bothered to shave for a couple of days. This was Tovey, and Suzie caught a full glare from his clear blue eyes. The look was of disinterest coupled with

171

arrogance.

'Tovey,' Lees-Duncan greeted him. 'People to see you. Tell you about Dulcie. Not good news.'

'Oh, yes?' Complete apathy.

Suzie stepped in, introducing herself and holding out the photograph of Dulcie, posing as Winifred Lees-Duncan at the Convent of St Catherine of Siena in Silverhurst Road taken in 1940. 'Is this your daughter, Mr Tovey? Your daughter, Dulcimer?'

Tovey raised his head and glanced at the photograph. 'That looks like her when I last saw her, yes. What you want to know for?'

'She has been living as a novice nun, a sister of the community of St Catherine of Siena.'

'Always bothering God, that one. What's happened now?'

'Mr Tovey, I'm sorry. Dulcimer was killed on Sunday. A flying bomb.'

Tovey gave a little laugh. 'Well, good riddance to bad rubbish is what I say, Inspector.'

It took Suzie's breath away.

CHAPTER FOURTEEN

'Mr Tovey, I understand your difficulties, but . . .' There Suzie paused, frustrated. Paused to get her breath and gain a little time because

172

she really didn't understand why Eric Tovey was taking such a stance, not cooperating, not even treating her questions seriously, distancing himself from the real matter in hand, the death of his daughter.

'But . . . you *have* to give me some reasons, some answers. Whatever happens you'll be expected to come to London with us, if only to formally identify your daughter's body; and maybe answer more questions as well.'

'Can't *he* do it?' Tovey snapped at her. 'Can't the God almighty John Lees-Duncan do it? He knew her as well as I did. Maybe better'n I did.'

Tovey had a distinct country burr to his voice, a quiet, nice, lilting accent that may well have been Gloucestershire. Suzie didn't know, wasn't good at accents, couldn't tell a Norfolk from a Berkshire—well, that wasn't quite true because she knew the Norfolk reasonably well with its distinctive stress on the aspirates. The only one she could be certain of was Mummerset, because an actor had once explained this hybrid ooh-aar bumpkin-like mode of speech to which actors resorted when they weren't conversant with the speech of a certain area. 'Hampshire and Berkshire are loud,' he'd told her, this elderly actor who was a spear carrier in Gielgud's accident-prone production of what he spoke of as 'the Scottish play', at the Piccadilly Theatre a couple of years ago. One of the Witches and their

Duncan had died on tour, the Banquo became seriously ill, and there were unseemly arguments and clashes of temperament about the sets and costumes. Tommy had dragged her to a party where she had met the actor, and she remembered him saying, 'If you haven't mastered a particular county accent, and you're playing the second gravedigger in *Hamlet*, then you'd most naturally play it in Mummerset.'

(Spear Carriers. That's what Tommy called the Squad. 'My Spear Carriers,' he used to say, arm stretched out, moving from left to right, a grand sweeping gesture. Proud of the Spear Carriers.)

'Boring old queen,' Tommy said about that actor on the way home.

'Possibly,' Suzie agreed, 'but I've learnt about Mummerset, and a lot of other things.'

'Feller was showing off.' Tommy was rarely happy about the fraternity whom he referred to collectively as 'that happy band of buggers'; didn't have time for them; rarely showed them any sympathy, and certainly believed the law was correct; didn't lose any sleep over charging them with lewd and perverted acts, getting them banged up in pokey for several years at a stretch, followed the current thinking.

After she'd broken the news to Tovey, Suzie stayed in the narrow kitchen with him, watching him chop the vegetables for his stew, making the right noises, she thought: asking if

174

she could do anything, saying how sorry she was to bring this sad news. He hardly took any notice, was monosyllabic, disinterested, and Suzie remained shocked by his 'good riddance to bad rubbish' remark; couldn't credit a father saying that of his daughter.

Lees-Duncan slipped away; she watched him walking straight-backed, striding through the small orchard, kicking a windfall apple, sending it broken apart sailing down into the kitchen garden, Howard Baldwin walking slowly in his wake looking lost and out of place, Sancho Panza to his Quixote.

Dennis Free stood just outside the kitchen: Dennis with his thick hair, impossible to keep tidy, parted on the left but raised in a great kind of coif, a mound, on the right which had a tendency to flop down over his eyes. Dennis claimed his hair was the most difficult part of his body. At school there had been jokes about it, and one master in particular used to get a laugh by telling him, 'Free, get your hair out of the ink.' The same master had caused jollity when, on the last day of a term, Dennis, the would-be dandy, wore a white-spotted blue bow tie, and was asked, 'What's the matter, Free? Got a sore throat?'

Dennis looked a bit lost outside the back door and Suzie wondered if he was missing Laura Cotter, off with Tommy's team in Sheffield. Word was they had a thing going, Dennis and Laura.

175

He had come into the cottage, Dennis, when she finally got Tovey's attention and they moved from the kitchen into the main body of the building.

Suzie now sat at a table in Eric Tovey's small front room, neat as his kitchen garden, old daguerreotypes of relatives on the walls, a framed looking glass over the little mantel, a stuffed sofa and two armchairs, blue geometric-patterned carpet, heavy dark curtains and the table at which they sat covered by a thick blue cloth. Dennis Free stood in the doorway.

It was in this setting that Suzie broached the question of why Dulcimer Tovey had entered a religious order under the name of Winifred Lees-Duncan.

'You'd have to ask her,' Tovey said. 'And it's a mite too late for that. She was always a tricky girl. Used to get ahead of herself.'

'She left you here on your own, though. Why was that?'

He did not answer straightaway. Then:

'She was her mother's daughter, that's why. Her mum left when Dulcie were ten year old, left her here for me to look after and I did my best. That's what Katie did. Walked out. I did my best.'

Suzie nodded encouragingly.

'But my best was obviously not enough. Not for her and not for her mother before her.'

'Can you give me any reason for her mother

leaving and why . . . ?'

It was this that set off Tovey's refusal to answer further questions. 'That's my business. Private. Personal, like my own thoughts on the matter. Not for any airing: not to you, miss, nor anyone else. They both left. I behaved proper but that made no difference. Katie left first, then her daughter ups and leaves when she reckons she's old enough.'

Her daughter.

'Your daughter as well, Mr Tovey.'

'I suppose.'

'There's a doubt?'

'She were her mother's daughter. I'm not going to answer any more questions.'

'I need to talk to you about her relationship with the others involved. With Michael Lees-Duncan and Winifred—Willow—Lees-Duncan?'

'You can ask, but I may choose not to answer.'

'Mr Tovey you'll be obligated to answer. It'll be a legal matter. You'll be put on oath and you'll have to answer. Possibly at an inquest. Maybe at a murder trial, I've no way of telling yet.' She looked up, straight into his face, saw the grey, placid eyes and the strained muscles at each end of his mouth. She saw the cloud pass behind his eyes and thought she could detect a sudden defeat as his lips parted then closed again. Resignation?

Finally he gave a small, sad smile. 'They

spent a lot of time together,' he began. 'Young Michael and Willow and my girl, Dulcie. Kath wanted her named Dulcimer because that's musical, even though Kath never knew the difference between a harp and a handsaw. I went in to see her down the Cottage Hospital and she said she were going to call the child Dulcimer 'cos it sounded melodic. But there wasn't much harmony about Dulcimer, nor much melody come to that. There was a lot of screeching.'

'This was when she was born?'

'August, 1913. Next year it was the war—the first one. Mr John was Young Mr John then. He went, all spruced up in his uniform marching off to do battle for King and country, like they sang—"We don't want to lose you, but we think you ought to go." I 'ad flat feet but plenty of others went and never come back. Mr John come back all right. Came back a captain then a major, must've been all of twenty, twenty-one, round there somewhere. Don't think he saw much action in the trenches, but he got some action in bed, 'cos young Gerald were born, what? '14? Then Miss Willow, '15 I reckon. Michael a year before that child of mine. Dulcie about the same age as Gerald. Then Willow.

'She were stunning, a smasher, Isabel Lees-Duncan, Isabel Hurst as was. Barely eighteen when she had Michael. Such a pity. Michael, Gerald, then Winifred-Winnie-Willow.'

'So what went wrong, Mr Tovey?'

'He come back a major, young Mr John. What went wrong? My Kath went wrong, miss.' He closed his mouth as though that was an end to it, shook his head, then nodded. 'About the size on it, Kath went wrong. Eventually like.'

A rapping at the kitchen door broke the moment and Suzie cursed to herself, wondered if she'd sorted it out properly in her head. Dennis nipped away, returning with a red-faced young uniform. 'PC Biswell, ma'am, up from Gloucester nick with a PC and another WPC. Sarn't Cox sent him over.'

The PC looked all of fourteen and must have had good intuitive powers because he obviously scented that his arrival was inconvenient. If he had not, Suzie quickly put him right. 'Stay by the back door, don't let anyone in or out without speaking to me. Go.'

Biswell murmured a 'Right ma'am,' and backed away as though he had just lit a fuse to a block of guncotton. Didn't like calling her ma'am either.

Suzie slewed back to Tovey. 'Your wife, Kath, went wrong?'

He nodded, eyes not meeting hers. 'Mr John came back changed you know. And Mrs weren't the same, Isabel. Not straightaway, mind. Took time. Ten years or so before her problem began to take root.' Like the butler before him Tovey lifted his cupped

179

hand to his mouth, brought up his arm and made a drinking motion. 'Kids all grew up together, played together, 'til the boys went off to school. Off to their boarding schools, public schools. Though somehow I didn't think it proper. Not right.'

Unhealthy relationship, John Lees-Duncan had said, and she didn't really understand what he was referring to.

Suzie, guessing part of it, again wondered how much she'd got right so far: the three Lees-Duncan children born across the Great War years—1914/18—and Dulcie, the gardener's daughter, growing up with them. An unhealthy relationship, two people had appeared to claim. The Lees-Duncan family undermined by some flaw in the mother. The gardener's wife departs, leaving her stolid, calm husband to bring up Dulcimer, who in the end escapes from a largely unexplained family chaos, making her way into a religious order using her friend's name (presumably providing a forged legal document demanding the nuns never contact the parents).

It was all too complicated. Not nearly enough information to piece the entire story together and, for that matter, did it have any relevance to the case in hand?

Suzie shrugged in her mind. Michael Lees-Duncan was somehow there, in a nunnery, when both he and Dulcie were killed, but Michael died from a knife, not from enemy action.

'Can I not ask you about the children? I mean the Lees-Duncan children and your . . . ?' she began, knowing Tovey would try to dodge the question.

'No,' shaking his head.

'I mean just how they got on. Growing up. The usual . . .'

'I'm not answering any more questions.' Irritated: she could feel true anger just below the surface. 'I've told you.' He stretched, looked at the ceiling then said he wanted to see to his evening meal. 'When you live by the soil, miss, you become dependent on it. It's part of you and you become part of it. We all return there one way or another. I can't get worked up about that girl dying because, as far as I'm concerned, she died long ago.' He pulled a wry face and stood up. 'Long before she left here I'd ceased to see her as the child I'd helped conceive. Certainly she was her mother's daughter. But . . .' he shook his head again, an act almost of despair, 'by the time she left, I couldn't recognise her.'

It was about as much as Suzie was going to get tonight. She told him she'd need more time to talk with him; she'd need him to come to London, and he laughed as if she was asking him to trek across the Sahara with her; so she once more said he'd have to identify Dulcimer Tovey; she'd be asking John Lees-Duncan to identify Michael. 'It'll be necessary,' she said.

Tovey nodded. 'When will this have to be, then?'

'Tomorrow, if I can organise it.' In her head she was telling herself that it would be better in London; in a proper interview room, after he had seen the body. Seeing bodies was often a good jolt to the system. 'I'll send someone over shortly. When I've arranged transport. Nobody's going to put you under arrest or anything. You've done nothing wrong, but you must assist us, Mr Tovey. You may prefer to have your legal adviser with you.'

'What, like Mr John and that pompous little beagle who runs round with him—Baldwin? Legal representative? He couldn't represent a Belisha beacon.'

She made a mental note of his telephone number written on the white circle at the base of the instrument, then walked away from the cottage across the walled garden, striding with a high carriage in the dusk that she could almost hear as well as smell; the uniformed PC—Biswell was it?—trotting along behind, and Dennis Free almost plucking at her sleeve, asking her how she was going to organise the interrogations of Lees-Duncan and Willow. She pulled away roughly. 'Shut up, Dennis. We're going to do this in London. We're going home: "Back to the shack where the black-eyed Susans grow."' He didn't have a clue; had never heard that old song.

She started talking almost before they were

182

inside the drawing room, through the French windows. 'Right. Mr Lees-Duncan, we're leaving now, but I'll telephone you later. You are required to formally identify your son, Michael, in London tomorrow. We will arrange transport and after the identification you will attend an interview, either at a police station, or at New Scotland Yard. Miss Lees-Duncan, the same applies. I shall require you to accompany your father. You can, of course, have legal representation— both of you—if you so wish, but we do not anticipate any charges, unless you resist my instructions. This is a police requirement. Thank you.'

Her team followed her outside, with the Gloucester constables trailing, looking dubious. The butler nodded respectfully to her in the hall.

'You leaving, madam?'

'Regrettably, yes, Sturgis.'

'Anything I can do, madam?'

'Make sure they're ready tomorrow. They'll be driven to London.'

'Very good, madam. Nothing trivial, I trust.'

She was aware of his right shoulder moving and a hand coming up. 'Perhaps these will be of use, madam. Young Mr Michael and young Mr Gerald.' He thrust two small photographs into her hand.

She gave him a little smile, smirk really. 'Thank you, Sturgis,' she said. They were dated pictures, around 1938 she guessed, but Michael was recognisable so she reckoned that Gerald would be as well.

Outside, their feet on the gravel in front of the house, she told the two PCs and the WPC that they could fit only one officer in the Railton, Dennis driving, but she'd see to it that the Gloucester nick would send transport back for the other two. Biswell elected to go with them. The remaining officers walked towards the main entrance to the drive, down the little avenue of trees, heads down, looking unused and unwanted.

'They'll be in the pub as soon as we're out of sight,' Dennis said, and Biswell, sounding a shade shocked, said they wouldn't because PC Sangster was teetotal and a Methodist preacher an' all.

Dennis chuckled. 'All drink should be thrown into the river,' he said, putting on a parsonical voice. 'Now, hymn number 28, "Let us gather by the river".'

Biswell asked how he could get himself transferred to the Reserve Squad at Scotland Yard.

'Drop enough clangers and the posting'll come through automatically,' Suzie told him.

When they reached the nick, Dennis asked if he should go back and pick up the Gloucester boys (his description).

'Let them wait,' Suzie told him. Then she instructed him to liaise with the duty sergeant and find a hotel for tonight. 'Nothing simple,' she added. 'I want something elaborate.'

'And organise their transport at the same time?' Dennis queried.

'Of course,' Suzie straight-faced, as though she'd remembered it.

'We spending the night here?' Shirley Cox sounded as though she'd just woken up, hadn't been listening.

'Give Dennis a hand, Shirl. I'm going to phone Billy, then the chief.'

Inside she spent a few minutes with DI 'Waiting' Gaimes who agonised for a while about which office she should use.

'If I can be of any help . . .' he said, almost cryptically, before leaving her in his office, then returning to see if she'd like tea and biscuits.

She rang the Squad's offices on the fourth floor of New Scotland Yard and got Billy Mulligan. They always had someone on duty and it was usually Billy whose marital status was a bit dodgy at the best of times. Billy often slept in the little bedroom off Tommy's office. She pictured him there now, seated at Tommy's desk playing with the model guillotine the chief had brought back from the Paris Exhibition in 1937, the walls decorated with original front pages from *The Police Review* and *The Police Gazette*, also an original wanted poster for Crippen and Ethel Le Neve.

'What's going on, ma'am?' Billy asked from

185

the comfort of Tommy's captain's chair.

'Precious little.' She sounded clipped and prickly, realised it and tried to calm down. 'I need two cars here in the morning, about ten'll do. Here in Gloucester.'

'Send me a couple of loaves and two small fishes and I'll do lunch for everyone at the Yard.' Billy always made heavy weather out of transport.

'Come on, Bill, it can't be *that* difficult.'

'Not more'n usual. And for an encore I'll nip over St Mary's Paddington and make their dead patients do the Post Horn Gallop.'

'Just organise the transport, Billy. They're prospective clients: John Lees-Duncan, his daughter and the head gardener, Tovey. Lees-Duncans know and they're all in the frame. Don't ask me how but they are.'

'Yes, ma'am.'

'Good. Ten o'clock at The Manor, Lees-Duncan's gaff, and have those bodies from the convent nice and laid out ready for their families to have a butcher's.'

'Ah.' The light dawned. 'Of course, ma'am.'

'You talked to the chief?'

'He asked if I'd talked to you.'

'We're staying here overnight. I'll let you know where as soon as Dennis's organised it.'

'Doubt if Dennis could organise the proverbial boozy party in a distillery, beggin' your presence, ma'am.'

'He has my confidence as well. Back

186

tomorrow, Billy.'

'Oh, your brother's been looking for you.'

'The Royal Marine?'

'You've only got one, haven't you?'

'What's he want?'

'Bed for the night, I think.'

'Ah.' Suzie grinned to herself. Young James was on the loose in London, she thought. 'If he rings back tell him, yes. He's got a key and I won't be back until tomorrow, lateish.'

There was a knock at the door and a young WPC came in with a tray—tea and biscuits. Dennis hovered in the background.

'Got us rooms. New Inn, Northgate Street: used to be an inn for pilgrims.'

'That's us all right, pilgrims. You fix the pick-up?'

'What pick-up?'

'The boy and girl in blue from here.'

Dennis frowned, said he'd do it now, and she phoned the Lees-Duncans, got Sturgis who fawned a lot but said he'd make sure they were all ready by ten. He also promised to advise Tovey. Then she tried The Royal Victoria in Sheffield. They rang Tommy Livermore's room but he didn't pick up, so she called the nick. They said he was in an important conference, which was code for interrogation so she told them her name and rank saying this was equally important. The WPC who was manning the telephone told her to hold, then returned and said Mr Livermore would be with her in a minute.

Suzie sipped the tea and ate a biscuit. There were two small sugar lumps in the saucer and, even though she'd given up sugar and sweets, she took a lump, put it between her teeth and sucked a dribble of tea through it, feeling the sugar dissolve as she sucked, the sweetness exploding in her mouth. She thought of Tommy then, suddenly, he was there at the end of the line.

'Suze, heart, what a lovely surprise.'

'Tommy.' She gave it her best erotic breathy delivery: two notes, up and down, rising and falling.

'Heart. What's new?'

She gave him a brief summary of the hints and evasions of the Lees-Duncan and Tovey families; of the identification of the masquerading nun and everything that went with it, the gardener's daughter using the Lees-Duncan name and the suspicions she had.

'Take 'em down the Tombs and sweat 'em.' Tommy did his atrocious New York accent. It was their old joke. B-movie thrillers often had cops taking suspects, 'down the Tombs'—the New York City prison (you could get buried there)—to be interrogated.

'It's what I am doing, darling. Gonna give 'em the toid degree.' The third degree was interrogation with physical encouragement—again spoken of freely in Hollywood movies.

188

'One question, though. Just to make sure I'm not dreaming.'

'Shoot.'

'Someone told us that Michael Lees-Duncan was in Mexico while his brother lived in Scotland.'

'Yes.'

'Who?'

'Who told us?

'Attila the Nun, wasn't it? No, her sidekick. Novice Mistress. Eunice. Sister Eunice.'

Winnie had two brothers, one of whom lives abroad, somewhere. In Mexico I think, Michael Lees-Duncan. The other—Gerald—last heard of somewhere in Scotland. That's how things stood in 1940 anyway.

'That's how I remember it.'

'Why do you ask?'

'Because John Lees-Duncan says both his sons walked out on him in 1939, and he didn't know where they were from that day. Says a friend saw Michael in New York later in '39, and he glimpsed Gerald in London in '42. That was it.'

'So where did Sister Eunice get her gen?'

'Exactly.'

'Only one answer.'

'Quite. Listen, heart, send me your interim report when you've written it up. And copies of the pretty pictures you had done, plus the one you got from Attila the Nun.'

'Roger. How're you doing?'

'A hundred and one suspects, plus a DS whom Woolly had on attachment here, having a look round, browsing. Bloke called Mungo.'

'Not Dave Mungo?'

'You know him?'

'Met him briefly when I was doing that work last year. With Curry Shepherd and the secret squirrels.'

'Maybe you should be doing the work here, heart. What did you know of him?'

'Too smooth; smooth as creamed potatoes . . .'

'. . . or a baby's top lip. Unless you blunder into something among the Lees-Duncans of this world you've still got a mountain of work to do—the holy sisters at the convent, then their place in Farnborough, and . . .' an afterthought, 'have you seen that other girl's parents yet? The cleric? Sister, Novice Bridget Mary. Harding was the name. Better get on and do that.'

'You're all work, Tommy.'

'Me? I'm a bundle of love, heart. I'm the prisoner's friend and I'm jolly well incarcerated by love for you.'

'You say the sweetest things, Tommy. And I love you as well.' Tommy, she knew, could be dead romantic when he put his mind to it.

'I should bloody well think so and all,' he said now. 'Sleep well and dream of me.'

'Of course, angel.'

'And don't forget to send me all the

190

paperwork.'

At that moment Tommy Livermore had no way of knowing that this request was going to turn the Doris Butler murder case inside out.

Dennis and Shirley were waiting just inside the main doors, protected outside by an anti-blast wall of sandbags.

'All aboard whose coming aboard,' Dennis said, raring to go. Shirley was hungry and said so. 'One of the WDSs says they do a good hotpot at the New Inn.' She licked her lips, overstating as usual.

They were almost outside when a police cadet came stumbling after them—'WDI Mountford, ma'am, there's a telephone call for you.'

It was her brother, James, ringing from a telephone box in Leicester Square, so he said. 'Thank heaven I've tracked you down, I'm harry flakers.' He sounded frantic, which didn't ring true. 'They've taken off the plaster. I can walk . . . Well hobble. Going to give me a new posting soon.'

'What d'you want, Jim?' All heart.

'Can I use the flat? I don't want to trail back to Newbury tonight.'

'You've got a key. I won't be back until sometime tomorrow. Use the spare room and for heaven's sake don't answer the telephone in the main bedroom, it's a bit iffy.'

'Trust me, sis. Great.'

It was only after she cradled the phone that

191

she realised her brother might not be on his own. She put her head back and laughed aloud.

*　　*　　*

SS-Gruppenführer Max Voltsenvogel had flown back to Berlin. He spoke to three people in the intelligence community, then went down to Rastenburg where the Führer was still directing things, ordering the arrest of the officers implicated in the bomb plot. There was to be a big show trial and it seemed that the Führer was more interested in vengeance than the slowly disintegrating situation in France.

It was not pleasant at the Wolf's Lair; in the summer, the log-built wooden buildings trapped the heat, there was the pervading sweet smell of rotting vegetation from the nearby marshland, and the camp was under constant attack from biting insects: gnats and mosquitoes. An unhealthy place.

Max wanted to see and be seen, and he was pleasantly surprised to note that the attempted assassination appeared to have given the Führer a temporary new lease of life. He was directing the search for the July plotters with a fresh vigour. More, he did appear to be making concrete plans to counter-attack the Allied assault along the coast of northern France. He looked older, his eyes glinted

192

feverishly, he had trouble with his left arm, but he could still give the impression of confidence, the certainty of victory.

(Only a few months later he disintegrated into a shuffling mockery of himself.)

'The winter will hold them up, just as it delayed our forces in Russia,' he claimed—though 'delayed' appeared to be a significant understatement. He also said the difficulty the Americans and British had experienced around Caen and other areas had completely thrown out their invasion plans. Yet below Caen the Allies were holding up armour, so allowing their other forces to head for the Seine.

Hitler's version of the situation was pie in the sky and this concerned Voltsenvogel. Initially he had maintained that they were 'going to get the thrashing of their lives on the beaches'. Now they were off the beaches. The fighting along the established bridgeheads was desperate, terrible carnage, but the six armies that had been landed in Normandy were making progress; and here was Hitler thinking about counter-attacking in the winter when they were hardly nudging September.

SS-Colonel Voltsenvogel drove out to the airfield and ordered his pilot to fly the Storch back to his headquarters: to Group Odin in Holland.

CHAPTER FIFTEEN

Lieutenant James Mountford, Royal Marines, came out of the telephone box his face blossoming into a wide smile, ear to ear, like a Cheshire cat, cream all gone. The jeep was parked five paces away, by the kerb, Leading Wren Emily Styles, wearing her Maren beret, sitting at the wheel in shirtsleeves, there in Leicester Square, dusk coming on.

'Upper St Martin's Lane, Styles,' he commanded, the goofy grin almost consuming her. 'Upper St Martin's Lane, and don't spare the 'orses. We have somewhere to rest our weary 'eads.'

'So we don't have to trail round hotels.' Emily pronounced it 'otels just like she'd been taught at the snooty school where they'd tried to educate her, without any real cooperation.

Emily Styles, tall, slim, leggy—she would hoik her skirt high on her thighs when driving—sumptuous in the upper areas, glossy brunette with a small, almost urchin, face, big brown eyes and a moist mouth, lovely lips. 'I've probably got a touch of the tarbrush,' she would say, looking in a mirror, licking the lips and pushing her nose up with a forefinger to better examine the nostrils. There was certainly a thickness there, and her lips suggested something of the Negroid

194

physiognomy even though she came from good county stock. She sometimes wondered if an ancestor had strayed in the colonies and now the secret was out.

That morning she had driven James from Newbury to the hospital near Oxford where the plaster cast was removed from his foot, and they had examined the wound in his shoulder, pronouncing it healed. Satisfied that he was heading towards fitness they gave him some remedial exercises and allowed him to take off the sling. He was told that he now had to get used to walking and using his arm. 'You'll be getting a new posting in a matter of weeks,' the surgeon commander said. 'We need all the able-bodied men we can find, though I don't see you back with your old unit for a few months. No more commando-ing as yet. Just get the foot and shoulder back in action, good man. Right, send in the next.'

James said, 'Aye-aye, sir,' which is the correct thing to say to surgeon commanders, with the red lines between the gold stripes of rank.

When he told Leading Wren Styles she asked, 'You going to practise on me, sir? Using the arm, I mean. Doing your remedial exercises?'

' 'Course I am.' Toss of the head. They had become quite chummy from the telephone calls and the drive to the hospital. Now James did not have to worry about what he was going

195

to tell his mum about tonight. Mums, he considered, still expected to be told everything even though he was a commissioned officer supposedly fit to lead great big hairy marines into battle.

He navigated while Emily drove, across to Trafalgar Square and on towards Charing Cross Station on their right—'I know the way now,' she yelled happily—left up St Martin's Lane, and at the top pulling up outside the Edwardian block of flats.

They had eaten earlier, in Oxford, a tiny café opposite the House. The café did wonderful egg and chips, and James pointed out Christ Church College opposite, starting to explain that colloquially it was referred to as the House. She waved him aside saying her brother had been up at the House. 1935–38, got an oar on his bedroom wall to prove it.

Now, outside the flats she screwed up her face and said, 'This is where I came in, sir.' Hopped out, disabled the jeep, removing the rotor arm, getting her little issue suitcase ('my ditty bag'), scooping up the cardboard box of supplies she had liberated from the Wrenery kitchens next to the hospital—eggs, bacon, a loaf of bread, pint of milk and a link of sausages the cooks said were gash—Navy for surplus to requirements, going spare.

James had his case but took the rotor arm and slung her navy raincoat and her jacket over his arm, peeping into the box. 'Well done,

Suzie didn't say if she had any food stored away.'

'Suzie? Your sister the cop?'

'That's the one. She nearly arrested our stepfather once. At least that's what she says. I wasn't there at the time.'

'Hope she doesn't bust in here and arrest us in the middle of the night.'

'She won't; she's on some Agatha Christie case out in the sticks.'

She stayed close to him as they went into the building. 'Don't have to help you up the stairs this time, do I, sir?'

'Don't have to help me cop an armful of bust either.' In fact it wasn't easy going up the stairs. After only a few hours out of plaster his foot was bloody uncomfortable.

'Don't know what you mean, sir.'

'Of course not.'

In the hall, just inside the door of the flat she said how nice it was. 'I thought that when I brought you here before. Roomy, isn't it? High ceilings. Great. Wonderful.'

He showed her around: the big drawing room she'd seen last time, with the phoney Canaletto over the fireplace, the kitchen—tidy and clean—the bathroom, where he thought it best not to mention what had gone on in there during the Blitz: the attempt to murder Suzie in that room, better keep quiet; didn't want to scare the pants off her. On reflection though . . . then the dining room with the Caroline table Mummy had bought for a song, just along from the two spare bedrooms, one with a big double bed, rust-coloured curtains and the two pictures his father had bought his mother on their honeymoon, big canvasses, dark autumnal woodland scenes; James could never see the point, too gloomy for his taste.

Emily in the corridor still loved it all, talking too quickly, too much, about the high ceilings, space, the mouldings on the dado, picture rails and the ornate lighting roses. 'Smashing flat,' she said, knocked out. 'Wonderful,' again.

'Needs decorating.' He looked at the outdated light blue paper with the little gold fleur-de-lys above the dado and the slashed crimson below: all faded and tatty now: old-fashioned trying to be up to date, the paintwork chipped and discoloured.

'Same everywhere,' she said. 'When the war's over I expect your sister'll do it up, get the decorators in; Sanderson's will be selling loads of new wallpaper.'

'And Jimmy will go to sleep, in his own little room again.' James sang a snatch from 'Bluebirds over the White Cliffs of Dover'. 'It's Mummy's really,' sounding distracted. 'Bought it with a legacy soon after she was married. When Daddy died and she remarried she never told my stepfather. We thought she was hanging on to it as a bolthole, just in case the marriage went wrong. Then Suzie sort of commandeered it, left home and took over.'

They were in the doorway of the larger of the spare rooms. 'Look. You have this one. Have the big bed. Enjoy it.' Edging her inside. 'I'll have the smaller one.'

She turned towards him, into him, looking up. 'We'll see,' long, long pause, 'sir.' Breathy, throaty. He took a step closer and thought, Christ, those big eyes could chew you up and spit you out. He could smell her, her hair, her body. Then she lifted her face and he bent his head to her.

At school, not so long ago, there had been a boy called Barnard, bit older than him but with a reputation of knowing about women. Barnard had said to him, 'Kissing's important. Chaps don't realise. Straight off they try to climb down a girl's throat. Not the way it's done. First time you've got to brush your lips on hers. Don't ever steam in and stick your tongue into her mouth. What you do is keep altering the pressure, keep moving your lips, then, just at the last minute, touch her lips with the tip of your tongue, just the tip. You let it run along her lips. Not wet and sloppy, but dry, sort of titillate her lips. Then, if she wants that, let her lead, get really into the kisses. That way you can distract a girl, they like that, and before you know what's what . . . Well, you're all over her and she's all over you.' As an afterthought he'd said, 'Don't go after her like a battering ram. This is a gentle loving thing. 'Cept when she wants it otherwise. Don't go crazy.'

So James did it, and Barnard was right. He let their lips touch, brush, held together by hardly a whisper, then let the tip of his tongue run outside her lips.

Her arms came up and she opened her mouth. He thought she was going to swallow him whole and suddenly he had an unusually large steel spigot between his legs. God, he thought. God, it's going to happen, and they were on the bed and he began to fumble with the buttons on her shirt.

'Let me.' She gently pushed him away and the buttons came undone and so did her bra. She slid the waistband of her skirt round and undid those buttons as well.

'They're not pusser's,' he said, staring. In the Royal Navy pusser meant one hundred per cent RN; correct; naval issue.

'Going to put me on a charge, sir? Have me up in front of the Jaunty for not wearing my blackouts?' She had a delicious giggle, like ice cream over treacle with a dash of honey, he thought, though that didn't make much sense. She spoke quickly, low and into his ear as she altered the position of her body. 'When I first joined the Andrew, we had this nasty little dykey petty officer.' The Andrew was the Royal Navy. 'She used to say, this petty officer, "I can see you're all wearing your pusser's lisles—our issue stockings—and I hope you're wearing your pusser's drawers. I don't want to see none of that fancy French lingeree." Well, darling sir, that's my fancy French lingeree.' She slipped them off and James could hardly contain himself. His hand rested on her pusser's lisle, just inside her thigh, then moved up. He felt her, like a soft excited bird under his cupped hand, while she took him gently with her fingers and, in one movement, put him where he should be.

'Welcome, sir.'

'Hall-o.'

They were off and he couldn't get over it. Oooh Lord, I'm actually doing it, he thought, actually doing it with lovely little Emily Styles.

'Oh, sir,' she breathed. 'Oh, darling sir.'

Oh heck. We're doing it. Wondrous. Magnificent. Makes you believe in miracles and everything.

'Oh . . .' they both said. 'Oh. Oh, and Oh.'

'Oh, sir.'

'Oh, Emily. Angel. Love.'

Then the repeated affirmatives, urgent, quite strident and a great rush at the end, like a factory whistle.

When it was over and they lay together, happy, all lovely and full of things, she said, 'Sir?'

'Cut it out.'

'What?'

'All this sir business. My name's James or Jim.'

'Darling,' she kissed him.

'Tell me about your first time ever,' she asked.

There was a long pause.

'Well, there was this Leading Wren who was driving for me . . .'

'You don't mean it.'

'Uh-huh.'

'You can't mean . . . ?'

'Yes.'

'That was your first . . . ?'

'Yes.'

'Let's do it again then; see if it's better the second time.'

'Yes. Wizard. But I've got to make a phone call first.'

'Who you phoning?' Suspicious.

'Mummy of course.'

'Diddums-wazzums.'

'Mummies have to be told.'

'You're not going to tell her . . . ?'

' 'Course not, but she'll want to know where I'm staying. Terrible worrier, Mummy.'

When he came back to bed they went off into another bout of what James was now calling fun and games. If it wasn't better than the first time it was certainly just as good.

They drifted. Dozed. Slept.

James dreamt of a meadow with long grass and wild flowers. Emily rose from the long grass and asked him to show her the place where people went. He asked where they went for what? and she said, 'To see the magic buns of course.'

They woke again and had another round of fun and games. 'Let's make it best out of five, eh?' he asked as they both drifted away again.

Then he woke, suddenly, sitting up to find that Emily wasn't in bed. He found her in the kitchen scavenging.

'What are you doing here at three in the morning?'

'Correction, sir. What are you doing in the kitchen wearing only your shirt and nothings?'

'Nothings?'

She flashed him, flipping up her shirtfront and giving a little rumba wiggle.

'Well, what are you doing?'

'Making a special.'

'What's a special?'

'Your sister has access to some terrific cheese. Black market, I'd say. Bloody sight better than the stuff on the ration, or even the stuff we get on the messdeck, which is like pusser's yellow.' Pusser's yellow was Navy issue soap. 'She must have about four years' rations, and butter by the barrel.' The ration for butter was 4 oz a week, while cheese was 3 oz.

'I know where the cheese and butter come from. She has a friend who's a farmer. It's all above board. All gash.' There was no way he was going to tell her that Suzie was living with her boss. Only a handful of police officers were well known to the general public through the newspapers, but Tommy was one—Dandy

203

Tom Livermore they called him in the Fleet Street headlines: DANDY TOM ARRESTS WIRE KILLER, one headline had claimed; DANDY TOM SMASHES VICE RING, another said.

'What's a special?'

'In those B-pictures, supporting films, people're always going into diners and places in New York and saying,' she rolled her shoulders and did an American accent—her version of an American accent—' "Gimme the special," or "What's today's special?" and the waiter says, "Same as yesterday's special," or "One special coming up, over 'n' easy." Well, I make my own specials. Hey, they've got salad cream, none of that snobbish mayonnaise. Salad cream's the stuff. And what's this, Kingscote Grange Piccalilli?'

'I expect it's home-made piccalilli.' James wasn't going to give away the location of the Home Farm.

'Great.'

'How d'you make a special, then, Em?'

'Em?'

'Why not?'

'Sounds as though I should be singing "Somewhere Over The Rainbow".'

'Just tell me how to make a special, then I can make them for you when you're feeling peaky.'

'Two slices of bread—I'm using our bread. Butter. Grate the cheese, mix in salad cream, chopped up piccalilli, horseradish and

204

whatever else takes your fancy. Spread mixture on bread. Make sandwich. QED. It's a great joke at home.'

'Quite easily done. Yes. Let's have a bite.'

They munched happily and Emily made some tea. Then James asked how long she could spin out keeping close to him with the jeep.

'Possibly another twenty-four hours. If I ring the chiefy and tell her we've been delayed. I've got some leave due. Should be OK.'

'Good. Let's go back to bed then.'

'When I've finished my tea. I suppose commandos specialise in sex.'

'It's always around. We learn to strip weapons, you know.'

'Highly charged.'

'There's even a part of the Bren gun that's sexual.'

'What part?'

'The Maiden's Delight.'

'Part of the Bren gun's called the Maiden's Delight?'

'Well, it's actually called the "body locking pin" but the lewd and licentious soldiery call it the Maiden's Delight.'

They were still in bed when Suzie returned late the following evening after a hard and taxing day, returning from Gloucestershire with the Lees-Duncans and Eric Tovey the gardener.

CHAPTER SIXTEEN

In the suite of offices on the fourth floor at New Scotland Yard the Reserve Squad had all mod cons, including an interview room complete with table and chairs bolted to the floor and a two-way looking glass so that people could see what was going on during an interrogation.

Suzie didn't want to use the room because Tommy rarely went near it: didn't hold with it. For important interviews Tommy preferred his own office. He even had a special chair, his 'awkward chair', he called it: a round cracked plywood seat on four unsteady legs and a curved, wobbly bamboo back. Once you sat on that chair you lost a whole wedge of confidence. 'Give 'em a nice room and an uncomfortable chair and they're yours for life,' Tommy would say. 'After ten minutes they'll start making things up, hoping they'll be able to leave. Rarely fails. Once they start making up stuff . . . well, you're halfway there.'

The chair was savagely uncomfortable: it numbed the buttocks, gave considerable pain to the lower back, put a crick in your neck and, after five minutes, started to produce symptoms of vertigo. People had been known to fall off Tommy's 'awkward chair' after a quarter of an hour because the legs felt dangerously unsteady.

Suzie had seen John Lees-Duncan's look when he came out of the hospital, having identified his son's body. The fiery Lees-Duncan now had a face the colour of powdered ash and appeared to be walking on eggs for'ard of the mainsail on an ancient man-o'-war. As she had previously predicted, it was time to put him to the question. Often the sight of the body of a loved one was enough to tip the scales, even if the loved one was not loved any longer.

Willow Lees-Duncan and Eric Tovey could wait. Dennis Free had organised rooms for them in a nearby hotel, overnight, but if push came to shove she'd stay in Dandy Tom's office for as long as it took. One of Suzie Mountford's strong points was patience.

She had cleaned out the other chairs and sat behind the big military desk, comfortable in Tommy's captain's chair, when Shirley Cox brought John Lees-Duncan into the room. He was followed, somewhat unwillingly, by the solicitor, Howard Baldwin, looking sheepish and uncomfortable.

Suzie simply pointed to the 'awkward chair', and Lees-Duncan sat down, leaving Baldwin standing disenchanted and fidgety. Suzie began to talk before Lees-Duncan even attempted to make himself comfortable.

'You'll appreciate that your son's death, and the manner of his dying, requires me to get a full statement from you, sir?'

'Depends what you mean by full.' The last traces of his arrogance still protruded above the surface, just willing to put up a fight.

'We'll require a full explanation of your relationship with your son—both your sons, come to that. We know you're supplying information to Sir Robert Vansittart at the Foreign Office, so I suppose we'll require some details of that side of your life as well, plus, of course, your links with the British Union of Fascists.'

Since '39 he's apparently disappeared a couple of times, gone off without warning, she'd said to Tommy speaking of John Reginald Palmer Lees-Duncan, informer to Robert Vansittart, Diplomatic Adviser to the Foreign Office. *They're unhappy about his sons as well—Michael and Gerald. Michael in Mexico, and Gerald living almost silently on the east coast of Scotland: very handy for the Firth of Forth, watching the naval traffic in and out. He (Lees-Duncan) didn't deny he'd had contacts within the Nazi Diplomatic Corps, their Army and the Luftwaffe.*

'If you want all that I'll have to make a telephone call.' A shade softer, not quite velvet, but the steel curtain was being dismantled. He turned towards the lawyer and smiled, almost benignly. 'Don't think I'll need you any longer, Baldwin.'

The solicitor suddenly looked happy, so

208

Suzie asked Shirley to take him down to the canteen. 'I don't suppose Mr Baldwin's averse to a cup of tea, Shirley.'

Baldwin muttered something about being partial to tannin stimulant, ha-ha-ha, and Shirley led him out.

'Go ahead.' Suzie rose, indicating the telephone on her desk. 'Make your call, switchboard'll get any number you want. I'll wait outside. Take your time.' She left the office, closed the door and picked up the phone in the ante-room, heard him give the number, listened to the brrp-brrp ring tone and heard the pick-up announcing a nonsensical acronym. Lees-Duncan asked for 'B2.'

'Putting you through, caller.' A bright chirpy upper-class accent.

'B2.' Eton and Oxford, probably military.

'Moonlight,' said Lees-Duncan.

'Right. Yeah?'

'I'm at Scotland Yard. My son, Michael, has been killed. Done away with. Murdered. They're going to ask a lot of questions.'

'Who're they, Moonlight?'

'Call themselves the Reserve Squad.'

'Yeah, well, some people incorrectly call them the Murder Squad. Tommy Livermore's lot. Tommy there?'

'Not at the moment. Chit of a girl's going to ask me the far end of nowhere.'

'Uh-huh. Right.'

209

'Just wondered how far I can go. What I can tell 'em.'

'Tell 'em the lot. They obviously have need-to-know, wouldn't ask you otherwise. Probably know most of it already. Tell them you're tied in with us. They'll be in touch if they need anything painting in. Good luck, Moonlight.'

Suzie waited until Lees-Duncan closed the line, returned her handset to the rests, counted up to fifty, went to the adjoining door, tapped on it, poked her head round, as though she thought he may still be on the phone.

'All done?' she asked brightly.

He nodded so she went back to the chair behind Tommy's desk and started, dead official—'You are John Reginald Palmer Lees-Duncan of The Manor, Churchbridge, Gloucestershire?'

'I am.'

'And this morning (she gave the date) you identified the body of your son, Michael Edward Palmer Lees-Duncan?'

'I did.'

'You had not seen the deceased for some time?'

'Not since 5th May, 1939.'

'You recall the date exactly?'

'Date that split up the family. Me sons left us on that date. Haven't seen either of them since.'

(And they haven't seen you, she thought— more to the point.)

210

'And the reason they left?'

'Difference of opinion.'

'What kind of difference of opinion?'

'It was a political matter.' Still not quite letting go.

'Because you were a fascist?'

'Possibly. Possibly because I was the wrong kind of fascist and because I wasn't a Nazi.'

So, Suzie thought. So, Lees-Duncan was a fascist but not a Nazi. 'Does that mean your sons were followers of Adolf Hitler?'

'Michael and Gerald, my sons, *were* Nazis. Members of the Nazi Party for all I know . . . They were certainly National Socialists in the Hitler mould, believed every turgid word he wrote in *Mein Kampf.* Thought the sun shone out of his bottom . . . if you'll pardon the expression.'

'But you're not one? Not a Nazi?'

'I admit to believing that a form of fascism was the only way to pull this country together, but I could never follow that little Charlie Chaplin moustache into history. Hitler's methods of National Socialism were not for me. All that play-acting, Ruritanian uniforms, banging of drums, beating up Jews, and other kinds of brutality. This pure race business, his Aryan nation idea, all a lot of humbug, far as I'm concerned. Wouldn't work for an Englishman—except with reference to the colonials of course.' He stroked an imaginary moustache.

211

'You can be strong and tough without descending to Hitlerite tactics. Went to take a look in '37 and was disgusted: first the ghastly uniforms, terrible colours, then the people who were wearing them. Oiks, yobbos, louts, hooligans,' spitting out the words. 'Yahoos to a man, uncouth Philistines. First thing I noticed at the railway stations: way they strutted around, bully-boy tactics everywhere.' He paused, smiling like the grim reaper on an early closing day. 'Then I got a glimpse of the four horsemen themselves: the fat oaf Goering with his fancy uniforms, chest full of medals he'd given himself; the little crippled Goebbels; the sadistic chicken farmer Himmler with his dreams and rituals; and, at the top, this funny little driven madman, Adolf Hitler. They were like a comedy quartet. One look and you knew it was all wrong. God knows why anyone ever took them seriously but they did.' Long pause. 'Eventually they did. Why we weren't ready for them I suppose. But over there people got carried away, the bright pigtailed fräuleins were all google-eyed, the diplomats bowed and scraped. You could see that the lunatics had taken over the asylum, but you couldn't quite believe it. But my God what a mess they've made: the slaughter, the deaths, the murders, the treachery. The Nazi ethic.' He made a terrible hawking sound in the back of his throat. Every word had been laced with disgust.

212

'And you fell out with your sons over it? Over Hitler's concept of racial purity? His general policy?'

Lees-Duncan gave a mirthless laugh. 'That and a few other things. Didn't hold with the way he was prepared to use brute force and ignorance. Didn't hold with his arrogance and idiocy. My sons said they wanted to throw in their lot with Hitler's Germany. I said should they do so I'd never speak to them again. Didn't for a minute think they'd fall for it. Didn't see how they could. But they left. Simple. Gone away. Mad as a pair of hatters.'

'But you remained a fascist? You were a member of Mosley's British Union of Fascists?'

'Outwardly. I was asked to give that impression. Mind you, I believe this country requires strong leadership: people at the helm who you can follow with confidence. People with strength of character. Educated people who won't jib at dealing with weakness and ignorance, who'll keep the masses in line.'

'You had given that impression for a number of years already, hadn't you? Being a fascist, going to house parties with card-carrying fascists; mixing with them; on friendly terms with Mosley and his people, proselytising for a fascist government.'

'Made it easier, yes. People in the Foreign Office wanted someone with his ear to the ground. Someone with credentials. I was that man. Ask them.'

'Who? Vansittart's people?'

'Him, yes. MI5 as well. They'll give me a clean bill of health. Individuals are another matter. You can't fool all of the people all of the time, as a shrewd political operator said.'

Shrewd political operator? Suzie thought they didn't come much shrewder than John Lees-Duncan. He had taken her in. Not just her but it was writ large in the records. More to it than that, she thought. His life was hardly an open book. There was something more that had come between him and his sons, or was there: maybe another problem that also engulfed Willow, and his wife, and possibly Dulcie Tovey as well. She still needed him to fill in the gaps: present the complete picture.

'And you had no idea what happened to either of your sons after 5th May '39?'

'Heard Michael was in the United States later that year, and that Gerald was seen in London, March/April '42. Told you that already.'

'And you were willing to allow this rift to continue? A separation from your two sons?'

'The difference between one political belief and another can be as vast as the difference between life and death. Doesn't mean to say that I *liked* it! Or that I was *happy* about it. Of course I wasn't, but what can a man do? In many ways I finally got the kind of fascism I approved of, with Winston and the generals

214

handling the country's affairs and the conduct of the war. That's a great kind of fascism.'

She nodded. 'And your wife. How did she take to separation from her sons?'

'Isabel never had the head for politics. Brought up in the country—horses, running around among the hay and going to hunt balls. Had a sound schooling but what good did that do? Kept her end up at parties, knew how to handle servants, arranged the flowers well, planned the menus. Not a political animal though. Never really understood men either. Got itchy when I strayed—like all men stray. Liked the drink. Became a dipso. Own worst enemy. Look at her now: morning passes in a rosy glow, has to take to her bed around three. Gets up later. Another half-bottle sees her through dinner. Knows how to pace herself, I suppose.' Total contempt in his voice. God help her, Suzie thought. John Lees-Duncan was possibly the most uncaring man she'd ever met, and if he was that, what price his children?

'I go now?' he asked, rising from the chair and stretching his legs, easing out the joints, pain in his eyes. It had been so easy, Suzie thought, too bloody easy.

Sit 'em in that chair and they'll talk, Tommy said; and Lees-Duncan had talked, spewed it all out with no hesitation, the reserve gone, no suppression, no side-stepping the questions. Too easy, she thought again.

215

'You've been most frank, Mr Lees-Duncan,' she said, knowing that he'd hidden more than he'd revealed, realising that was his job, being something he was not and living off it. 'We'll talk again.' What she was really saying was, don't go anywhere. I have plans for you.

'Daddy rode over Mummy like a bloody traction engine rolling out the tarmac,' Willow said later, when Suzie finally faced her with the big question. But before then she talked to a contact with MI5 and even managed a word with the man who she'd heard speaking with Lees-Duncan—B2. 'We don't tell old Woolly that much,' B2 said. 'Bit loose of mouth. Better let him think some of our people, like old Moonlight're not quite kosher. Stirs up the Branch. Keeps them on their toes.'

She painstakingly wrote her report, typed it and put a carbon in an envelope addressed to Tommy, enclosing copies of the happy snaps of the dear departed.

A short talk with Willow unearthed nothing she either knew or suspected, so she left the WAAF officer in the charge of Shirley Cox while Dennis shepherded Lees-Duncan and his gardener to the private hotel they often used near Whitehall.

She walked into the flat in Upper St Martin's Lane just after ten-thirty to the tinkle of laughter coming from the larger spare bedroom.

CHAPTER SEVENTEEN

'Hold the front page, heart,' Tommy said, on the telephone from Sheffield.

'You've got a scoop have you?' Suzie had just finished talking to Willow Lees-Duncan: a long, frustrating session, it was twelve noon and she felt fed up and far from home.

'May even have a result, heart.' He sounded calm and loving. 'Now this is what I want you to do.'

Her eyes opened wide as she listened. 'But, I . . .' she began.

'Hear me out. Now . . .'

'Didn't I send all that?'

'You sent the pretty pix and your report: four pages of it. Nothing else.'

Indeed, her heart had done a nice little arpeggio when she heard his voice on the telephone, but she went off him a bit when he began carping.

'Tommy, you're carping,' she said.

'Possibly, heart, but I think we're nearly there.'

'At your end, maybe, but I feel I'm fighting with a black man in a coal cellar at midnight here.'

'Don't get tetchy with me. Just do the job. Oh yes, I miss you like buggery.'

'Good,' she didn't say aloud.

'Just do it.'

'Yes, darling.'

'Rinky dink,' Tommy said. Then, 'Probably see you tonight.'

'Tom, I—' But he'd put the phone down.

For a moment she thought about the interview, glanced at her notes. The only intereresting exchange had come suddenly, unexpected. 'Michael,' Willow had said. 'Funny, Michael . . .'

'What was funny, Willow?'

'He was such a rackety, devil-may-care boy except when it came to politics. He would laugh, joke, pull the most extraordinary japes and hoaxes, then if you turned to the politics of National Socialism he became totally serious, humour went and he was absolutely committed. It was like switching off a light bulb.'

Suzie wondered what Tommy would make of that, and wondered what he was up to.

In Sheffield he had started the morning by telling Ron Worrall to take a couple of DCs and do a final search of Doris Butler's house and garden. 'Turn over every blade of grass,' he said. 'We need a murder weapon.' In spite of previous searches they hadn't found a thing that could have been used to batter Doris to death.

Ron went on a bit because he'd already been up Bluefields Road twice, cleaning the place out, going through it like a dose of salts.

'Once more won't hurt,' Tommy told him. 'I'm off to see the RTO with that bugger Mungo.'

Dave Mungo was still not his favourite person; Mungo, the sergeant DCS Woolly Bear had sent over from the Branch, put him covertly into Sheffield nick; it really irked Tommy, who felt it had been done on purpose, not a word to him, not from either Chief Superintendent Bear nor the local DCS Berry whom Tommy thought of as an old friend. Some friend, wandering around with his eyes, ears and mouth closed tight as a badger's armpit. Tommy Livermore was well put out and determined to cause Dave Mungo some grief.

'It's not Mungo's fault,' Berry had said. 'I should have spoken up. Just didn't cross my mind.'

'Maybe it's not Mungo's fault, but life isn't fair, is it?' Tommy smiled his terrible smile and told Mungo that they were off to see the Wizard, 'The wonderful wizard of the railways, and his little friends the Military Police sergeants.' If the truth be told, Tommy was pretty much obsessed by the three shady servicemen who had attached themselves to Doris Butler in the days before her death. He was deeply suspicious of these men—the Frenchman, Henri Maisondel; the Pole, Stefan Korob; and, finally Gittins, Stanley Gittins, corporal in the 1st Battalion, Suffolk Regiment. The last had arrived in mufti which was most unusual. Tommy somehow thought they all added up to being sinister even though Mungo had told him they had been checked out by the MPs, giving the impression that they had proved to be clean as a bath full of Lux washing powder. Mungo, Woolly Bear's man in Sheffield, had said the local Military Police had taken a good look at them.

MPs took a look and they came up smelling of roses?

You'll have to talk to them, sir.

Who? The MPs?

The Frog and the Pole, and the corporal sir. The MP section at Sheffield Victoria followed them up. I think they're Lux clean.

Tommy didn't believe a word of it, that was why he was going over to Victoria Station, Sheffield, to check it out: taking Dave Mungo with him, watching him like a hawk and giving him a nasty case of the shakes if he had his way.

The Railway Transport Officer at Victoria Station was a little major with a voice like a turkey, all gobble, and a nasty squint which made him stare straight over your left shoulder when he was looking you in the eye. His name was Austin and he had some sort of power complex, monarch of all he surveyed, including his two Military Police sergeants who were big men, hewn out of off-cuts from Stonehenge.

'You're a civilian far as I'm concerned,' he gobbled at Tommy. 'I'm not obliged even to speak to you, let alone answer questions.'

'Oh, I think you'll find I can do all manner of nasty things to you if you refuse to cooperate, Major Austin.' Tommy smiled, the seraphic smile this time, taking in little Adrian Austin and the two MP sergeants all decked up in their white webbing, red caps, lanyards, revolvers and all. He then used his twelve-bore shotgun method of questioning, swinging from left to right and scattering questions, blasting full on at both of the sergeants and the peptic major. The questions probed into their own knowledge of Doris Butler, their personal interaction with her, and the manner in which they viewed her during the time she worked as a civilian clerk to the RTO.

In all there were ten Military Police NCOs attached to the RTO Office, but it so happened that the pair on duty—Sergeants Carmichael and Thompson—had done a large percentage of daylight shifts, therefore coming into contact with Mrs Butler more than most.

Almost straightaway Major Austin revealed he had felt some suspicion when he discovered Mrs Butler was, as he put it, 'a fluid German speaker', information that exposed the unfocused major as a dimwit of proportions equal to his rank.

'Didn't just speak Kraut, either,' Sergeant Carmichael volunteered. 'What worried me was she began nattering in Frog and Pole to the two other geezers. Then, what followed, well . . .'

'What exactly followed?' Tommy asked.

'Well, what we discovered. When we looked into the backgrounds of Maisondel and Korob,' Sergeant Thompson said in a clever-pocket voice, his head wagging from side to side like a child who knows all the answers.

'And what did you discover?' Tommy caught sight of Dave Mungo's face falling through several thousand feet to a low, dodgy area where they could shoot him down in flames.

'Don't forget the Official Secrets Act,' Major Austin said quite quietly at which point sergeants Carmichael and Thompson clammed up so tightly that Tommy wondered how they managed to breathe.

'I'm sorry, sir,' Mungo added with a smooth shrug. 'Mr Bear, sir.'

'I'll be back,' he all but snarled.

*   *   *

Ron Worrall stood in the little clearing of grass and bushes on the north side of 65 Bluefields Road. There was a young elm tree among the bushes to the front, the tree from which the bark had been picked. Slightly to the rear a poplar stood to attention—one of five that ran proud in a line along the back of the houses.

Ron was fussy about his appearance, almost as fussy as Dandy Tom: liked to show a good inch of cuff, nice links, and the polished brogues which were, this morning, scuffed and dirty.

They had turned the house inside out, knowing it had all been done before: opening drawers, taking stuff out, then repacking, bottom drawer first like thieves so they didn't have to close them straightaway. They'd rooted around under the stairs, gone through everything in the kitchen, cutlery, pots, pans, utensils; then the DCs cleared out the coal shed outside, just to the rear of the back door. DC Bones and DC Trickman.

He'd brought a pair of uniforms as well as the two DCs and they'd worn overalls to do the coal. 'Not a sausage,' Bones told him when they were done and knew they'd have to take scrubbing brushes to their hands to get out the ingrained coal dust.

'I wasn't looking for sausages, more like fire irons,' Ron said, unsmiling.

Now they were traversing the lawn behind the house while Billy Bones examined the flowerbeds.

Ron looked around him, then up just as a breeze hit the poplar and sent the leaves shimmering enough for him to go on looking at what he first thought was probably an irregularity—a branch out of alignment, slanting straight up, the other branches folded back like a closed umbrella. He stepped sideways, still peering up, head back, neck aching. It was too thick to be a branch and seemed to be jammed close to the trunk some six feet from the tree's base. Easy to overlook. If it was anything it had already been missed.

Poplars are not trees for climbing but Ron sussed out two of the lowest branches that would possibly bear his weight. Balancing on the balls of his feet he craned upwards then sprang, arms stretched out, hands clasping the branches where they forked from the trunk. He flexed his arms and pulled upwards so that his head came level with the slender branches.

Reaching up with his left hand, he grasped another branch two and a bit feet higher; then the right hand, feeling the strain of his weight, a grazing of his palms on the rough wood, flexing again and pulling his chest upwards against the springy branches and leaves. Again. This time the object was revealed and just within reach. It had no ornamentation which dated it after 1887 when truncheons decorated with coats of arms and individual markings were all recalled. This one was probably smooth crocus wood, around 15 inches long, a truncheon with a leather thong at the handle.

Taking his weight on the left arm, Ron reached up, grabbed the thong and held the weapon dangling from his own wrist as he clambered down to the ground.

There was a lot of discolouration, dark, almost rust coloured with raised particles sticking to the wood. Worrall had no doubt that this was the weapon that had bludgeoned

Doris Butler to death. He called to the other men, giving instructions so that Billy Bones came over and held a large cellophane evidence envelope under the truncheon, allowing Ron to drop the weapon into the bag and so hold it safe from contamination. Whoever had battered Doris to death in her kitchen had crept out to the hiding place, then tossed the item gently into the tree where it had luckily slid among the branches, snagging itself almost hidden against the trunk.

'Might never of found it,' observed Trickman.

'What goes up must come down.' Ron said. 'Lucky throw.'

'Yea,' Bones agreed.

The two uniforms in their blue overalls still moved up and down the lawn, searching.

CHAPTER EIGHTEEN

Mungo was still with Tommy when they arrived back at the Central Sheffield nick. 'I'm going to London and you're coming even if I have to crush you into my suitcase,' Tommy told him. 'And when I've talked to your guv'nor you could find yourself on permanent traffic duty . . . in the Orkneys.'

'Most restful, sir.' Mungo's face didn't show a flicker.

Tommy said he should get his overnight bag. 'I'm not going to see Woolly Bear without you, Mungo. I want you there when he lays his nasty bits of secret news on me. And don't go playing hide and seek round the nick because I'm not leaving without you.'

'Ears, sir,' said Mungo in a passable imitation of Detective Chief Superintendent Bear.

There was good news and bad news waiting when Tommy got to the little office they had given him: two chairs, a plain table for work, two telephones and one of the amusing *Careless Talk Costs Lives* posters on the wall—the one with Hitler and Goering on a bus sitting behind a pair of yattering women. 'Reminds me of you, heart,' he'd said to Suzie when describing his surroundings to her.

First was the bad news, Brian came in to say he'd heard the chief wanted him.

'We're going up to town, Brian. Get the Wolseley juiced up.'

'The Wolseley's u/s, Chief.'

'Well, get us a car from here.'

'None available, Chief. I've been dashing around like the proverbial blue-based fly trying to get one. No can do.'

'How long to get the Wolseley operational?'

'Two to three days.'

'What the hell's wrong with it? Sprung a leak?'

'Something like that. Needs a new rotor arm

226

and they're muttering dark prophecies about a rebore.'

Tommy thought for a minute, said *he* needed a rebore, and added that they'd have to go by train. 'Myself, Ron and that bugger Mungo.'

Brian went off to check the trains and Ron Worrall came in with a smile that could have got an award. He held the bagged truncheon up like the Chancellor of the Exchequer holding his dispatch box for the cameras before making his budget speech.

'Another sixpence on fags?' Tommy asked.

'No, the Holy Grail.' Ron tried for a wider smile. 'The murder weapon.'

Tommy had collected bits of naval slang from Suzie's Royal Marine brother. 'Shave off!' he said. Then once more with feeling, 'Shave off! Stroll on!'

Ron told him about the drama of finding the truncheon.

'Stroll on,' Tommy repeated. Then he asked about prints. All the film scripts had coppers talking about 'dabs' which they just didn't like and certainly didn't do. They always spoke of 'prints'.

'There's plenty of gore and possibly flesh on it. Where there's muck there's money, Chief.'

'We'll do it properly. You come with us, Ron. It can go over to the Bureau as soon as we get in, then you can ride it over to Hendon.'

'Chief,' Ron acknowledged. The Fingerprint Bureau was part of Scotland Yard itself. A former inspector general of the Bengal Police, Edward Henry, had been appointed Assistant Commissioner (Crime) early in 1901. A few months later he set up the Bureau, continuing the wonderful work he had begun in India. Hendon, the site of the Police College, was also the home of the Forensic Science Laboratory. The College had been closed for the duration when the war broke out in '39, but the laboratory remained, despite the mistrust of 'scientific policing' in some circles.

Tommy was fond of telling people that when the famed Lord Trenchard, 'Father' of the RAF, had become Commissioner of the Met in the Thirties he was told by eminent doctors that they were dead against police-paid scientific experts giving evidence in court. They said the public and the judges wouldn't accept such evidence.

'I don't think there's much doubt that the blood and flesh on that truncheon belong to Doris Butler,' Tommy said, then picked up and opened the large envelope that had come from the Yard addressed to him. Suzie's reports and the photographs spilt out onto the table just as Sergeant Mungo came in with his overnight case.

'Crikey,' Mungo peered at the picture of Michael Lees-Duncan, 'Stan Gittins doesn't look so good.' He scowled. 'Positively peaky.'

'Who?' Tommy looked up at him, frowning, then down at his finger touching the edge of the photo of Michael Lees-Duncan looking only half alive even though he was actually dead.

'That's Stanley Gittins.' Mungo said. He was telling them that this was Stanley Gittins, corporal in the 1st Battalion, Suffolk Regiment, friend of Doris Butler. Probably the last person she had been seen with.

'Of course it is,' said Tommy feeling the best he'd felt all day. Jackpot, he thought. Bingo, reaching for the telephone to ring Suzie.

Hold the front page, heart.

Got a scoop, have you?

May even have a result. Now this is what I want you to do . . .

*   *   *

It was towards the end of August that the bad news came to Max Voltsenvogel. The pink flimsy paper he held in both hands trembled unnecessarily, so he lowered his elbows to the desktop and looked above the paper at the young Unterscharführer Schmidt, his servant, his shadow and, sometimes, his conscience. Now the man's steady blue eyes appeared to be holding Voltsenvogel's like a radar beam trying to detect movement. It was a quiet benign battle of wills.

'This came direct?' Voltsenvogel asked

quietly.

'Less than five minutes ago, Herr Gruppenführer. In the normal traffic we get around six o'clock. It was sandwiched between an aircraft test transmission and a series of BBC Overseas rubbish. *Flaubert would like to speak with Lapin. The willow still weeps in Henley-on-Thames*. You know the kind of stuff, sir. It's clever to piggyback on top of those radio messages. The British are too arrogant to monitor those broadcasts.'

'I'm surprised London still needs to send the messages, now they're actually here, on the ground.'

'It is not altogether a pessimistic situation. Some would say it was evidence that they are not in control of their so-called resistance forces.'

Voltsenvogel smirked. 'General de Gaulle's resistance forces, you mean.'

Schmidt nodded with a tight little smile, followed by a small shrug and a knowing look.

Voltsenvogel knew that what he held in his hands was genuine information. It was also bad news. 'So we must consider that Bellwether (he used the German word *Leithammel*) is dead?'

'That's what it says, Herr Gruppenführer. He's dead.'

Voltsenvogel nodded and ground his teeth, moved his head in a sideways turn, as if winking, then cursed. Bellwether had been the weak link from the beginning. 'Always had private agendas, Bellwether.' He looked at the little corporal as though he was blaming him, personally, for the news of his agent's death. 'These Nazis who're intellectually transformed are like Roman Catholic converts: more holy than the Pope himself: more of a fascist than the Führer. At least we have the Ram.'—*Der Widder*.

'You said some time ago, Colonel, that much depended on him—on Bellwether. Now he has come unstuck.' Schmidt's eyes showed no sign of moving away, steady as a barmaid's hand on the pump, Voltsenvogel thought. The boy had nerve. Was it paranoid of him to suspect the young man? He hardly thought so. His byword was that you should suspect everyone, especially those who bring bad news and this was bad news for Operation *Löwenzahn*: Lion's Teeth.

'You don't get more unstuck than dead. But, yes, we have the Ram,' Voltsenvogel repeated. In his heart he felt the two agents had been wrongly named. Bellwether should have been called the Ram, while the Ram should have been called Bellwether. Why in heaven's name had Bellwether killed the woman? She was a good, dependable little cog in Voltsenvogel's English part of the organisation: someone who couriered, and looked after agents for the odd night. 'Our bed and breakfast girl,' Schmidt called her. Someone for them to talk with.

231

Damn Bellwether. What had happened? She'd probably looked at him the wrong way, or made a remark he took to be disparaging. He was always a little unhinged, apt to fly off the handle. Become violent. Fool.

The room in which Voltsenvogel sat had originally been planned as the main reception room of this long low bungalow, built in 1938 for a doctor who had his eye on retirement. As soon as you entered this room you were aware of the beautifully sprung and polished natural wooden floor, while the varnished panelling doubled the price. There were four high windows set in the outside wall, and two more in the shorter end wall, for the room was on one corner of the house. The casements were wooden, beautifully crafted and fashioned with great care. Once a show place, the interior, under the SS, had become vulgar and cheap. The curtains were a heavy silk, the colour of the bottom of a pond, which meant they did not match any other colours in the room, making the cream sofas look dingy and clashing unpleasantly with the three big throw rugs, and the heavy peach-coloured wallpaper, chosen by the doctor's wife herself. Now also the pictures and decorations were not in keeping with the design of the place—Hitler photographed at his desk looking gravely into the camera, like a provincial schoolmaster, another of Reichsführer Himmler, looking exactly what he was—a chicken farmer—and a painting of the Brandenberg Gate in fog that would have not been out of place on a cheap box of chocolates.

The bungalow stood in a small patch of ground—a couple of acres—made into a pleasant formal garden just outside the small town of Huissen, some ten kilometres west of Arnem. Intelligence Group Odin—Voltsenvogel's own overdramatic nomenclature of his unit—had used this spacious home as their headquarters for a little over a year now.

When he really owned to it, Odin had been conceived by Voltsenvogel as early as the summer of 1940 when, as a member of the RSHA—the Reich Security Administration— he had been trained and posted to Department VI, the Foreign Intelligence division. The plan itself had not formed until it began to flourish in the past two years. But the germ of it had been seeded into his mind back in the early summer of 1940 when nothing could go wrong for the Führer and the armed forces of Nazi Germany.

Voltsenvogel's face was closed, showing nothing. 'The Ram,' he said again. Then, in English, 'You are looking after the Ram, friend Schmidt? Taking care of him? Preparing him?'

Kurt Schmidt replied in English, fluent, a cultured accent—what the British themselves would, incorrectly, call an Oxford accent.

'Night and day. I don't let him rest.' It was the accent and the man's knowledge of colloquial English that gave Voltsenvogel occasional doubts. Only a week ago, the corporal had said he thought the officers who had tried to kill the Führer—the 20th July plotters—were 'round the bend'. He had the British slang off to a T, and that had worried Voltsenvogel.

'What,' the SS-Gruppenführer asked now, 'would have happened if von Stauffenberg's bomb had killed Hitler? Tell me that, Schmidt. What would it have achieved?'

Schmidt held out a hand and tipped it from side to side. 'Maybe the enemy would have sued for peace: a few thousand lives saved.'

Everyone was conscious that the battle was hopeless. The slow progress of the Allies would have no effect on the final outcome. Everybody in Voltsenvogel's small command was jittery, straining as though they could hear the raucous sounds of battle from the west.

'When you cut off the head, the body dies, yes?' Voltsenvogel nodded. 'Well, we shall see. Tell the Ram that his time is nigh.' He sounded like a cheap evangelist thumping his Bible, and knew it, the spectre of a smile around his lips, not even rising up his cheeks.

'In those words, Colonel?'

'In those words exactly.' A dismissive nod. He wondered if it would work in reverse, cutting off the head. He thought it would cause the Allies to flinch, shrink back and in that moment take their eyes off the ball. The Allies were all so obsessed with the goodness of their cause. It was partly the Jewish question. We would never behave like that, we *could* never carry out such barbaric acts, they would say to each other. So what was Hamburg and the firestorms? What Dresden? What Cologne? Voltsenvogel thought, 'Don't tell me the Allied leaders didn't know what they were doing?' Men, women and children consigned to the bombs and the flames?

Cut off the head and the body dies. We'll see.

As he reached the door, Schmidt said there was one further thing, 'A secure message on the cipher machine. For you only. From your friend SS-Obersturmbannführer Erich Lottle. From Peenemünde. The beanpole adjutant. Remember him?' For a moment their differing ranks disappeared.

'Unzip it for me, Kurt . . .'

'But it's for you only. Your eyes.'

'As the Yankees say, who's counting?'

When Schmidt returned with the message neatly typed he told his superior officer that Lottle was showing off. 'The signal came, forwarded by OKL—Luftwaffe Headquarters. He's letting you know what an important man he is.'

Voltsenvogel read the message and chuckled. 'Yes, he's showing off. We talked about the British cryptonyms—*Diver* for the

Fe103 and *Big Ben* for the A-4 rocket—the *Vergeltungswaffe Zwei*. I suppose he's trying to be witty.' He read aloud, 'Big Ben will chime in Paris on 7th and London on 8th.'

So, the big A-4 rockets would be fired at Paris on 7th while the attack on London would begin the following day, 8th September.

Voltsenvogel said something about trying to kill that walking nose General de Gaulle in Paris. 'I suppose he's still there.' Paris had fallen to the Allies on 24th August.

General Charles de Gaulle was not universally loved. The tall Frenchman was one of the few generals who, in the days before the great tactical German victory of 1940, when the Panzers and Stukas swept across Europe, had preached the kind of warfare demonstrated by that Nazi Blitzkreig. To the dismay of the French General, Staff de Gaulle, as early as 1938, had wanted all the troops under his command to be mechanised and foresaw the fast leapfrogging of armour combined with swift, hard-hitting air power.

At the time of the Allied retreat from Dunkirk, de Gaulle slipped out of France, before the French surrender, and took command of the Free French forces in England. In this capacity he did not make himself a beloved figure among his fellow allies. 'There, but for the grace of God goes God,' the British Prime Minister, Winston Churchill, was reported to have said of him, while in Nazi-occupied France he was found guilty of treason and sentenced to death. But a couple of weeks ago, he had led his troops into Paris, liberating the French capital.

Voltsenvogel picked up his telephone and asked his field switchboard to get him the commanding officer of Luftwaffe unit KG200, Oberst Heinz Heigl. He would either be at the battle group's headquarters at Rangsdorf, on the placid shore of the Rangsdorfer lake, only a short distance from the centre of Berlin; or at the Führer's headquarters at Rastenburg, the Wolf's Lair.

KG200—Kampfgeschwader 200—was the most secret unit of the Luftwaffe. Formed only in February, from a nucleus of two large technical wings, KG200's official job was to evaluate aircraft for warfare. As such they had bases all over occupied Europe, and even deep into Russia. Bomber and fighter Staffels rarely knew when they shared an airfield with a KG200 unit.

KG200 were equipped with every known type of aircraft serving with the Luftwaffe, and also had access to captured RAF, USAAF and Russian aircraft. This was their secret side: their vast collection of British, American and Russian aircraft. They had airworthy DC3 Dacotas, Spitfires, Lancasters, Stirlings, Mustangs, Thunderbolts, Wellingtons and many more. KG200 flew B17 Flying Fortresses stuffed full of radio equipment, shadowing the box formations of the Fortresses that daily bombed German targets. The KG200 Fortresses would follow and report on height, speed and course of the American bombers. They flew Sterlings, Beaufighters, Mosquitos and Wellingtons, tagged to the end of British bomber formations, creeping up on individual aircraft, catching RAF airfields off guard as aircraft were landing.

A Lancaster would be making its final approach to its home base, the crew relaxed and relieved they had completed another mission intact. Then, out of the night would come a Beaufighter or a Mosquito, hammering bullets and canon shell into the big bomber, sending it sprawling onto the runway in flames.

KG200 had many tricks up its deadly sleeve using captured Allied aeroplanes, literally flying under a false flag.

When Oberst Heigl came on the line, Voltsenvogel sounded almost lighthearted. 'Heizi,' he chirped. 'It's Max from the Research Department.'

'So, what are you after this time?'

'I've got a holidaymaker who needs a seat on one of your planes. We need a good pilot, one who'll get him safely into the glorious English West Country. Last time we used a Grasshopper I recall.'

'The Grasshopper could be difficult, but I've got a nice little Stinson. The L-5, what they call the Sentinel. Land and take-off on an

English cricket pitch. When do you want it?'

'Sometime after 8th of next month: say the 10th or 11th, depending on weather, of course.'

The Sentinel was a two-seat, high-wing monoplane that the Americans used for liaison work, for taking senior officers around.

Voltsenvogel knew exactly where there was a flat stretch of ground ideal for the Sentinel, close to the rail track that ran from Exeter to Exmouth in Devon, glorious Devon.

As Schmidt left the office, Voltsenvogel called after him, 'Tell the Ram he'll be taking a little trip around the 10th or 11th.'

'He'll be delighted,' said Corporal Schmidt, then, showing off his versatility, he broke into song—

When Adam and Eve were dispossessed from their garden up in heaven,
They planted another one out in the west,
T'was Devon,
T'was Devon, glorious Devon.'

*　　　*　　　*

When Schmidt returned, around thirty minutes later, Voltsenvogel was standing looking out of one of the big windows.

'I've talked to the Ram,' Schmidt told him. 'He seems nervous. Jumpy. What if this doesn't go properly, Herr Gruppenführer?'

Voltsenvogel shrugged. 'If something goes

wrong and the thing doesn't work then it doesn't work. There's no point in being concerned. We're not fanatics, Schmidt, my friend. I believe in the Führer and in the National Socialist Party. I believe in the Führer's way of running Germany, the Third Reich. But, if he's wrong then he's wrong. We can do nothing about it. I don't believe in fanaticism. Understand?'

CHAPTER NINETEEN

The truncheon found by Ron Worrall close to Doris Butler's garden turned out to be the goods. The fingerprints belonged, indisputably to Michael Lees-Duncan, and after three days the forensic lab came back from Hendon with the news that the blood, at least, matched that of the late Mrs B.

Tommy had not gone home to Suzie: stayed in his big office on the fourth floor of Scotland Yard waiting for the forensic results, spending the nights on the unspeakably uncomfortable camp bed, and the days reading up on Suzie's assessment of the situation vis-à-vis the Lees-Duncans and the Toveys.

He was amused to find out about Lees-Duncan's courtship by the security service: more than amused to discover that they weren't sharing much with 'Woolly' Bear and the Branch. In theory the Branch was a kind of mailed fist for MI5, but it seemed to be a fact that they didn't like sharing with their friends in the Met.

She had gone for Tovey immediately after he had identified the body of his daughter, Dulcie. 'I felt he was more vulnerable than Lees-Duncan,' she wrote: adding that she had already worked out what had probably happened: pieced it all together from the two conversations and her own observation. Tommy felt proud of her as he read the transcript.

DI MOUNTFORD: Mr Tovey, you've identified your daughter's body, so now I have to return to the questions I started in your cottage, back in Churchbridge.

TOVEY: I told you, I 'en't answering no more questions. You can ask as long as you like, but I en't answering.

Later she told Tommy that he almost spat it at her, a fine spray of spittle hanging in the air and dropping to the table between them. 'It didn't matter,' she said, 'because you didn't have to be Professor Joad to work the whole thing out anyway.'

Professor Joad was a household name, appearing weekly on the BBC's *Brains Trust*, a hugely successful programme throughout the war. Joad was greatly imitated because he had what amounted to a catchphrase. When asked a question he would come back with, 'It all

depends on what you mean by . . . whatever.'
Comedians found him a natural. Later Joad
was to fall from grace by being caught
travelling by train without a ticket.

The transcript continued:

DI MOUNTFORD: Look, Eric . . .

TOVEY: No need for you to be familiar,
miss. No need at all. I am Mr Tovey.

So, the transcript continued for several
more pages of cut and thrust of questions and
parry by Tovey who, to use Suzie's description,
'hurled the words back at her like throwing
bricks'.

'Or, perhaps, darts?' Tommy Livermore
queried.

She told Tommy that she should have hit
him with her version of the truth straightaway.
Hit Tovey, that was.

'And what is your version?' Tommy asked,
and she looked at him as though he was half
daft.

'Two families . . .' she started and Tommy
muttered, 'Both alike in dignity.'

'Families lived cheek by jowl: one a servant,
the other the master . . .'

'I hardly think Eric Tovey thought of
himself as a servant. Gardeners don't. The
garden is always *their* garden; the flowers are
their flowers; the veg is *their* veg.'

'OK, Tommy, but they still lived cheek by
jowl and the kids all grew up together. Then
both the wives flipped. One ups and leaves

home, the other takes to the bottle. I haven't worked out the dates yet but I reckon the reason was the same.'

'And the reason was . . . ?'

Kath went wrong, Tovey had said. Then Lees-Duncan had commented on his wife— *Poor Isabel.*

'Dulcie wasn't Eric's daughter. She was John Lees-Duncan's daughter.'

'Prove it.'

In her head she heard Tovey again—*(John Lees-Duncan) knew her as well as I did. Maybe better'n I did.*

Then Willow—*Daddy rode over Mummy like a bloody traction engine rolling out the tarmac.*

'Lees-Duncan's almost admitted to it,' she told Tommy. 'No, I can't really prove it, but I know a man who'll give evidence.' She thought of the butler, Sturgis, and prayed that he would give up some of the family secrets.

'You may know it to be true,' Tommy had said. 'You may know it, but if you can't prove it . . .'

'Tommy, the meanest intelligence could . . .' She stopped. *The meanest intelligence.* Lawks, one of her dreaded stepfather's favourite expressions. She was ashamed of herself for using it.

'I think you're right, heart. There's little doubt. But we're going to have to get something solid. One of 'em's got to admit it out loud and in front of witnesses.'

243

This was after Tommy had finally curry-combed all the paperwork and returned to the flat in Upper St Martin's Lane.

'I'm cock-a-hoop,' he said, coming into the sitting room. James Mountford looked up from reading the official-looking letter that had just been delivered to him by dispatch rider.

'It's good to be back,' Tommy rubbed his hands together briskly, dropping a file of papers onto one of the side tables, the photographs of Michael and Gerald Lees-Duncan spilling out from the papers. 'So how're you, young James? How's the foot?'

'Lot better, Tommy.' He came over and peered at the photographs. 'Pair of right Harrovian thugs you've got there, all right.'

'Not sure about the Harrovian bit but they're certainly a pair of thugs. That one's no longer with us, by the way,' touching the picture of Michael Lees-Duncan.

'Sorry to hear it.'

'I'm not. Bloody murderer. One of the reasons that I'm cock-a-hoop. Solved my murder up in Sheffield.'

'Well, I won't be around for long.' James eased himself into a chair. 'Got my marching orders.'

'Oh. Good. Suzie around?'

'Not back yet, Tommy. Want to hear about my posting?'

'Let me guess: they're sending you to Brazil,
244

where the nuts come from.'

'I'm to be OC the Royal Marines Detachment at George Street. How about that?' George Street was shorthand for the Cabinet War Rooms, the underground bunkers, fashioned from the chambers below the Public Works Building on the edge of St James's Park and Horse Guards Parade. Only relatively few people were aware of this sophisticated shelter, but Tommy was obviously one of them.

'You'll have to be smart on that one. You'll be up to your arse in generals and cabinet ministers, not to mention the prime minister.'

'Absolutely. I'll have my fingers on the pulse of history.'

'Well, you watch it, laddo. Fingers near the pulse of history sometimes get burnt. And you have to be ready with the odd bon mot.'

'Such as?'

'You know the kind of thing—"the lights are going out across Europe, we shall not see them lit again in our lifetime." Good stuff like that.'

'I think I'll leave that to Winston,' James said, sounding most serious, and at that moment Suzie walked in.

'Ah-ha, the good old English Tom is back home at last.'

'Just dropped in for a saucer of milk and the odd fish bone.'

'Super to see you, Tommy.'

James hardly acknowledged his sister, still

245

staring down at the photos. 'You say this one's dead?'

'Shut up.' Tommy sounded like a bad ventriloquist.

'Well. How?'

'Tell you later, old boy. Got adult things to do now.'

She walked across the room to him, conscious that she was being provocative in the way she moved, and he took her into his arms, one thigh between hers as he hugged and kissed her, whispering in her ear. 'I have a nice present for you, Suzie darling. When you've got a minute.'

She looked over at her brother. 'We have a lot of business to discuss. See you later, brother dear.'

'He said he was cock-a-hoop.'

'Did he now.' She led Tommy away, his face wreathed in smiles, as they say.

'Cock-a-hoop.' She gave him an arch look.

'Plenty of one and not much of the other,'

'Oh, Tommy!'

Later, in their bedroom she raised herself on one elbow, looked down at him and said she'd done as he had asked.

'I know, heart, and you're magnificent.'

'No, Tom, I'm talking work. I did as you asked: about the Haynes family. Mr and Mrs and little Doris who became Doris Butler. The late Doris Butler, née Haynes.'

'Solved the murder.' Tommy grinned and

246

looked self-satisfied.

'So you said. You want to hear what I discovered? It's interesting, I promise.'

'Go ahead. But nothing would surprise me about Doris Butler now.'

'She was German.'

'I wondered.' He sat bolt upright as though a trap had been sprung behind him. 'She was. Really?'

'So were her mum and dad. Came over from Frankfurt in 1932. Changed their name from Hahn. Carl and Lottie Hahn. He was a qualified chemist and of course it was long before Hitler came to power. Lottie Hahn was originally Charlotte Fisher.'

'Related to Jeremy, I suppose.'

'Tommy, shut up and listen. This could be important.'

'Oh, it is, old darling. It's very important.'

'So important I think your friend Berry should know about it. His investigation originally, wasn't it?'

Tommy nodded but didn't say anything.

'Berry should be out doing traffic duty in the Kalahari.'

'He sounds hopeless.'

'Outside the Yacht Club. No, the Kalahari hasn't got a Yacht Club, has it? I'm thinking of the Gobi.'

'In a minute you're going to tell me that you're personally going to make sure Berry never handles a case again.'

247

'You're right. I'm going to see to it personally.'

'But they were German—at least he was, so I suppose Doris was . . . technically.'

'A German murdered by a pro-German. Well, pro-Nazi. I have a theory about what they were up to.'

James was just greeting his Maren friend when Suzie and Tommy finally emerged, dressed and more or less in their right minds.

'Shan't be late. Emily's got to get back by midnight or she'll not get use of the jeep again for some time.'

'This a regular thing with the Wren?' Tommy asked.

Suzie said it seemed to be and he grunted. They went out to eat—the Savoy, Tommy's treat, but were back in bed again by midnight.

Just as Suzie was sliding into sleep, Tommy stirred. 'You talked to the parents of the other dead novice, heart? What was her name? Parson father? Harding, was it? Sister Bridget Mary?'

'There hasn't been time, Tom. I've been up to my ears with the bloody Lees-Duncans.'

'Do it tomorrow then. And what about the third one? The one in hospital. Sister Monica?'

'Tomorrow, Tommy.'

Bugger, she thought, then of course couldn't get to sleep: tossing and turning all night with Tommy snoring like a doodlebug all the time.

248

CHAPTER TWENTY

Suzie dozed off at around five and woke with a start at seven feeling depressed and anxious, knowing immediately that she would have to go to the convent today.

Urgently.

Worse, the nuns seemed to be blessed with second sight. As she was organising transport—Tommy had to be at the Yard all day, 'Dealing with bloody Berry,' he said ominously—when Billy Mulligan came on the line. 'Message for you, ma'am.' The 'ma'am' sounded heavily laced with friendly insolence: Billy always thought of Suzie as a kind of superannuated schoolgirl—at least that's what Suzie thought.

'It's them nuns . . .' Billy said.

'Yeees?'

'Nun called Monica. Was in hospital after that doodlebug at the convinct. Wants a word.'

'She's out of hospital then?' She was sure he was taking the mickey.

'So it would seem, ma'am.'

'Tell them I'll be in today. The chief's okayed Brian to drive me and I'd like to take Shirley.'

Billy said Brian and Shirley would pick her up in half an hour. Tommy was making his own way in, but his parting shot was that she'd better remember the other parson—'The one out near Bedford Park. Nun's father. Sister Bridget Mary's Pa.' Tommy never missed a trick.

Memory like a Hefalump, Suzie thought.

'Leave the talking to me, Shirl,' she told Shirley Cox as they arrived in Silverhurst Road. 'Take notes. Check and double-check. OK?'

Mother Rachel and Sister Eunice were waiting for her. Suzie had telephoned before leaving home and the gatekeeper led them straight to Mother Rachel's office: the big room with the tall windows looking down on the cypress-flanked path to the chapel.

The scent of the place came up and whacked her in the face: the mixture of polish, incense and an almost tangible calm, taking her straight back to her schooldays at St Helen's among the sweet rise and fall of plainsong and the quiet-spoken nuns who taught her. Quiet-spoken, that was, until tempers became frayed. The English teacher, Sister Mary Joseph, whose tones rose to a screech and who was not averse to rapping you across the knuckles with a springy twelve-inch ruler. Indeed there were passages from Shakespeare that always brought back a sharp agony to Suzie's fingers. They said you couldn't remember pain, but she'd like to differ.

Both of the nuns were standing by Mother

Rachel's desk, all traces of bonhomie gone, replaced by sober, almost gloomy, expressions. Sister Eunice was red around the eyes, as though she had been weeping.

Mother Rachel took a step forward and placed Suzie's hands between her palms. 'We're so glad it's you, my dear,' she smiled, but without any twinkle. 'We were concerned that it might be your colleague, Mr Livermore. He seemed a rather stern person and we were worried for poor Sister Monica.'

Stern? she thought: must remember to tell Tommy what an effect he's had on the nuns.

Mother Rachel gestured towards a chair, and Suzie seated herself. Shirley Cox had moved a wooden stand chair into a corner and now sat there, quietly, as though not wishing to be noticed, notebook on her thigh, pencil poised.

'And it's really all my fault,' wailed the Novice Mistress, her voice catching in a little sob.

'Don't be foolish, Eunice. It's as much my error as yours.'

'What error?' Suzie asked.

'The day of the doodlebug,' Mother Rachel began. 'That Sunday morning, early. We were both spending the weekend at our Farnborough house, the house of the Holy Family. You may recall . . .'

'I recall it very well.' In her head she had a picture of Mother Rachel's anger on

251

discovering nobody had warned her about the V-1 and the deaths here at the Mother House.

There are forty-five sisters in the convent and nobody had the wit to telephone our house in Farnborough, our house of the Holy Family, to inform us of this tragedy.

'Early that morning we watched the postulants being driven away from the Holy Family. Starting on their journey to this convent, to prepare for taking their final vows. Three of them. A precious trio.' The Mother Superior's voice rose as she rapped out the names, 'Sister Bridget Mary, Sister Theresa and Sister Monica. All three were novices actually. We watched them board the little bus that had come over from here, driven by Mr Taylor. We watched them.' She was screeching now. 'One two, three,' a long pause, 'four.'

Irreverently Suzie thought of the popular song: *We three, we're all alone . . . My echo, my shadow and me.*

Then the full significance hit her: four of them, starting their final journey towards death. Suzie gulped.

Sister Eunice said they both knew well enough that there were only three going to the Mother House. 'Yet we stood by as four sisters boarded the bus. Stood there and waved to them.'

'Didn't question them. Didn't see what was wrong. Four not three,' the Mother Superior all but shouted. 'And neither of us recognised the fourth. Sister Michael, so called. No wonder we didn't recognise her. Neither of us was alert. It could have been Hitler getting into that vehicle.'

'If we had questioned the fourth there and then this would never have happened.'

'If we'd just realised there was a fourth.'

'But we stood there,' Mother Rachel's lips were pursed. 'We stood there. Like Patience on a monument.'

Suzie felt a reminiscent springe in her right knuckles. She knew too well how it could be. One quick distraction, a moment slipping from concentration. But, she argued with herself, playing devil's advocate, these were disciplined women, holy women, used to meditation and prayer both of which demanded extreme attentiveness. Would their minds so easily slide from the fact of the situation? She decided they would. It could happen to anyone.

'And Sister Monica?' she asked, returning to the task at hand.

'Well, you know she was terribly injured.'

She nodded. To be truthful she only remembered that Sister Monica had been unconscious and they had not been able to see her at the hospital.

Sister Eunice said Monica had suffered broken ribs, a broken arm, head wounds and severe shock, and Mother Rachel continued. 'She's still not sure what she saw and heard. I think some of it seems like a dream to her.

Indeed, some of her memories are so extraordinary, so unpleasant, contain such heavy mortal sins, that . . .' She foundered for words, stuttering slowly to a stop. 'To my old mind it's almost unbelievable. I mean, I knew that Theresa had lived a full life. We had a long talk when she first arrived here. A lot of women are concerned about their past lives— if they're fit to become members of the order, if they've lived in the world for a long time, partaken of the fruits of life. My personal view is that the more they've experienced the better religious they'll make. But you must hear for yourself.'

She seated herself behind her desk and pressed a bell-push near the telephone. A moment later there was a knock at the door and a nun, wearing a white veil, as opposed to the grey of the order's habit, appeared, pushing a wheelchair in which Sister Monica sat—a small woman, slight, hunched, shrunken, and with a dreadfully pale face, except for her left cheek which was seared red raw, puckering the skin.

Sister Eunice introduced the white-veiled nun as Sister Constance, adding that she was one of the four trained nursing nuns belonging to the order.

'And this is Sister Monica,' Mother Rachel said, and Monica flinched, looking as though she was trying to get her body through the back of the wheelchair.

Suzie offered her hand and told her who she was, looking into the little nun's pale grey, frightened eyes. The handshake had no grip to it and the nun's palm was cold and damp.

'I think we'd better leave you alone.' Mother Rachel shepherded Eunice and the nursing nun to the door, turning back and stooping towards Sister Monica as she passed the chair.

'Sister, there's no need to be afraid of Miss Mountford. She understands. Just answer her questions as truthfully as you answered me.'

Monica gave a small nod, barely perceptible; Mother Rachel sounding somewhat condescending.

'There's no need to be any way frightened, Sister Monica.' Suzie told her as soon as the door closed behind Mother Rachel and the other two sisters.

'I . . . I'm not frightened of you.' The voice was, like the person, slight, piping, pitched high. 'I'm just . . . well, I'm just frightened all the time. It was so horrible and, to be honest with you, I can't sort out what I remember and what I dreamt. Some of it is so awful that I can hardly believe it's true.' She gave a nervous little glance behind her, as if checking that Mother Rachel had left the room, and Suzie saw that she was forcing her hands down into her lap as if trying to stop them shaking.

'Tell you what,' Suzie began, 'let's just take it one step at a time. You do know that you

255

had a man with you, dressed as a nun?'

'Oh, indeed, yes. Sister Michael.'

'How did that happen? How on earth were you taken in? Or were you not taken in?'

'Sister Michael just appeared, joined us at the door as we gathered to leave. Some of the sisters were outside close to the little bus Mr Taylor had driven from the Mother House.

'Sister Theresa explained who she was. She said, "Sister Michael has to come with us." And she said something about showing us the ropes. That stuck in my mind because it was an odd expression for her to use. And I remember thinking that I hadn't seen Sister Michael before. I wondered about Theresa as well. She always seemed to harbour a lot of anger.'

'And you just accepted her, Sister Michael?'

'I hardly looked at her. I was simply conscious of a tall nun, in the habit of the order. It was only later that . . .' She swallowed audibly and moved uncomfortably in the wheelchair. 'Theresa seemed to take charge. I think both Bridget and I were a little cowed by Theresa. She could be, well, explosive. There was a lot of anger buried in Sister Theresa, God rest her.'

'So nobody queried her presence?'

'It would seem not. We didn't take much notice of anything. I wonder if you understand. This was a very serious time for us, the three of us. We were to take our final vows. Our

256

minds were supposed to be on the great steps of poverty, chastity and obedience. In a week's time we would make our dedication to the order, and be confirmed in our future lives, wedded to the rules of our order. The bishop of Oxford, Dr Kirk, was coming to conduct our Professing celebration. It's a huge step and the days leading up to it are very special. We were holding ourselves apart. That's why it seemed all the worse, what happened.'

'Yes. Yes, I understand. Tell me what happened when you arrived at the convent.'

'We were allotted to cells and we made our way to them, maintaining silence. No, Theresa left us. She broke the silence. She said she had to see Sister Sophia in the kitchen. Something about food she was not allowed to eat—it was a medical thing. No fat or something. I think she'd seen a doctor during the previous week.'

Handy, Suzie thought. Nipping into the kitchen and probably concealing a knife in the folds of her voluminous habit.

'We were told there was ten minutes before refectory. The midday meal. I spent the time in contemplation. In my cell. Then I heard the sound of the flying bomb, that horrible burring engine noise. I was frightened and then I heard something else.'

'Yes?'

'Raised voices. A huge argument. Theresa and another voice, deeper, like a man's voice and Sister Theresa shrieking, wild, most angry.

257

The two noises appeared to merge together, the engine of the flying bomb, scoring across the sky, then the shrieking of Theresa's angry voice.'

'And . . .'

'And suddenly the doodlebug's engine stopped. Well, you know how frightening that can be. Waiting for the wretched thing to glide down and explode.'

Suzie nodded. Of course she knew. Just like everyone knew. The burring pop of the engine and the sudden cut-out that meant the bomb had ceased its flight, lowered its nose and come hurtling down to explode. It seemed as random as the ball on a roulette wheel. It *was* frightening. Far more terrifying than the aircraft, the bombers flying in and releasing their cargo, aiming at given points. These V-weapons seemed haphazard, making individual deaths a hit and miss business. James had told her that he had been on the parade ground at Deal and a flying bomb had puttered its way, right over the barracks. 'We tried not to show fear,' he said. 'But we must have wavered, because our colour-sergeant shouted. 'Stand still there. That's nothing to do with you.'

'I ran out of my cell. It was next to the one allotted to Sister Michael. She was almost in the doorway and it was then that I saw she wasn't a woman. That Sister Michael was a man, and Sister Theresa was screaming at

258

him.'

'Did you hear what she was screaming?'

Monica squirmed uncomfortably. 'That's the most difficult thing. I really don't know. I heard something, but I find it very difficult to believe it was real. It's more likely I heard something devilish in my head after I'd lost consciousness.'

'Tell me anyway. Tell me what you think you heard.'

'I thought I heard Theresa scream, "Michael, you have manipulated me all of my life!" I know it's madness, but I can hear that still. Plainly. Then she seemed to shout, "Michael, you seduced me. You made me commit a mortal sin and you made me twice guilty! You knew what was between us. You knew we had the same . . . " And I thought she shouted "father". "You knew we had the same father!" Then she rushed at him and I saw something in her hand, something silver. She leapt towards him, shouting, "Traitor! Traitor!" and at the same moment Bridget Mary came out of her cell and ran towards Theresa. As she did so, there was this terrible sensation, as though we were surrounded by fire. The air was singed and seemed to be drawn away, as though there was no air to breathe. I felt pain and I passed out with a huge roaring in my ears, like a massive thunderclap.'

Unbidden, words from one of the psalms

came into Suzie's head. She could almost hear them being sung in the chapel at St Helen's years before, when she was a child:

Thou shall not be afraid for any terror by night: nor for the arrow that flieth by day;

Nor the pestilence that walketh in darkness: nor for the sickness that destroyeth in the noonday.

A thousand shall fall beside thee; and ten thousand at thy right hand: but it shall not come nigh thee,

*   *   *

Words particularly apt at the moment; words that came as a comfort to people facing the bombs and flying bombs; people who were concerned with what the Nazis may still have up their sleeves.

'I couldn't have really heard her scream all that, could I, Miss Mountford? It must have been some dream, a nightmare popping out of my subconscious. I mean Sister Theresa and this man, Michael.'

'Sounds like a dream to me,' Suzie lied. 'Who knows what tricks the mind can play when you've just been almost blown to . . .' She was going to say, 'blown to buggery', but amended it to 'blown to bits'.

'Must have smuggled him into the place in Farnborough,' Tommy said as he read Suzie's notes. ' "You knew we had the same father." '

Well, that's what we thought, but how the hell did she think she'd get away with it? If it hadn't been for the V-1 she'd probably have been sentenced to death: swung for him, because it seems horribly premeditated. She had to hide him in the Farnborough House overnight; dress him up; pass him off as a nun going to the Convent of St Catherine of Siena. Then she sneaks off, gets herself a knife and slashes him with it. This wasn't a spur of the moment thing. I suppose we'll never know the full story—like so many murders. But we've got means, motive and an eyewitness.'

He went on reading, then started to leaf back through the pages. 'What was it she said about Sister Theresa? There was a lot of anger buried in her?'

Suzie nodded. 'You really think the incest element was enough to drive her to kill another human being?'

'Obviously. That's what happened. What I really wonder about is the murder of Doris Butler. We have the evidence but no motive.'

'Unless there was a link with enemy agents—I mean the Frog and the Pole, and we know Michael Lees-Duncan's politics. He was a fascist: he admired Hitler.'

So they wrote a detailed joint report that was mostly educated deduction from the few facts available—Tommy did the full analysis of the Doris Butler killing without reaching into realms of fantasy over motive.

261

And there it might have remained but for events over which nobody had any control and which finally threatened to swamp the Mountford family.

CHAPTER TWENTY-ONE

The adjutant at Peenemünde, SS-Obersturmbannführer Erich Lottle, had told Max Voltsenvogel there was to be a rocket attack on Paris—using the new A-4 rockets, the V-2s—on 7th September.

Nothing happened.

He had clearly said that Paris would be targeted on 7th and London on 8th.

Big Ben will chime in Paris on 7th and London on 8th.

When no rockets arrived near the Eiffel Tower Max Voltsenvogel became annoyed and irritated. He rang Peenemünde but the adjutant was not available.

That morning two of the *Meilerwagen*, the mobile launch platforms, each carrying one of the big A-4 rockets, hidden from view by camouflaged hoods, drove to a prepared site some two miles from the Belgian town of La Roche-en-Ardenne, thirty miles south of Liege. The rockets were accompanied by the tanks containing the propellants, and a *Feuerleitpanzer*—an armoured fire-control vehicle. The A-4 rockets belonged to *Lehr & Versuchs* (Training and Experimental) *Batterie 444* of General Kammler's Vengeance Division. They were quickly gassed up and raised above the launch platforms which stood on specially reinforced concrete platforms. The rockets were adjusted and set to be fired at Paris.

Finally the order was given and the first rocket engine ignited and throbbed up to launch speed. The rocket rose a couple of feet then the engine cut out and the big projectile thudded back onto its site. It wobbled and swayed but did not topple over.

The second rocket fired with similar results. When the tail fins had cooled both rockets had their fuel and propellants removed, and it was later found that the accelerometers on both weapons were faulty, causing the engines to cut out prematurely. Indeed, a large proportion of the A-4s were substandard and failed to launch, broke up or exploded in mid-air. Enough fired normally however, and the A-4s aimed at London on the following day were in good working order.

At a little before twenty minutes to seven on the evening of Friday, 8th September 1944, a dull, drizzling evening, Frank Stubbs, caretaker of Stavely Road School, Chiswick, was walking across the school playing fields with Army Private Frank Browning, who was on leave and going to see his girlfriend.

Without warning both men were hurled into the air, landing twenty yards away. Browning died instantly but Frank Stubbs climbed to his feet, shook himself and saw immediately that houses on both side of the street, alongside the playing fields, had been demolished. In all, two people were dead and twenty more injured, trapped in the rubble of their houses.

Emergency services arrived quickly, followed by two RAF officers who set about examining the crater, thirty feet wide and ten feet deep, in the middle of the road. The RAF men retrieved shards of shrapnel from the crater which they carried off in their briefcases.

Later, some high-ranking Civil Defence people came to the site, together with a pair of US Army Air Force officers. When asked what had caused the explosion one of the Civil Defence men replied that he couldn't be sure. 'It might have been a gas main,' he said.

A few minutes later another rocket landed in Epping.

So the V-2 rockets were first nicknamed 'flying gas mains', and the V-2 assault on England began. From then until the following March the unstoppable weapons fell on London in a terrifying new Blitzkrieg, causing death, damage and, worse, a severe shaking of morale.

Max Voltsenvogel now set Operation *Löwenzahn* in motion. His remaining agent, the Ram, was put on readiness. 'The new attack with the rockets will give you a chance to escape, and get back to us here,' he told him. 'Failing that you must make your way across Europe to Berlin. With rockets falling all the time, the enemy will undoubtedly see your attack as one more piercing rocket hit. They won't be looking for an individual so you'll make good your escape.'

The following day the aircraft arrived from KG200—the L-5 Sentinel landing in a field close to Voltsenvogel's headquarters. Just after eleven o'clock that evening, with a KG200 pilot called Adolf Grief in the left-hand seat and the agent code-named the Ram—*Der Widder*—beside him, the L-5, still with its USAAF markings, took off. Four hours thirty-five minutes later Grief—a brilliant navigator—crossed the English coast just west of Sidmouth, letting down, with the engine throttled back and flaps extended, until they saw the twin pinpoints of light shining towards them, activated by a pair of agents Voltsenvogel had sent over many weeks before.

Grief switched on the big landing light for a couple of seconds, so that he could see the flat stretch of ground ahead. Moments later he touched down, quickly coming to a halt as *Der Widder* pushed open the small flat, hatch on his right, climbed onto the wing, hauled out his baggage, then slid down onto the sweet-smelling early autumn grass as the little aircraft revved up, turned, then with a roar bounced over the flat earth to become airborne again, having been on the ground for less than ninety seconds.

The Ram grabbed his gear and set off swiftly towards the railway line that would take him to his destination.

*   *   *

The rain of A-4 rockets now fell regularly on London and the south of England causing death, damage and renewed fear to the civil and military populations alike.

The V-1 flying bombs had been bad enough, but at least with them there had been some small warning in the buzzing and popping motor. Now the big rockets caused great consternation, arriving without warning, just the terrible thunder of their explosion, usually the double crump made from the breeching of the sound barrier followed by the horrible crash, crump and blue-tinged flash of the explosion as the one-ton payload impacted.

Tommy Livermore and Suzie Mountford, trying to bury their fears, assumed the nonchalant habit of copying Mother Rachel's and Sister Eunice's skit of Germans in Berlin.

The ground would tremble and the thud of the explosion rock walls and windows and Tommy would say, 'Vot vos dot?' while Suzie would quickly reply, 'Dot vos a bomp.'

The British public had no idea that some of the War Cabinet had expected worse. The intelligence reaching England in the weeks before the assault was of a much larger rocket—the V-2 was 46 feet high and carried one ton of explosive in the warhead. Initially the military analysts expected a warhead in excess of four tons, a possibility that had even Prime Minister Churchill fearful and alarmed.

Later, the prime minister wrote, 'This new form of attack imposed upon the people of London is a burden heavier than the air raids of 1940 and 1941. Suspense and strain were more prolonged. Dawn brought no relief and cloud no comfort. The man going home in the evening never knew what he would find; his wife, alone all day or with the children, could not be certain of his safe return. The blind, impersonal nature of the missiles made the individual on the ground feel helpless. There was little that he could do, no human enemy he could see shot down.'

The general public, tired and drained after almost five years of war, were shocked and dragged down by this new terror. The news following the June invasion had been good and most people saw the defeat of Germany in sight. The new terror, coming by day and night, defeating weather and seemingly random in its effect, was a dreadful blow that set already frayed tempers on edge, and scratched at the thin veneer of many people's outward calm. Morale was low and it was several weeks before the authorities allowed the truth to be circulated about the new menace. After all, France had been retaken and the rockets could now only be launched from Germany itself or from the flatlands of the Low Countries.

So, it was in this time of jumpy apprehension that Suzie headed for the leafy road of large Victorian houses, abutting on Bedford Park to seek out the Reverend Father Aubrey Harding, father of Sister Bridget Mary, killed by the V-1 before she could take her vows at the Convent of St Catherine of Siena in Silverhurst Road.

He was a small man, running to fat and with sad eyes that reflected his demeanour. ('So short,' Suzie told Tommy, 'that I think he'd have trouble cutting a decent cabbage for himself.') Father Harding, after the manner of High Anglican priests, wore a tailored soutane, the badge of his High Anglo-Catholicism, and moved in a precise manner, as though every action was part of a ritual of life.

The big house with its heavy furnishings had belonged to his wife, and was his place of retirement. 'I suppose I'll sell it once this wretched war is over. I can't afford to be sentimental over bricks and mortar.'

He had retired in 1942 from a parish in the Midlands and returned to London with his wife who was killed in a bombing raid later that year. Now he helped out in a nearby parish and, as Mother Rachel had said, took retreats at the convent where his only child had intended to spend the rest of her life as a nun.

He appeared to be immensely proud of her and of her vocation. 'People don't always understand the calling to the religious life. It is a hard and often difficult path: praising God, living apart—teaching in the case of the holy sisters of St Catherine. It was her desire from her teens to somehow serve God in this way. If the priesthood had been open to women— perish the thought—she would have put herself forward for ordination. But, God had another path and He's taken her to Him.'

Suzie thought that, for a man who professed a belief in happiness and life following death, Father Harding was in many ways a sad man who rather enjoyed the self-pity which came with the loss of wife and daughter. 'All I had has now gone for ever,' he said ushering Suzie into a neat study lined with mahogany free-standing book cases with fussy leather trim along the shelves. In one corner there was a huge old roll-top desk, in the other a prie-dieu set facing a crucifix. A chiming clock stood on the mantel, flanked by brass candlesticks and further decoration came in heavy religious pictures: Erasmus, Christ being taken down from the cross, a chocolate-boxy painting of

Our Lady and another of some young female saint—Suzie couldn't place who she was.

The priest gestured her into an easy chair as he sank into its twin in front of the fireplace (complete with fire irons with devil's-head handles), and lit a cigarette without offering one to Suzie who took her own blue paper packet of Players from her bag, selected a cigarette and lit it with a match. Even then, he didn't apologise for his rudeness.

'I simply came as a representative of the Metropolitain Police to offer our condolences.' Suzie leant forward. They had not allowed any hint of Michael Lees-Duncan's death as a disguised nun to seep out into Fleet Street or the wider world. She was there ostensibly to offer the Met's commiseration; in reality to see if he could give them any further information.

'Nothing bothering your daughter was there, Father?'

'Bothering? Why? No.' Naturally the old priest couldn't get the drift of Suzie's question. But, as she was leaving—after Father Harding had made her kneel with him and pray for the repose of the souls of Sister Bridget Mary and her companions—he grasped her arm and said, 'But, yes. Yes. The last time she was here, Bridget was most concerned for one of her colleagues—no name, no pack drill, what?' And it came out, some morbid story about this friend's past life, and how she so regretted it and how she was plagued with the desire to

270

murder the man responsible. 'Whoever it was, it seemed to me that the woman needed the services of a psychiatrist as well as a priest.'

Suzie nodded calmly, knowing exactly who he was talking about—Dulcie Tovey driven half mad by the knowledge that she had committed fornication with her own half-brother.

There was a distant rolling roar and the ground throbbed beneath Suzie's feet while Father Harding looked up, alarm in his eyes.

'Dot vos a bomp,' Suzie thought. V-2s could be heard over thirty miles away.

Back at the Yard she talked it over with Tommy and they came to the conclusion that for a religious woman it was the kind of sin that could drive you to the edge of dark madness: had indeed done so.

Laura Cotter had now returned from Sheffield so Tommy, out of the goodness of his heart, sent her and Dennis Free to Farnborough to the House of the Holy Family where the novice nuns had spent much of their time before returning to Silverhurst Road, and their deaths. 'I want to know how Michael Lees-Duncan insinuated himself into that party,' he said. When the couple returned—full of their plans for marriage—they brought with them a good picture of what had gone on.

The House of the Holy Family turned out to be a large, pleasant 1920s villa, set back from the road and screened by a stone wall and

271

trees. A gravelled drive ran right around the house, the kitchens of which were at the rear. 'The kitchen staff had orders to be generous to any vagrant coming to the back door,' Dennis told them. 'And the morning the nuns were leaving they had a man begging at the kitchen door—on that Sunday. Didn't seem like a vagrant but they gave him a bacon sandwich.' (The holy sisters received more than the usual bacon ration. Dennis said they had a God-fearing butcher.) 'This bloke at the kitchen door asked for Sister Theresa by name and Poppy—that was the cook I got all this from . . .' (Here Laura gave him a suspicious look, a sneaky look up from under her eyelids and Dennis told her there was no need for her to be jealous because Poppy was a Ten Ton Tessie type and Laura knew what he, Dennis, thought of chubby women—couldn't abide them.)

Anyway, Poppy had gone up and fetched Sister Theresa down to see the man. 'Oh, she knew him all right,' Poppy said. 'That was obvious, 'cos she went chalk white . . . no. No, I didn't see him leave, but he must of done 'cos there was no sign of him later.'

'There you have it,' Tommy said. 'Premeditated. Dulcie must've decided what she was going to do. Madness, of course. Like a fever. Dress him as a nun, get him to Silverhurst Road then do away with him. Only thought that far. Didn't work the rest of it out.'

272

Tommy Livermore did not like to leave loose ends dangling so he went off to Gloucester, with Ron Worrall in tow and, as he said, 'Put Lees-Duncan to the question.'

To Suzie's chagrin he returned with a nod from both Lees-Duncan and Tovey.

'Don't know if they'll sign anything when it comes to it, but they both blinked. Sure as eggs are eggs, Lees-Duncan is Dulcie's father. Absolutely no doubt.'

Suzie was not so sure about the blinking. She knew Tommy of old: he would never admit to a failure.

But, the following week there was confirmation of their suspicions; plus some of the reasons. When it came, the end was quick and dangerously violent: an end that, had it been a success, might have made a grave difference to the last months of the war.

CHAPTER TWENTY-TWO

Before taking up his new posting, Lieutenant James Mountford RM was instructed to report to Eastney Barracks, Portsmouth: the Royal Marines Barracks of Portsmouth Division. There, he was told, he would be familiarised with his new duties in the CWR—the Cabinet War Rooms, Winston Churchill's bunker, ten feet below ground level under the New Public

Offices building, hard by Horse Guards Parade and St James's Park.

He had been stationed in the Officers Mess at Eastney only once before. Just after being commissioned, completing the Royal Marines OCTU at Thurlstone in Devon, Jim Mountford had been sent to 'Pompey'—as Portsmouth was known to the Royal Navy and Royal Marines, and practically everybody else—to be initiated into the arcane world of mess etiquette.

While preparations were being made to complete the training of many military personnel before Operation Overlord, the invasion of Hitler's Fortress Europe, this group of young officers were taught essentials such as the ritual of taking snuff after dinner: being passed the beautiful silver snuff horn with its four implements hanging on chains from its outer side. You tapped on the lid with the tiny hammer; raked the snuff with the silver rake; placed a spoonful of the powder on the indentation below the apex of thumb and forefinger of the left hand; divided it in two— one for each nostril; closed the lid, took the snuff and brushed off the excess with the rabbit's foot. This, and the correct way to pass the port, were still seen as part of an officer's training. Jim always thought that the Royal Marines were covering their rear. Having made these men into officers they felt they should make absolutely certain that they had chosen gentlemen.

Now, Jim reported to the adjutant and was told he would be promoted to captain, 'Purely on a temporary and unpaid basis, young Mountford,' the adjutant said. 'Don't get any ideas above your station. It's simply that the post requires a Captain of Marines. Winston demands that and he'll probably call you "my good boy". That's what he appears to call his male secretaries. He's God, Mountford, remember that as well.'

The prime minister, Mr Winston Churchill, was thought of and spoken of as 'Winston' by practically everyone—though not to his face of course. Jim Mountford soon got used to that and noticed that NCOs and other ranks often spoke of him as 'Winnie'.

Captain 'Hank' Hennessy, the officer who had been in charge of the Royal Marine detachment at the CWR—now leaving to take up sea duties—arrived the next morning and took Jim through the job in detail. 'You're going to have a dozen men under you,' he said. 'Plus the excellent Colour-Sarn't "Tubby" Shaw, and I see from a signal just received that they're posting another sarn't to you.' He held the flimsy signal form up to the light, squinting at it as though looking to make sure it wasn't a forgery. 'A Sarn't Harvey. Can't think why because Colour-Sarn't Shaw knows the drill, you won't go far wrong with him. Good type. Salt of the earth.'

The marines at CWR, including himself, would be dressed in Number Ones—blues—at all times, and worked in four-hour shifts, twenty-four hours a day. The dozen men were relieved every six weeks for a second twelve men who carried on the four-hour-stint routine, turn and turn about. The Captain of Marines was not relieved. He soldiered on, twelve months of the year with the occasional spot of leave.

'The job is to safeguard the prime minister; his cabinet; the service advisers and staff. But we put the prime minister first. Initially the unit was designed as a fighting force to repel any German attack on the bunker. Shouldn't see that as a problem now, but it's as well to keep your fellows on the qui vive. You should be aware of who is in the bunker at all times, and what they're doing.' Hank Hennessy laid a conspiratorial forefinger along the side of his nose.

Men were posted at significant points in the warren of offices and rooms. A couple of men were usually outside the Cabinet Room itself, and there was always somebody close to the Map Room and one outside Mr Churchill's private room.

Hennessy told him that, while things were still fairly busy and urgent in the CWR there was not the pressure that had existed during late 1940 and early 1941 during the Blitz. 'And, of course it was hectic as all hell in the weeks leading up to D-Day,' Hennessy said. 'But don't be worried about upsetting people. If necessary follow individuals if they roam around, particularly at night. Better safe than sorry: that's the watchword.'

James Mountford left Portsmouth, most conscious of the extra pip on his shoulder, and wary of the new and important job he was about to take on. Also, he was not a little excited, because he, James R Mountford, was to be close to the centre of things, guarding the legend, Winston Churchill, and all those who had worked so hard to save Britain from becoming enslaved under the Nazis. Heady stuff for a twenty-one-year-old recently commissioned officer.

On taking over command of the Royal Marine detachment of the Cabinet War Rooms, James had done another swift flanker. He had quickly discovered that the unit was entitled to a jeep and driver and, by way of sucking up to the adjutant at 'Pompey', he had managed to get Leading Wren Emily Styles assigned to them as the detachment's driver. It was Emily who drove him to George Street on his first day when he learnt that he would be given a bed in what they called the 'Dock' below the CWR. Emily was found comfortable quarters in the New Public Offices. 'Bloody sight more comfortable than mine,' Jim later complained.

Colour-Sergeant Shaw turned out to be an

277

old-school Royal Marine NCO; stiff bearing, correct attitude, pride seeping out of every pore of his skin. Slightly portly, as his nickname implied, Colour-Sergeant Shaw could be relied on in any circumstances. Jim knew the type and was grateful for his presence.

'We had a long quiet period here, sir,' Shaw told him. 'But Winnie's back to holding Cabinet and War Defence Committee meetings down here. Done that since the buzzbombs and these rockets. The V-2s.' They were standing just outside the New Public Offices building, and Colour-Sergeant Shaw signified the CWR with a slight nod of the head. 'It's an honour to work here, sir. See all the great figures passing through. Help them. Give them a hand. Get to serve men like Winnie, the . . . er . . . the prime minister, sir.'

He said he would introduce the men to Captain Mountford at the six o'clock parade, and Jim said he was looking forward to it. Gave the colour-sergeant his best beam: ear to ear.

'You'll eat in the War Rooms Canteen, sir.' It was almost an order. 'I've heard it's not bad. Some grumble, but when didn't men grumble about food? I hear there's a lot of tinned soup and sausages. Nothing wrong with sausages, though, sir, and I expect they ginger it up, ring the changes with "Herrings-in" from time to time.' 'Herrings-in' was a Royal Marines treat,

278

short for herrings in tomato sauce, served hot or cold, often a staple for Saturdays when a lot of people wanted to go ashore. In the Royal Marines you went ashore even if you were based ashore in what was often termed a stone frigate, or shore establishment.

'Know anything about the new sergeant they're posting to us, sir?' Shaw asked him later. 'I don't think I've served with him before. Have you, sir? Name of Harvey.'

Jim said he had not, and it was readily obvious that 'Tubby' Shaw was intrigued by the new posting. 'I've been here almost two years. Now, when the end's in sight, they send me some help.'

'You know what it's like, Colour-Sarn't. Chap'll probably get claustrophobic.' People always said that all postings were strange: a good cook was sent to a MT unit, while a skilled motor mechanic was remustered as a cook.

Harvey arrived at noon the following day, just as Jim was starting to find his way around the underground bunker with its single long narrow corridor, and ceilings crossed by thick, red-painted metal girders that reinforced the roof. It would be easy, Jim quickly discovered, to get claustrophobic because the main problem with the CWR was space, and it was difficult to envisage how they had managed when the whole of the Prime Minister's Office had been permanently down in the War

279

Rooms in 1940/41.

Even now, when the main threat was still from the skies there was a hum of activity that seemed to spill from the rooms, spaced along each side of the corridor. People's voices could be heard and the telephones constantly rang, runners and messengers pushed their way along the central passage, avoiding the big plain map storage chests and aware of the hiss of the compressed air that sent message capsules along the Lanson tubes, from office to office. Everyone was used to the Lanson equipment as it had been a regular feature all over the country in larger shops and department stores before the war—flinging accounts and cash to the girls who sat in till booths saving shoppers from queuing or paying their bills at a till. The Lanson tubes distanced the shopper from the sordid financial part of the transaction. Now, like most things, the Lanson system had been called up for war work.

At around eleven-thirty Colour-Sergeant Shaw took a phone call from Harvey who was at Paddington Station having travelled from Exton via Exeter. Jim immediately authorised the jeep to pick him up.

'Cheeky bugger,' Emily told him that evening when they managed to slip away for a quick drink in a pub where they weren't known. 'Tried to pinch my bottom as we arrived in George Street. Made some remark about me probably being an officer's groundsheet. Not very nice.'

'He'd better stop that or he'll find himself up the creek without a paddle,' Jim assured her.

Harvey had a shy smile. It was the first thing Jim noticed about him, a shy, unassuming smile and grey-green eyes, the colour of the North Sea. He was tall, well set-up as you would expect a Royal Marine sergeant to be. But Jim immediately knew that he'd seen Sergeant Harvey's face before.

'We served together, somewhere, Sarn't?' he asked. 'Commando Training Unit? 41 Commando?'

' 'Fraid not, sir. No. Most of my war's been spent at sea.'

He was efficient and got on with his job, soft-spoken, but firm. Men would instinctively obey him without question.

'Good NCO,' Colour-Sergeant Shaw said. 'Knows how to keep the lads happy. You heard about the Cabinet Meeting tomorrow, sir?'

Jim Mountford *had* heard about the meeting but he just nodded. No point in showing his NCO that he was as excited as a schoolboy. Tomorrow afternoon at three o'clock he would see Winston Churchill, the living legend, the one who had told them all that they'd fight on the beaches and that they'd never surrender, when Jim was a schoolboy and Britain faced a hungry, trained and well-equipped German army at its gates. At that time nothing had stood between them and defeat: annihilation if you thought about it. But Winston had made everybody feel there was not just a chance but a certainty of victory. At that time, nobody had doubted the growling, gravel-voiced leader. They believed him and that was what was required.

Now, young Mountford would be entrusted with Churchill's safety. The thought was enough to pop the buttons on his Blues jacket. Jim squared his shoulders and felt proud, knew his mother and sister would be proud, and probably his stepfather—the Galloping Major, whom he loathed—would also be proud. Fuck him, he thought.

Then Tommy Livermore turned up without warning. 'Thought I'd look you up, old sport. Make sure you're OK.'

'My sister sent you, didn't she?'

'No. 'Course not, Jim. I came because I've never been down here. Always wanted to see it.'

This was in the morning of the day of the Cabinet Meeting. They would all be here this afternoon. Three o'clock. Fifteen hundred hours. 'Well, you've seen it, now you can bugger off,' Jim told him.

'Don't be like that, James. Let me have a look round.'

So Jim introduced him to Colour-Sergeant Shaw and Sergeant Harvey, took him along the passage, let him peep into the Map Room and the PM's bedroom, with the little tin jerry under the bed. Tommy smiled, winked and mysteriously said, 'Bingo'.

Then he thanked James, a shade too effusively, and left, giving James plenty of time to be at the CWR entrance from the basement of the New Public Offices, halfway along the main corridor, when the prime minister arrived at just after two-thirty in the afternoon.

He had already saluted the CIGS, Sir Alan Brooke—Colonel Shrapnel as he had once been called—on his arrival, and received a blistering salute in return, one that made Jim ashamed of the sometimes lazy way he responded to salutes; he had also been aware of Anthony Eden and Stafford Cripps as they arrived with a number of other important people, civilians as well as high-ranking officers of the Army, Royal Navy and the Royal Air Force.

When he arrived, the prime minister gave Jim a beaming baby-faced smile and addressed him by name. 'Captain Mountford, I presume.' He thrust out a hand. 'Welcome to the CWR. Now, look after me well. I'm not as young as I was and my detective's on sick leave.'

'No, sir,' James said, surprised that the great man had taken the trouble to acquaint himself with his name. 'I mean, yes, sir.'

'Good boy. Walk me to the Cabinet Room.

'Make sure we're not disturbed,' he said

283

with another smile as they reached the door to the Cabinet Room at the far end of the passage.

Jim saluted again and was aware of Sergeant Harvey leaning past him to close the door and saying loudly, 'Very good, sir. I'll do it straightaway.' He closed the door and Jim noticed that Harvey was still holding the Cabinet Room keys he had taken to unlock the room earlier on Jim's orders.

'I'd better get them, then,' Harvey said as he caught Jim's eye.

'Get what?'

'The PMs cases. He just asked for them. From his car.' Harvey started to hurry down the passageway to the entrance, past the prime minister's bedroom/study on his right, and the big plant room containing the electricity and air-conditioning generators and subsidiary equipment on the left.

Jim looked round for Colour-Sergeant Shaw but he was nowhere to be seen. He could have sworn that the prime minister had not given any orders to Sergeant Harvey.

But a few moments later he saw Harvey return, lugging two great heavy metal cases, followed by Emily Styles using both hands to carry a third case. Harvey was breathing heavily under the exertion of carrying the cases and, as he came abreast of the Cabinet Room door, he called back to Emily, 'Leave that one out here, in the passage. He doesn't need that

284

yet.' Then, in an even more commanding voice, 'There. Leave it outside the door! There!' Pointing.

As he opened the door and slid the metal cases into the Cabinet Room, Jim Mountford glimpsed Winston Churchill half turn from his heavy wooden chair, looking puzzled, but before he had time to say anything, Harvey slammed the door and James heard the clear sound of the key turning in the lock.

Sergeant Harvey had locked the prime minister and his War Cabinet into the room.

And also at that moment Jim realised where he had seen Harvey before. His photograph, next to that of his brother, sliding out of a file that Tommy Livermore had brought into his sister's living room. Gerald Lees-Duncan.

Pair of right Harrovian thugs you've got there all right, Tommy.

Not sure about the Harrovian bit but they're certainly a pair of thugs. That one's no longer with us, by the way,

Jim Mountford shouted. 'Stop him! Stop Harvey now!' and felt the man's fist come up in an attempt to strike him in the face, felt the metal from the keys in Harvey's hand and realised that he had more than one key clasped in his fist: a whole bunch.

He saw Emily make an attempt to grab the sergeant who brought his fist up again and hit her hard in the face. She gave a grunt and fell to one side, hitting the wall and crumpling into

285

a heap. Blood on her face.

Jim grabbed for his pistol in its leather holster and tried to drag it out but changed his mind as he set off in pursuit, his brain teeming with the possibilities. What was in the cases? He stopped pursuing Harvey and shouted down the corridor. 'Colour-Sarn't Shaw! Spare keys! Spare keys to the Cabinet Office and the main door! Now! Quickly!' Then he heard a rattling from inside the Cabinet Room and heard the prime minister growl, 'Open this damned door. Get us out of here at once. What's in these damned cases?'

Jim dragged out his Smith & Wesson .38 revolver and shouted, 'Stand back, sir. Out of the way, I'm going to shoot out the hinges,' and when he heard Churchill's distinctive, 'Good man. All clear,' he put two rounds into each hinge, top and bottom, close to the wooden jamb, splintering the wood and twisting the metal hinges.

One of the two marines on duty outside the Cabinet Room helped to pull the door away, and from inside Admiral Cunningham, the First Lord of the Admiralty, finished the job.

Colour-Sergeant Shaw was at his elbow now. 'The main door's open, sir. He left it open.'

'Get the prime minister out, Colour-Sarn't. Now! All of them. Quickly. Get them out, this is bloody dangerous.'

'What is this, young Mountford? Is it a

286

Nazi plot?' Churchill gave his distinctive pronunciation of Nazi—'Naazzzy plot.'

'I very much fear it is, sir. Please move out. Fast as you can, sir.'

'Good boy. Good boy,' said the prime minister as he headed along the passage to the door that would lead him into the Public Offices building.

Jim looked at his watch. It was just five minutes to three. 'Come on,' he shouted to those of his squad who were already in the main passageway. 'Let's get these damned cases outside. They probably contain explosives so don't tarry. Get them away into St James's Park.' He grabbed the nearest case and lugged it along the passage, feeling a terrible strain on his hands and arms. The case must have weighed a good hundredweight, and he felt his arms creak in their sockets. Two of his marines were heaving on the other case, and another couple of the lads had their hands on the one left in the passage.

Colour-Sergeant Shaw leant over to help him, but Jim motioned him away. 'Help the young Maren,' he ordered. 'Get her out, Colour-Sarn't.'

Emily was groggily trying to get up as Shaw reached her. Then another of the marines arrived to assist Jim with the case. They both grunted and groaned as they half carried, half dragged the metal case out into the basement of the Public Offices building, then up and out into the afternoon sun.

As they emerged, Jim saw, first, Tommy and then his Suzie. Behind them were several uniformed police officers surrounding Gerald Lees-Duncan. 'Get out of the way, Tommy . . . sis . . .' he yelled. Then to his men, 'Get everyone out of the way! Get those cases out into the park! Away from the buildings!'

People had crowded around to see what was going on and the marines had to shriek at them, physically driving them back.

Exhausted by his exertions, chest heaving, arms strained in their sockets, Jim managed to get the message to Tommy, and some of the uniformed police broke away, shouting at the sightseers, urging them to get out of the way. Jim heard somebody yelling, 'UXB. Unexploded bomb! Get the hell out of it.'

They dragged the case across Horse Guards Road and onto the grass of St James's Park. The two marines dragging the other case from the Cabinet Room had left it on the grass, and Jim, panting and heaving told his companion to drop it and get away. The third case was now nearby, and Jim began to run back towards Horse Guards Parade, shouting to everybody to take cover. He saw Tommy and Suzie drop to the ground and the small knot of police officers hustle away the captive, Gerald Lees-Duncan.

Then the cases erupted, the sound of each explosion merging into one thunderous roar.

It was exactly three o'clock.

By this time Jim Mountford was flat on the ground near his sister. The noise battered his eardrums and he felt the shock wave. As it dwindled away he heard his sister say,

'Vot vos dot?'

And Tommy replied, 'Dot vos a bomp.'

He thought they were both mad.

CHAPTER TWENTY-THREE

Tommy said they were damned clever, the bombs. 'If it had worked the PM and the whole Cabinet would have been wiped out. Immediate thought would have been that it was a V-2 rocket. Would've shaken everyone rigid.'

'There'd be no metal, though. No traces of a rocket,' Suzie countered.

'Nobody was going to look *immediately*.' Tommy did his all-knowing and omnipotent look. 'Would've given brother Lees-Duncan time to slip away. The three cases made a crater about thirty feet across. The things went off right on three o'clock. Most efficient timer.'

Jim asked if they knew what the explosive was.

Tommy said it was plastique as far as they could make out. 'The new stuff. C-4 I think they call it. Pounds of it, with nails and bits of old metal mixed in.'

'So where did that come from?'

'That's the one thing lacking at the moment. Maybe we'll knock it out of him in time.' Tommy shook his head. 'I don't know what we're going to do with him. General view is we'll never get him in front of a judge. Nobody wants to admit that we allowed an assassin to get that close to Winston.'

'There are other things we'll never know.' Suzie looked at him archly.

'Such as?'

'Such as did Dulcimer lure Michael to his death or did Michael just want to see if he could get her out of that nasty old habit.' She chortled, overdoing it a bit.

'You took your time getting there,' Jim grumbled to Tommy.

'Well, I thought you'd have the fella in irons. I recognised him straight off. Tipped you off; said "Bingo". Did everything. Ball in your court.' Tommy had started pronouncing 'off' as 'orf'.

'How did he work it?' Jim was still in the dark.

'Turned up, out of the blue, at Exton. Royal Marine Camp down near Exmouth. It's the Pre-OCTU—as you know—and a holding unit. They had nothing about Harvey. But, amazingly, within an hour of him being there they found a signal posting him to the CWR.

Bloody Jerries were light on their feet. I've seen the paperwork and it all looks first rate. Genuine as a five-quid note. Must've landed him near Exton somehow. He arrived on the train platform, as I say, out of the blue. Went to the guardroom and was in.'

The next day some decisions were made and Tommy went over to see Mother Rachel and tell her that the business of a man being found dead in the convent would not get into the press. They were keeping quiet about it.

'Thank the Good Lord for that.' Mother Rachel was as ecstatic as her position would allow. 'I was dreading headlines in the *News of the World*. It would've been a terrible scandal. MAN FOUND IN CONVENT HORROR.'

By way of a thank you, Tommy and Suzie were invited to the nuns' evening meal on the following Sunday. Tommy grumbled of course, didn't want to go, but in the end it was a most enjoyable evening: Fresh poached salmon ('Poached in every way, I believe,' Mother Rachel said with a twinkle), new potatoes, garden peas and a strawberry mousse. 'You mustn't think we always eat like this,' Sister Eunice whispered to Suzie who nodded sagely.

After the meal they went into chapel for the sisters to chant the divine office, and Suzie was in her element because the slow rise and fall of the plainsong brought back memories of her childhood and the time she had spent at St Helen's when her father was still alive.

After chapel it was announced that there was to be a special entertainment, and they all sat in the Sisters' recreation room, while Sister Agnes did her famed impression of an elderly canon reciting 'The Charge of the Light Brigade'. Sister Cleo did her conjuring tricks, and very good she was: making silk handkerchiefs change colour, producing billiard balls from the air and linking solid rings together.

'Don't know how she does it,' said Tommy.

Last of all, Mother Rachel and Sister Eunice did the two Germans in an air raid shelter—

'Vot vos dot?'

'Dot vos a bomp.'

How Suzie and Tommy laughed: a shade hysterically.

'So, what's next?' Suzie asked when they got back to the flat above Upper St Martin's Lane. 'Tommy Livermore going to do his contortions, is he?'

'Well, if you don't mind I've instructed the banns to be read in the chapel at Kingscote, and in the local parish church.'

'Tommy!' she squealed. After all, they had been quietly engaged since 1941, and Tommy had occasionally blown hot and cold about it. 'Oh, you really have done it? We're to be married?'

'Of course. If you don't mind.'

'Oh, yes please. Yes very please.'

Smiling, Tommy leered quietly in her ear. 'Get up them stairs,' he said.

'Tommy.' She gave him a curious look. 'We haven't any stairs and it's get up *those* stairs. What's happened to your grammar?'

'Heart, it's get up *them* stairs. That's the way the brutal and licentious soldiery indicate their need for connubial congress. "Get up *them* stairs," they say.'

'Dirty beasts,' Suzie said with a broad smile, as she headed towards the bedroom.